Cover Your Tracks – *Morwenna Blackwood*

About the author

When she was six years old, Morwenna wrote and endless story about a frog, and hasn't stopped writing since.

She's the author of bestselling noir psychological thrillers, *The (D)Evolution of Us, Glasshouse, Underrated,* and *Skin and Bone*, has an MA in Creative Writing, and can usually be found down by the sea. Morwenna has also written a number of short stories, and a collection of poetry.

She often thinks about that frog.

Acknowledgements

In the same way that stories are inextricably linked, so I ought to thank everyone and everything that has touched my life ... is how I started the acknowledgements for my debut novel, *The (D)Evolution of Us,* and it's as true as ever.

And, as ever, my thanks go out to my family, close friends, and the Northmoor/Costa/darkling writer-friends I've made along the way. I'm so very happy you're all in my life.

However, particular thanks go out to Dad, this time.

And shout out to Roland – you've inspired my MC's look; and on that note, it's either serendipity or some spooky coincidence that your code name is Agent Orange.

This story has been a long time coming …

For Dad

Cover Your Tracks

Simon, 1984.

It's a cliché of a scene; the police officer I spoke to on the phone was right. A thick rope tied to a branch of a gnarly old tree, and dangling from its other end is a middle-aged man, dressed in jeans and a lumber shirt. On the ground a little in front of him, among fallen acorns, lies the plastic milk crate he'd kicked away when he'd reached the point of no return. Critical mass. The half-empty bottle of amber-coloured spirits by the foot of the tree must have helped him along his way.

A weird sort of detachedness comes over me as I regard the man. It occurs to me that I should be shocked, or upset, or something, but all I can think about is the fact that he's still hanging there. Presumably, someone comes to take the body down and wheel it off to the morgue before they allow the press in, don't they? But I keep forgetting that I'm in the South-West now. Things are different in the countryside. Usual rules don't apply, I suppose because no one's watching. No one cares but the locals.

My sight drifts in and out of focus as I watch the dead man swinging slightly in the cold wind, and I wonder for the umpteenth time whether I've made the right decision moving down here. Despite myself, I take my hat off in respect – for the dead man, or my former life, I'm not sure.

"Blimey, boy!" The policeman pronounces it *bey*. "You're either made of strong stuff or you're a serial killer in disguise!" The rotund, moustached man pulls a cigarette out of his pocket and tilts the packet in my direction. I smile and reach out to take one, but he pulls the packet back, uncertainty flitting across his face. "Actually, are you old enough, boy?"

It's become an automatic response to laugh and make light of it when people say things like this. I expect the growing knot of seething fury I keep locked up in my stomach will give me an ulcer one day.

"Yes, I'm 21, Officer. Mr Locke wouldn't send the YTS lad to a suicide."

Mr Locke – Derek – is the editor – or, rather, the commander and chief – of the Eskwich Gazette, the local rag I work on now. I could have taken the job I was offered in Winchester, or even tried to make it in London. But I went for the chief reporter's position on the *Swansbourne Gazette*, and moved down there, and then the *Esky Gazette* called me – although that doesn't count as being headhunted, according to my father – and now I take a train and a bus here and back every day for the privilege of a few more pounds a year. I ought to get a place here in Eskwich, really, but I enjoy living in my little flat above the chippy – it's comforting, somehow, listening to the sea, and the trains going past. It makes me feel like I'm not that far away from Charlotte, like I might spot her standing repentant and resplendent on the platform one day, her Rapunzel hair whipping round her head in the ocean breeze. Deep down, I know that's never going to happen. She's the reason I moved away.

"You can put your cowboy hat back on, boy," the police officer says with a laugh. "It's not going to make *him* feel any better!"

My feet are taking me closer to the dead man. I have this morbid fascination to see the expression on his face. I read a William Burroughs story that said when you top yourself like this, you get an erection, but the man's checked shirt is hanging over his crotch, so I can't tell.

"Not too close, boy," the officer calls, crunching over the gravel to join me. "This is a crime scene, you know." I supress a laugh at his sudden seriousness. I bet this is the most exciting thing that's happened to him in years.

"Crime scene? It's a cut-and-dried suicide, surely? We just need to find out who the man is, contact his relatives, and then try to find out why he did it …"

The police officer cuts me off. "I think you'll find it's *us* that need to do that, boy – not you news hounds! And things aren't always what they seem, you know!" He puffs out his already expansive chest and blows cigarette smoke in my face. Lambert and Butler – the same brand my boss smokes. I pull my Stetson back down over my hair.

"Okay, so why I am here before the Serious Crime lot?"

"You only had to drive up from Esky, boy. The big guns are coming down from Exeter."

We're at Eskwich Junction railway station – an inappropriately named place, if you ask me, because it's actually several miles from Eskwich – round the back of the platform and the station building, in a kind of gravelly wasteland that was probably used for loading back in the day when this was a busy place with a thriving freight yard. Only main-line passenger services stop here now, and rumour is they're going to close the station altogether soon. Nettles, brambles, and teasel are already reclaiming this area, and clearly, rooks are roosting in and around the old sheds. I mooch about for a bit, kicking up dust, wishing I'd been able to drive up in a car of my own, instead of having to borrow Trish, the deputy editor's. It's peaceful out here. No HSTs have been through. All you can hear is birdsong, the occasional car passing, and a low rumble from somewhere.

"What's that noise, Officer?"

"Call me Al, boy, for God's sake! And it's Poultry Packers," the man replies, with a tone that suggests he's baffled that I don't know.

"Poultry Packers?"

"Yeah. The abattoir over there." He points a meaty finger to some grey industrial buildings a way behind me on a hill. "We're lucky the wind's blowing the right way – bloody stinks out here normally!" A thought occurs to him. "How can you work on the *Esky Gazette* and not know what Poultry Packers is?!" He tilts his head and looks at me as if seeing me properly for the first time. "You're not from round here, are you, boy?"

Since we're the only ones out here, and neither of us is doing anything useful, I consider telling him what he wants to know. It might be good to get in with this man – it might lead to exclusive stories. But then he might react in the same way the other lads on the paper did – he'll presume I'm *posh* and won't want to give me the time of day. Blow it – he'll find out regardless. I opt for the brutal truth.

"No, I'm originally from Winchester," I say, watching his eyes for prejudice. "I moved down here when my girlfriend told me she was pregnant with my mate's baby."

"Ooh," Al says. "I feel for you, boy, I really do. My wife – soon-to-be ex-wife – did something similar. Can't trust women as far as you can throw them. You're better off out of it, if you ask me."

"I'll drink to that!" I mutter, eyeing the bottle of spirits, its contents gleaming in a shaft of sunlight. "What's that?" I inch over and pick up the leather wallet that's near the bottle, partially camouflaged by ferns and fallen leaves.

I've opened it up and fished out Geoffrey Kerslake's British Rail ID card before officer Al can tell me to drop it.

Taking the stairs up to newsdesk two at a time, I stumble into the office leaving the door to slam in the through-draft. Having mentally composed the story in the car on the way back into Eskwich, I want to get it typed up while it's still fresh in my mind. I rip a sheet of paper from the thick pad by my telephone and feed it as gently as I can into my typewriter, which clicks and squeaks in protest as I do so.

"Do I detect the whiff of an interesting story happening in Esky?" Trish deposits a mug of muddy coffee on one side of me, a heavy cut-glass ashtray on the other. I throw her a thankful smile and plonk myself down on my chair.

"Yes," I say somewhat breathlessly, "the apparent suicide of a train driver is opaquer than they're letting on, and I want to get the basics down before I do some digging."

"Intriguing!" Trish declares, pursing her lips in approval, her eyes twinkling. I cringe internally, wondering if the twinkle has something to do with the fact that I used the word *opaquer*. "Then I'll just leave this here." She moves off, long, pleated skirt swishing. I look down at the cigar she's placed in one of the dips in the ashtray.

"What's that for?" I can't help but ask.

"Our esteemed editor, Mr Derek Locke, has decreed that this October shall be the month we all get a pay rise!"

Everyone in the office who isn't on the phone cheers, and I laugh along, until Steve, the YTS lad, slaps me on the back with his skinny hand, saying, "Yeah! Even us newbies!" The boy doesn't look any older than 14, but he's puffing his way through a Cuban like the rest of them. I bite my lip and shoot him a tight smile that is at juxtaposition with the dislike I know is smouldering in my eyes. The fact that this little upstart who makes the tea and does a bit of photocopying thinks he's on a level with me, who came straight in as chief reporter, really grates on my nerves.

"Are you old enough to be smoking that?" I cringe at myself again, for echoing PC Al, but the jibe is out before I can stop myself.

Steve glares at me. "Fuck off, Shirley," he mutters, skulking over to Larry, newsdesk's veteran, who seems to have taken the youngster under his wing.

Shirley. Another addition to the ball of repressed rage in my stomach. I was *blessed* according to my mother, with my grandfather's curly, ginger hair, so my colleagues have given me the nickname, Shirley, as in Shirley Temple. Back home in Winchester, I'd been Agent Orange to my friends, which had at least been a cool nickname (Dave and I had loved James Bond, that's how the nickname originated). My bloody hair. It's not even wavy strawberry-blond. It's thick orange corkscrews, and I've hated it ever since I reached the point of self-awareness. Personally, I don't get it: it's hair, that's all. I could call Steve's dogshit-brown; Larry's nicotine-white, but apparently, those colours are acceptable. Being ginger in Devon is a curse.

Nia, 2022.

I've known Matt forever. I've known his mum, Misty, for just as long, but – and I know this sounds harsh – if I never saw her again, I wouldn't be that bothered. Whereas if I never saw Matt again, I'd fall apart. Me and Matt were born within hours of each other – our mums were on the same labour ward at Esky Hospital. The shared shock of giving birth and then suddenly having a little human to look after forever more resulted in them becoming close friends and me and Matt growing up together. My earliest memory is of being at a playgroup in this big, cold, church hall, eating cut-up apple and drinking mini bottles of milk through stripy plastic straws, and playing trains with him.

Everything changed when we turned 5. As me and Mum lived in Exeter, I couldn't go to the same school as Matt. Mum said she tried really hard, but the authorities said that roots didn't account for anything, and that if she'd moved to Exeter and we were living in Exeter, then I had to go to school in Exeter. Matt lived in Esky, so he had to go to school there. We could still see each other, Mum said, and I would make new friends who I could see after school every day, without having to get on a bus or a train or both, or having to ask someone to come and pick us up. She said that when she phoned Misty, I could speak to Matt. I was a little kid. There was no way we were going to sustain our relationship with phone calls. We argued, me and Mum, as I grew up. I said she should sell the house and buy somewhere in Eskwich. We'd always spent most of our time there. There was nothing keeping us in Exeter, except for the fact that she wouldn't leave the house. She said she *couldn't.* Mum kept saying that I'd understand when I was older, but she never gave me anything more than that. I began to hate her. Eventually, our mums realised they couldn't sustain their friendship with phone calls, and our visits to Eskwich became sporadic. Now we could read and write, Matt and I became kind of pen pals. Life in Exeter grew on me, but I loved receiving his letters. And I loved hearing the trains going past our house all the time.

Matt and I had both been obsessed with trains when we were little, but as we grew up, it became apparent that I loved them because I enjoyed travelling all over the country on them, while Matt loved them because he obsessed over making a little replica country with little replica versions; which is another reason why we drifted apart, I suppose: I wanted to go out and touch the world, while he wanted to hold it in his hands.

I left Devon – with the intention of it being for good – when I was in my late teens. I only returned after Mum died. She made me her executor, so I had to come back and sort everything out. My intention had been to sell the house, cut any remaining ties and bugger off to New York or something, but when, for the first time in years, I catch sight of our old home on Beaufort Road, I know I'm never going to leave it again.

It's something about the smell of the place. Walking into the front room from straight off the street, it's like being physically lamped round the head with nostalgia. A jolt passes through me, and my eyes well up. I make my way through to the kitchen, put the kettle on, and sit at the circular, pine kitchen table while I wait for it to boil, and find myself singing Nik Kershaw's *Wouldn't it be Good to be in Your Shoes?* I take my cup of coffee – Mum didn't like mugs – up the stairs and into my old room. I sit on the bed, forgetting how springy the mattress is, and nearly spill my drink. I nearly spill it again at the sound of a train rushing past outside, and then I just sit cross-legged on my old bed for bloody ages, watching the passenger and freight services going by. When my legs cramp, I go downstairs and make myself another coffee, and a plain cheese sandwich with the last sliced white loaf Mum ever put in the freezer. When I bite into it, the bread hasn't quite defrosted from its 30 seconds in the toaster. I eat it anyway. Apart from the trains, it's eerily quiet.

I leave the house and walk the few minutes to St Thomas' and catch the next train to Exmouth. Mum and

Dad used to do it, apparently, before I was born, so I do it out of some weird kind of sentimentality, or to feel spiritually close to Dad, or something, I don't know – he liked doing it, and I'd been with him in Mum's belly when they did it, so it's the nearest thing I have to a family tradition. Sometimes when I feel down, I get on the train to Exmouth from wherever I am and spend the day on the beach or in one of the sad, seafront cafes if it's raining. Ironically, I feel grounded and secure at the seaside. The vastness and otherworldliness of the ocean makes me put my life in perspective – I'm insignificant, but essential at the same time. It sounds really lame, but it makes me feel whole. And I imagine my dad looking out at the sparkling, crashing waves and over to Swansbourne, Teignmouth, Brixham and that big rock at the end that I always want to call Berry Head, but I don't think that's the right name, and I imagine I'm looking at it all with him. Then I berate myself for being wistful. It's easy to love someone who's not there, and never has been. My dad could have been a complete bastard for all I know. Mum had been deliberately vague about him my whole life, and now she's gone. It feels like there's a hole there, but how can there be a hole if there was never anything but words to leave one?

I've got all the way up to Orcombe Point in a kind of daze, and realising where I am and how far I've walked in the heat, I buy a vegan latte from Bumble and Sea – the little eco tea shed halfway up the cliff face at Orcombe Point – and go and sit on the sand with my back against the sea wall and sip it. Bad choice – the creamy liquid burns my lips. I'd ordered it on autopilot. I remember a friend telling me years ago, when we were at 'big' school, and she went to Corfu when the furthest I got was Saunton Sands, that hot drinks cool you down, and, yeah, there's probably some scientific truth in that, but I could have done with an ice-cold can of Coke, even if its effect is only psychosomatic. I get to my feet and look back over the sea wall to the tea hut. The queue is massive now. I'll have to make do.

It's one of those longed-for July days when there isn't a cloud in the sky and the ocean ripples blue. The beach is packed, and people are parking all over double-yellows, and even the pedestrianised area at the end. I'd seen a couple of police riot vans in town, and on the way up, but they can't get up here – the road has become a crawling car park. The air smells of sun cream and barbeque smoke, with occasional whiffs of BO and weed. I can't hear the sea for all the shouting and laughing, the clashing strains of music, and the relentless hissing and puffing of people inflating paddleboards. It's disappointing. Why can't people just be quiet? Intermittently, there's an explosion of gull cries when one of them finds an unattended picnic. I love to sit and watch when this happens, because people show who they really are: you get the ones who watch and laugh as the birds chuck stuff around and fight with each other; the ones who dash over and try to frighten them off; the ones who look around to see if they can see anyone who looks like they might be the owners of the food; and the ones who watch, and then encourage their toddlers to run screaming at every bird they see. Oh, and there're the ones like me, who sit there and regard the chaos with a wry smile. Let the gulls eat, I say. They're the avian equivalent of humans, after all.

I grab my DM sandals, ditch my empty coffee cup in one of the recycling bins, and mooch down to the sea. The tide is miles out – the groynes and flags exposed in all their rusty, barnacled glory – and I kind of wade through the deep, dry, golden sand, pick my way over the inevitable thick line of washed-up seaweed, shells and driftwood, and enjoy the easier terrain of damp sand, which gently and then steeply slopes, becoming ever more saturated, until I'm following rivulets down to the surf, careful not to stand on the bubbly bits which are some sort of creatures, apparently. The chill of the water shocks me, but only for a moment. I know that if I brace myself and steadily make my way further in, I could happily swim for hours in just my bikini. Those people in wetsuits and those weird plastic daps make me laugh – this is as warm as the sea around the UK gets! I curse myself for being so impulsive and just getting on the train, because now I have an urge to swim, but nothing else to wear.

Leaving my sandals above the tideline, I go as far in as I can before the waves hit my jean shorts. I curse myself again for my lack of foresight, and wonder if anyone will notice if I swim in my bra and pants. The water is clear, and there are hardly any rocks or bits of seaweed around me. Movement catches my eye, and I watch a shoal of minnows flit by. Straight ahead, a cormorant bobs on the waves before disappearing – presumably the minnows went the wrong way. Once when I was swimming – I mean properly swimming, not just doing a few strokes and floating about – I dived down to try to see a cormorant under water, but I'd been over in Swansbourne and the visibility was crap because the sea can get really violent there, so it wasn't the uplifting, David Attenborough documentary-type moment I'd been hoping for, although

I'd got a buzz from being under water near a fishing cormorant. Today, I scan the surface for the bird, but it must have dived again, so I dip my hand in the water and splash my face, then return to the beach, grabbing my shoes, and deciding to risk the walk round Orcombe Point to Sandy Bay. If the tide turns and comes in when I want to come back, I'll just go over the cliffs – I haven't done that in ages. Also, I need the loo, and the pub at the top of Sandy Bay has to be closer than the minging block of loos halfway between the cliff and the lifeboat station.

There are loads of people milling about, excited dogs charging all over the place, and pockets of teenagers lurking on the rocks with cans of beer, so I don't feel scared that the tide will cut me off before I get there. The cliffs on the other side of Orcombe Point – usually part-hidden by the ocean – are enormous; their ruddy expanse is crumbling in the wind, reflected in the rosy sheen on the sand. I'm suddenly compelled to run, but there are groups of young lads around, and I don't want to look like a weirdo. Not that they'd pay any attention to me – a wobbly-fleshed, bloated 38-year-old – and not that I want them to! I hate myself for not being able to get these kinds of culturally ingrained thoughts out of my head. I fix my eyes on the ocean and concentrate on trying to walk like a normal human being.

There's a lovely middle stretch to this walk where there's hardly anyone about. People who've parked their cars along the mile or so of promenade I traversed earlier don't want to leave their stuff for too long; the old people and their yappy little dogs are scared of the length of the journey back; and the holidaymakers at the caravan park at Sandy Bay are mainly only there for the beach and the beer anyway, and most of them have young kids who'd be bored after five minutes. So, I slow down and enjoy this bit. I inhale deeply and stretch my arms in great arcs. The ground is flat, and the sun beats heavily on my shoulders. I'll have to buy some sun cream when I get there.

Sandy Bay is packed. It's worse than at Orcombe Point because even when the tide's out and there's this much sand exposed, the beach isn't half as wide. Also, there's a great thick strip of drying seaweed near the beach bar and the path down from the holiday park – no one wants to sit in that stinking mass. I meander through prone bodies on towels, tents and inflatables, my gaze on the bar. A nice cold San Miguel would go down a treat, but there's nowhere to sit, and anyway, I need to get sun cream from the shop, and go to the loo!

Listening to people chatting as they carefully descend the killer-steep path, it seems as if the whole of Birmingham is here. A little girl jumps at the crack of a rifle – I bet none of these tourists banked on there being an army camp on the cliff next door. I wonder if Haven declare it in their holiday brochures. I'm out of breath before I reach the bend in the path, and I can feel the sweat trickling down my back before I make the top. That's why I only ever wear white or black tops in the summer. Somehow, it's okay for blokes in red or light grey T-shirts to go round with massive dark patches under their arms. Not so for women. The whole thing is ridiculous. When I was in my twenties, I went through a period where I refused to shave my legs – an act of defiance against the Barbie doll version of perfection. I say 'period' – after ten days I felt so disgusting I couldn't bear it anymore, and I've shaved at least every other day since.

The loos are surprisingly clean, so I give myself a bit of a sponge-down with cold water and paper towels before making my way over to the pub. There's a sign on the wall – no beachwear, no topless men. Presumably topless women are fine. The pub isn't actually a pub – the sign says South Beach *Café* – and its mostly terraced tables with a panoramic view of the bay, and a kind of wrap-around seating area under the veranda. Inside, it's dark, and mostly restaurant. The whole place is done up like a child's idea of an Australian beach bar – all curved slats of wood put together like someone found them washed up on the shore, with palm trees dotted about, even inside. The bar is totally incongruous – a slate-grey L bordering a square of grey floor tiles. The pumps are spread out along it in a way that suggests massive queues, and there's a big metal water bowl for dogs at one end, and a low table bearing wicker baskets full of straws, crayons and colouring sheets at the other. It's so functional and depressing that I'm about to go straight out and just grab a can of Coke from the shop next door, but the barman clocks me, so I look at him and smile vaguely, but it's Matt, and he beams at me, yelling, "Happy birthday!"

It's so full of love that I burst into tears.

Simon, 1984.

It's okay, it's Friday; it's okay, it's Friday is my silent chant as I force my legs up Bampton Street. The batteries in my Walkman ran out before the bus pulled into Eskwich, so I don't even have David Bowie to help me through the day, unless I pop down and ask Marie on reception if she's got any in the stationery cupboard. I'm at the deep blue side door of the Gazette offices now, and I punch in the access code. It makes me laugh that the whole point of a newspaper is its news stories, but the reporters have to go in through the side door, up a steep, narrow stairwell, and sit in a dingy, beige office where the air comprises more nicotine than oxygen; while it's the girls in advertising who get to enter through the ornate, blue-panelled glass doors and into the bright, clean reception area. I suppose it's to draw people in. Who wants to look at a load of sweaty blokes hammering away on typewriters when you could be watching Marie and her crew clicking about in their stilettos and pencil skirts? Maybe it *is* all about the advertising.

My hand is on the worn brass knob of the door to newsdesk when Lee shouts up to me.

"Si! Thank God it's you! I've got a bit of a problem in the darkroom again …"

I know what he's hinting at, and I cringe internally at the thought. "Sorry, Lee, I'm late and Mr Locke will go ballistic ..."

"Don't give me that, boy; you're always the first one in! Get down here and help me!"

I hesitate. Lee's smiling, weathered face wrinkles into a pleading grin. "There's a pint in it for you..."

Cursing myself, but laughing at the same time, I clomp back down the stairs to where Lee stands at the door to his darkroom. It's closed. "Ready?" he says.

When he opens the door, it's like the third plague of Egypt. The room is black, but it's not black because the lights are off and Lee's developing some pictures. It's black because it's swarming with flies. My skin crawls, and I want to call Lee all the names under the sun, but I can't for fear of getting a mouthful of insects. Lee's the only photographer on the Gazette, and he has worked here for so long that the darkroom is his territory and his alone. So, he stores his fishing bait in here because his wife won't let him keep maggots at home. And when there's a power cut and the electricity goes off – as it did yesterday – the freezer defrosts and the maggots become flies. The only reason Mr Locke doesn't fire him for it is because Mr

Locke never finds out, because some poor sod – usually me – gets called in to man the flyswatter while Lee props the front door open and raids the cupboards for fly strips.

Within fifteen minutes, most of the flies are dead or have escaped out of the front door, and Lee and I are in hysterics. Christ knows what the people in the flat opposite must think!

"Over the Moon at half five, then, boy?" he calls as I ascend the stairs. I just laugh and nod and shudder as a rogue fly buzzes past my ear. *It's okay, it's Friday,* I tell myself again. *It's Friday. I'm over the moon.* Then I open the door.

Nia, 2022.

Matt tells me to wait in the bar for an hour until his shift finishes. I protest – the tide will have turned by then, and I don't fancy the coastal path when it's getting dark, but he says he'll shout me dinner and drop me home.

That's the difficult thing with Matt to this day – he's a lovely guy, he really is, and he'll make someone an amazing husband … just not me. I love him – he is my best friend – but I don't love him like that. I mean, I'm not *in love* with him. Or anyone. I've had the odd crush, growing up, and I've been out with a few guys – and I'm definitely not gay, or bi-curious, or anything – but after a couple of weeks, I don't want to do the sex thing. I don't like it, don't enjoy it, don't understand what all the fuss is about. I recently heard the terms *asexual* and *aromantic*, and I think that might be me. I tried talking about it with a guy once, but he just called me frigid, and dumped me.

Anyway, eventually, Matt finds me out on the terrace, and pulls a chair round close to me. The chat of the tourists at the tables around us blurs into white noise; all I register are the cries of the gulls, and the occasional crack of a gun somewhere in Lympstone Commando. I smile, but automatically shift my chair back a bit. He drops his head and gives a tight laugh. He's ordered us both a burger and chips. He tells me that mine's a veggie burger, and it's so sweet that he's remembered, that I don't correct him and drop the vegan bomb. I'll just have to suck this one up for old time's sake, especially after the chair thing. I say a silent *sorry* to the cows.

"Well, if you've got the food, I'll get the drinks in," I say, standing, but Matt grabs my hand and sits me back down.

"Don't be silly!" he says. "This is my treat. Also, I get a massive staff discount. What are you having?"

I hate it when men ask me what I want to drink. I always feel like I should have wine or a bottle of fruity cider or, if it's summer, Pimm's or a cocktail. The thing is, I get really thirsty. I've been tested for diabetes and everything, but the doctor reckons it's a side effect of my meds. I'm thinking about that pint of San Miguel I wanted from the beach bar earlier. If I'd have bought one there, it would have come in a plastic glass. If I get one here, it should be in a nice, cold, proper pint glass. And this is Matt, my friend forever, the person who knows me better than anyone else in the world. If I can't be myself with him, then there's no hope. Ha! There's an irony! And it's such a beautiful day. And I'm 38 – I can drink what I want. "I'll have a San Miguel, then, please!" I say, and Matt nods and dashes off to the bar to get our drinks before our food arrives.

He's gone for ages, so presumably there's a queue at the bar and he's stepped in to help. When he returns, he's looking flustered and hot. He's carrying a pint and a half-pint of lager. He smiles and places the half-pint in front of me. It's in a plastic glass. I shoot Matt a quizzical look. "I know the West Country is the arse end of England, but I had thought glass had made it down here!"

"Oh, yeah, I know." Matt looks embarrassed. "We're not allowed to serve drinks in proper glasses outside the bar area. It can get a bit rowdy here of an evening," he says.

"Don't worry about it – I saw a load of riot vans heading for Orcombe Point earlier. I guess it's people having parties on the beach down there, and there can't be much going on up here of an evening," I say, looking around. There's a little shop, a toilet block, and a couple of kids' play areas, but that's about it. If you have young kids, I guess it's the South Beach Café until bedtime becomes unavoidable, or bust.

The squaddies let off another rat-a-tat-tat of – presumably – blanks, and the juvenile gull picking the remnants of a meal on a table just down from us takes flight. Matt doesn't bat an eyelid. I guess you become habituated to it. Our food arrives, and I select a nice, fat chip and dunk it in tomato sauce. "It's funny, isn't it?" I comment, waving the chip around, not looking for an answer. "We're sitting here all relaxed with a beer and a burger, and one of those guys could have lined us up in his sights. They could just pick us off, right now – boom! – and that would be it."

"Yeah, but they are here to protect and defend us," Matt replies, snorting into his pint. "It's their job. I think killing off tourists would be frowned upon in military circles. In most circles, actually."

"Yeah, but they could say it was an accident. It must happen all the time."

"And why would anyone want to bump you off?"

"I don't know. Because they can?" I pause and drain my glass. "You know if you apply to be an RSPCA officer, one of the last things you have to do to qualify is shoot a cow. Maybe it's like that. Just to see if you are able to do it if and when the time comes." My eyes flick to Matt, whose own are wide and incredulous.

"Seriously?" he says. "They seriously make you kill a cow? Like, look it in the eye and shoot it dead?"

"Yeah," I return, with an emphasis that suggests even to me that I think I might have made this up. "They take you to a slaughterhouse, get a cow off a truck – you know, one that's about to be killed anyway – and make you shoot it. It's fucking hardcore." I twist my empty glass on the table. "But it's a better outcome for the cow, though. Imagine what it feels like to walk into an abattoir …"

Matt picks up his burger, looks at it, drops it back onto his plate and pushes it away.

"I see your outlook on life hasn't changed much in … however long it's been!" Matt laughs. I bet he knows exactly how long it's been, possibly down to the hour. He swigs his beer, swills it about and drains it. "Having another?" he asks, standing. I nod and smile.

"A proper one this time, if you don't mind!" I wink at him. His face lights up, and he springs away off to the bar. Bloody hell. What on earth possessed me to wink?

Simon, 1984.

Geoff Kerslake. The name rings a bell. I mean, both names are common enough around here, but I'm sure I know him – or know of him – from somewhere. I'm sitting in my armchair, by the window that looks out over the station, marvelling again that the guy who owns the cafe downstairs rented out a flat with a sea view for next to nothing. It's Saturday afternoon, and I've just got back from work. I quite like working Saturday mornings, just me and Trish bumbling round the office taking a few calls, going through the press releases, doing a bit of editing and tidying up. Mickey does the sports reports, but he just pops into the office after the football to type things up. Then on Monday, we all work like stink to meet the Plymouth deadline, the paper's out on Tuesday, and everything starts again.

Saturdays have always felt a bit magical to me – I suppose because of the promise of Saturday night; not that I ever go out. But I hear the good folk of Swansbourne in the streets, going from pub to pub, getting chips on the way home, talking, laughing, crying. Sometimes I turn the lights off and watch them all from the crack in my curtains.

Mostly, I want to be them, but when I'm having a bad day, I remember that Saturday night when I was out with Charlotte in Winchester. She'd seemed a bit distracted, twiddling the stem of her wine glass but never sipping from it, smiling and saying *yeah* in the wrong places because she hadn't been listening, and then when I came back from the bar with another round, she wasn't at our table. I presumed she'd gone to the loo; I presumed she'd gone to the loo and got chatting to someone, like women do; I presumed she'd got chatting to someone and they'd asked her to meet their friend, or something; and I finished my second cigarette, left our drinks at the table, and walked round the pub, and she wasn't there, and I shouted through the door of the ladies, but she wasn't there either according to the group of girls who were comparing lipsticks, and I went in the beer garden, but she wasn't there, and I went outside and up and down the street, but Charlotte had disappeared off the face of the earth. None of my so-called friends had seen her, and they gave me that pitying look, slapped me on the back and told me to forget about the bitch and come and have a few beers with them. I told them to fuck off. My best mate, Dave, came up to me at that, and took me off to the bar. He told me I was better off out of it, that Charlotte had never been right for me, and he ordered us Pernod and blacks. And when we'd had a few, and had started talking about football, and work, and stupid things that we'd done at school, he said *I know how it feels, Si, I really do, but she was always waaayy out of your league; her mum dropping her off in that Porsche 944! And there's you and your dad in that Rover! He's still driving it now, isn't he?! It was never going to happen, Si; not in a million!* His mouth laughed while his eyes did something else, and he slapped me on the back again, and even though I could see that he was trying to comfort me, thought he was being a good mate, I felt like punching his lights out. And then when I found out what had really been happening, and I went round with the express purpose of punching his lights out, he'd disappeared, too.

Consequentially, I'm reading the paper and watching the trains and the seagulls, with *The A-Team* theme tune just starting up on the telly, in a flat that smells of fish and chips. In fact, this week's *Swansbourne Gazette* will probably be wrapped around someone's cone of chips later this evening. Geoff Kerslake. The story died – all that became of it was a couple of paragraphs in the Obits. Poor bloke. So much for interesting news happening in Eskwich. The YTS lad, Steve, delighted in taking the piss out of me. Although, you could write a bloody saga on why someone topped themselves. Funny, what makes the news.

Nia, 2022.

Me and Matt sit and chat, and watch the sea and the tourists, and it's so easy to be with him, that I can't stop smiling. It's like we pick up where we left off, and the forgiveness we feel to each other floats around us, unsaid but present, with no hurt attached. Matt's my best friend;

he's always been my best friend, and I've missed him. I want to hug him, but I know he'd misinterpret it.

"I'm so sorry about your mum, Nia," he says, when there's a pause.

I just smile, in a sad kind of way. "So am I. I should have visited more, but I just couldn't, you know? It's so ironic. I never knew my dad, but his absence made him more there than if he had actually physically been there, if that makes sense. And lovely as Mum was, I *knew* she knew more about him disappearing than she let on. And it was just so frustrating living with her with all her lying – and before you interrupt me, yes, refusing to tell someone the truth, for whatever bloody noble reason you might have, is lying! Ugh!"

The familiar anger rises in me again, and Matt reaches out and touches my arm for the briefest of moments. I flick my gaze to meet his eyes, and there's something in them that I can't read. I ought to say, *you look like you want to say something* as a prompt, because he does, but my anger gets in the way and the moment passes. Matt drives me all the way back to Exeter, and says he'll pick me up on his way through to see his mum tomorrow. She'd love to see me, he says, grinning. "And you can give me the tour of Esky, too, if you like," I smile. "Have they got the internet there, yet?"

"Cheeky cow," Matt laughs. "There's a McDonald's now, so I'll treat you to lunch, if you like!"

"Ooh, I'll put my best dress on!"

And with that, I get out of the car, unlock the front door, and stand there watching and waving until his car disappears round the corner.

The next day, Matt makes good on the tour of Eskwich, including all our old haunts. By eleven, we're up by the canal, killing time, psyching ourselves up for the visit to Matt's mum's.

Matt takes his vape out of his pocket and drags on it. The air's so still that when he exhales, he cocoons us in a cloud of sweet-smelling smoke. Ordinarily, I would have made a fuss and flapped it away, but today, I take a deep breath in. "Remember when we used to sit here and smoke Marlboro Lights before youth club?"

Matt shoots me a tight smile. "Ha! Yeah, course I do." He turns to face me, but I refuse to take my eyes off the greenish water. In my peripheral vision, I see him open his mouth to say something, but he decides better of it and takes another drag. Things unsaid cloud around us, like the smoke.

Dropping my eyes to the tow path, I reach down and scoop up a handful of red gravel. I examine it, rolling it round in my palm with my thumb. Then I pick out the biggest stones and chuck them one at a time into the canal and watch the ever-expanding circles of ripples.

Matt scoots closer to me on the bench, throws his right arm round my shoulder, and gives me a dead leg with his left. "You know I love you, Nia," he smiles. I can't bear this. I screw my face up and punch his arm.

"Ooh, you've been practising!"

"Fuck off!"

I inch out of his embrace, and the moment of mirth is over in a nanosecond. We sit silent for a second. Then, very quietly, Matt says, "I remember the time we came here after you had that big row with your mum." The silence that follows builds painfully, but just when the pressure subsides and I think the moment's passed, Matt adds, "And the night you ran away." He's not looking at me. He's watching his trainers make patterns in the ruddy gravel.

In spite of myself, I tense up. I know he's noticed. Matt flicks his eyes to the side, silently urging me to speak. A man with tattooed legs cycles past, his dog trotting alongside. The dog tries to stop and sniff at my hands, but his lead drags him away. I throw the remaining dirt into the stagnant water and smile at Matt. "None of it ever brought my dad back, though, did it? And this isn't either. Come on." I get up off the tree-stump bench, step clear of the vape smoke, and stride off down the path.

It's a short walk to Matt's mum's house. We reach the canal basin in a couple of minutes, then turn down onto Canal Hill, and then first right on The Avenue, which is no longer an avenue, because the council have cut down the tall pines and oaks that once lined it, to make way for these random *Grand Designs*-type places. In fact, with the exception of the dilapidated – but still beautiful – old police station, The Avenue looks like any other posh street in Eskwich. At my anger-driven pace, we're at Misty's in no time. She rents out the top floor of their once-grand Victorian house, to Danny – one of Matt's railway mates – who I'm hoping isn't in, or they'll be up there on his model railway together shooting YouTube videos for the rest of the day. They have their own channel, and it's doing pretty well – Matt says they've got nearly a million subscribers! Hats off, but I don't see the attraction of fiddling about making a miniature world and then sitting there watching trains go round and round. It's no wonder Danny wears glasses. When I'm with them, I just let my eyes go out of focus and my mind wander, which isn't a good thing, these days. I'm either dwelling on my dad, or on the fact that we're all in our late thirties now, and are still living our lives like we've just turned 20. Danny jokes about it, calling me and Matt *perpetual students*, which annoys me, especially when he's the one renting rooms in his mate's mum's place; but then he has got a kid, so maybe it's fair enough. And to be honest, it's a relief to be talking about something trivial.

Matt has a key, but he always knocks loudly on the front door before opening it and calling *hello* down the hall.

"Oh, Matthew, how many times?! You don't have to do that! This is still your home – it always will be!" Misty dashes out of the kitchen to greet us, followed by the tall, lolloping figure of Danny. Bloody hell. He grins at us from under his mop of shiny black hair, waving a slab of what looks like chocolate cake. He's not wearing his glasses. Maybe he got contacts.

"Good timing, mate!" he says with his mouth full. "Your mum's just done some brownies!"

Now he's said it, I can smell the warm, rich aroma emanating from the kitchen, and Misty, Matt and I kind of drift towards it.

Matt makes coffee, and Misty sits back down and gestures us to help ourselves. Danny shoots out a skinny, tattooed arm and grabs another – the biggest one on the plate. Misty rolls her eyes at me, and all I feel is a surge of embarrassment. She must notice, because she says, "So, what brings you two here on a Tuesday afternoon?" She says it over-brightly, a flutter of a smile passing across her face. It dawns on me that she thinks Matt and I have come round to announce our engagement. Bloody hell!

Matt sits down, pulling his chair closer to Danny's, making an unsaid point. Then, out of the blue, he says, "Actually, Mum, I wanted to ask you why you always used to tell me not to go into the woods at Dad's."

Simon, 1984.

I'm standing in the space between two coaches wondering why the train's stopped. The conductor's just announced that we're pulling into St David's, and I just saw by the fact that we passed the industrial estate and the abattoir that we are pulling into St David's, so I immediately pulled on my Stetson, grabbed my holdall, and, knowing the platform would be on the left, I'd made for the door. And now we've stopped. We never stop here. I glance at my watch. I'm going to miss the bus in a minute!

It was Mickey's idea. He said that it would probably be quicker for me to jump off the train at Exeter, because the 55B stops right outside the station. It would save waiting in St David's for ages before going on to Eskwich and again waiting ages for a connecting bus to fiddle round all the country lanes on its journey into town. If we don't move in a minute, I'm going to have to sit back down and go on to Eskwich anyway!

I look out of the window over the roofs of the terraced houses below the railway line and gaze over the city to where the green wavy line of hills meet the hazy blue sky. The picture seems faint again. I take off my glasses, wipe them on my jacket and put them back on. No difference. Maybe I ought to make an appointment with the optician. Crackled words spit out of the Tannoy. There's congestion at the station, and we have to wait for a platform to become available. It's already hot, especially standing by the window. I remove my hat and lean my head back against the coach wall. I take a deep breath. Today's going to be a scorcher, according to the weather girl, the humidity oppressive. My palms are sweating and my heart's racing. Again. This tends to happen on a Monday morning, because it's the busiest and most important day of the week. I feel the tension building in me from about midday on Sunday. And I can't be late, because most of the guys on the newsdesk hate me enough already. Straight out of university with a first-class degree in English, straight out of *Winchester* university with a first-class degree in English, straight out of *Winchester.* The other reporters – with the exception of Heather and Trish – chose their careers by picking a YTS scheme out of a hat when they finished school, and their parents told them they either got a job or moved out. And there's me, headhunted and straight in as chief reporter. *Bloody hell, Si – get a grip on yourself.* Today is a bad day.

I remove my glasses again – they're sliding down my nose anyway – close my eyes and allow my head to flop to the left. When I open them, I'm staring into the upstairs window of one of the houses. It's oblong with pale blue curtains. Before I can look away, a girl with long, dark, curly hair rips open the curtains and shrugs off her quilt. She kneels on her pillow, which is right up against the glass, and shoves open the small top bit of the window. She stays like that, kneeling on her pillow, with her arms on the window catch. She's wearing a crop top and cut-off jean shorts. When I bring my eyes back to her face, she's grinning at me. I feel the rush of shame, my cheeks burn; I avert my gaze, but only for a second. I can't help looking back. She's smiling – she knows what I'm feeling. I put my Stetson back on my head and raise it to her. She laughs. I laugh. There's a jolt, and I stumble, and she laughs again, while I just want the floor to swallow me up, and my train eases its away into St David's. Suddenly panicked, we hold eye contact until the light's wrong on her window, and then I'm left bereft.

Nia, 2022.

It wasn't until I started school properly that I realised everyone else had a daddy. I suppose it was because I was always with Mum, or with Matt and his mum, or at playgroup; and at playgroup it was just mums with their children, and the two ladies who ran it – all the dads were either working, down the Job Centre, or sitting at home in front of the TV waiting for the pubs to open. In the 80s, raising children was still very much women's work.

Our teacher, Mrs Hamer, put the grey-topped desks together, sat us all around the outside, and bunged a load of coloured tissue paper, Pritt Sticks, crayons and pictures of animals and rainbows and the like that had been cut out of magazines, in the middle. She put a folded piece of card in front of us and told us we were all going to make Father's Day cards for our daddies. I remember feeling very confused and very sad, because everyone else had enthusiastically grabbed handfuls of stuff and were busily fighting over glue sticks, and I had no one to make a card for. I sat there and watched them. Amid the chaos, my teacher came over and asked me why I hadn't started, and if she could help me think of an idea. She selected a cartoon drawing of a lion and said maybe I could make jungle leaves out of the green tissue paper. I said, *lions don't live in the jungle,* and *I haven't got a daddy.* Then I cried, and she took me off and gave me a cup of Kia-Ora and a cow biscuit.

Mrs Hamer escorted me out to meet my mum after school, instead of letting me join the free-for-all in the playground like usual. I remember being annoyed, because it meant I couldn't splash in the puddles with Matt, or get a sneaky climb of the scramble net, and I remember the concern on Mum's face as we approached her. Mum held my hand while Mrs Hamer spoke softly to her so I couldn't hear what she was saying. Mum smiled, but not in a happy way, and when we got home, she took my coat off, took my packed lunch box out of my school bag, put the TV on for me and went off into the kitchen to get me a snack and a cup of tea for her, like nothing was different. Except I felt that things were very different, and that Mum wasn't in a good mood.

I climbed down off our pin-stripey sofa and wandered out into the kitchen. Mum had the backdoor open and was lighting a cigarette off the hob. "Mummy," I said, "how come I don't have a daddy?"

Mum pulled back from the hob, the tip of her cigarette glowing red, and moved over by the backdoor. She always said she couldn't stand people smoking indoors – it made their clothes smell, which I always thought was funny, because her clothes always smelled of smoke, but I didn't say anything.

She smiled at me. "Mummy, are you sad?" I asked. A little sob escaped her, and she crouched down, her arms open for a cuddle. I ran into them and hugged her, but she only hugged me with one arm, because she was still holding the cigarette and didn't want to burn me, I supposed. We stayed like that for a while. I could have hugged her forever. She was warm, and she smelled mainly of Pears Soap. "Oh, Nia, you're freezing!" she said, rubbing my goose-pimpled arms and pushing me back into the kitchen and away from the wind and rain blowing in through the open door. "Let me finish this, then I'll tell you about your daddy. I've got a photo of him somewhere. Then we'll have sausage, chips and beans for tea – does that sound like a good idea?"

"Can we have custard afterwards?"

Mum laughed. She made custard from scratch, whatever that meant, and used to go mad because the powder always went everywhere. "Yes, all right, we'll have custard," she said, smiling. I skipped back into the front room to watch *James the Cat*.

Mum shut the door and came and sat and watched the end of *James the Cat* with me. She was cold, and smelled of smoke and rain. When the programme had finished, she got up and switched the telly off. We sat smiling at each other on the sofa for a bit, and then she came closer and put her arm around me.

"I haven't said much about your daddy, Nia, because I didn't know him for very long, and he disappeared before you were born …"

"What do you mean, he disappeared? Like magic?"

Mum smiled sadly at my gesture of magic – making a little poof of air with my hands. "Kind of," she said. "A very sad sort of magic. The police tried to find him, and everyone was looking for him, but he just sort of disappeared off the face of the earth."

"Why?"

"I don't know, NiNi. I don't know. Sometimes bad things happen and we don't know why. But we still have each other, don't we?"

I can't remember what happened next – it must have been all too much for me to deal with at 5 years old. Mum might have put the telly on, and we probably watched

Button Moon together, like we usually did. We definitely would have had the custard.

Years later, I saw the photo. I'd been reading in my room – I think it was *The Whispering Statue,* my favourite Nancy Drew book – and I heard a weird noise. I tiptoed out of my room, across the tiny hall. Mum's bedroom door was ajar, and I pushed it a bit further open, hoping she wouldn't hear the sound of the wood across the carpet. If she did, she didn't turn round. Her shoulders were shaking, and I thought for a minute that she had hiccups, but then she let out a sob, rummaged up her sleeve, pulled out a tissue and blew her nose. As she did so, a thick book with a shiny green cover fell from her lap to the floor. The thud of it landing made me jump, and Mum spun round, her eyes puffy and red, the irises watery blue.

I'd never seen Mum cry before. She wiped at her wet face with her hands, but they were trembling, and she sobbed again, and turned away. In tears myself, by now, I crawled up onto the bed and wrapped my arms around her. She tried to laugh, but she sobbed again, her face cool and salty on mine. I was crying hard, and she flipped into mum-mode, dried her face on her sleeve, patted at my tears with her other sleeve, and stroked my hair, until we'd both calmed down. I felt sleepy, but Mum said, "I was crying because it would have been your dad's birthday today, and I'd been looking at some old photos. Would you like to see them?"

Mum picked up the glossy album and started turning the pages reverently. I snuggled close to her on the bed, and saw prints of her as a child, of me as a baby, of much-loved pets now deceased. There were even a few of her and Matt's mum in gardens, babies and glasses of wine in hand. I laughed at the disgusting wallpaper and carpets, at their silly long collars and flared trousers, and marvelled at how pretty my mum had been, which made her laugh in turn.

We got to the last page, and she still hadn't pointed out my dad. I started crying again, but she pulled back the brittle film that covered the photos and pulled one out from behind the one of her holding me, just after I'd been born.

It was of a tall man on a beach. I recognised the cliff in the background as Orcombe Point. The man was wearing a dark grey cowboy hat, but you could see bright orange curls poking out from under it. He had a pale face with muddy green eyes and a small, nervous smile. The man wore a shirt, and smart trousers, over which was a very long dark coat. The way it billowed out in the evident gale that had been blowing that day, it looked more like a cloak. He had weird, but very cool ankle-boot shoes. Something about him reminded me of Inspector Gadget.

"He looks like Inspector Gadget," I told my mum. She laughed.

"It's funny you should say that, NiNi. His friends used to call him Agent Orange!"

"Agent Orange? Like secret agent? Wow! Was he a secret agent, like James Bond?"

Again, Mum laughed. "No, NiNi, nothing as exciting as that! Your dad was a journalist. His name was Simon." Mum put the photo back in the album. Something told me I shouldn't ask her why she kept it hidden.

"Simon." I rolled the word around in my mouth. It sounded like a good, strong name. "What's a journalist?"

"A journalist is someone who finds out the news, and writes the articles in the newspapers." Mum stood up and kind of ushered me downstairs. She wanted a coffee or a cigarette. Probably both.

Halfway down the stairs, something occurred to me. "I've got some news!" I exclaimed.

Mum shot me an enquiring, amused smile. "My apple pip has come up!"

"Come up? What do you mean? Has it got leaves?" Mum filled the kettle by letting the tap run into its spout.

"Yeah!" I said.

"Ah. It's *sprouted*," said Mum.

"'Sprouted'," I echoed. "My apple pip has sprouted and it's going to be a tree soon! Can that be in the paper?" I nodded my head as Mum waved the Kia-Ora bottle. She smiled.

"No, NiNi," she said kindly. "That's not a story for the newspaper. It's important news to us, but not to everyone else."

"Why not?! Trees are important. Paper is made out of trees, and birds live in them, and me and Matt like climbing them. Trees are very important. And they should be in the news." I stamped my foot, but took the beaker from Mum and had a long drink. Crying makes you thirsty.

"Ah. You may think so, but you're not the editor," said Mum, unlocking the back door and pushing it open. She went to the cooker and turned the gas on. I hated the smell, but loved the whoofing noise it made when it turned into flame.

"What's a editor?"

"*An* editor is the person who decides what news stories go in the paper." Mum took a hard pull on her cigarette and stared into our yard. Mould was creeping up the whitewashed walls again, and the snowdrops in the plant pot were turning brown. We heard the sort of hiss of the rails that told us a train was on its way, and the black cat that had been skulking along the top of our wall dashed over to the shed, jumped down and hid in my old Wendy house as the HST shot by.

"So *an* editor decides what the news is?"

"Yes."

"Well, I'm going to be an editor when I grow up so I can tell people about trees!"

Simon, 1984.

When you open the door to the newsdesk in the morning, the air is stale with the previous day's cigarette smoke. If I'm the first reporter in, which is most of the time – Derek always opens up, although I don't know what he does when he gets there – I always push the sash windows up as far as they'll go to try to get some fresh air in. The cleaners come in at about six every evening and empty the ashtrays and hoover and stuff, and I presume they open the windows too, but they can't be in there for any more than half an hour, and that's just not enough to clear eight hours of eight people chain-smoking. And I'm one of them – the worst, according to some, because I smoke Panamas. Panama cigars. You can think with a cigar. You can puff and contemplate, and when you've finished contemplating, you just light the thing up again. I tried cigarettes, but they just burn away, and it was costing me a bloody fortune. Nevertheless, I do my bit and try to fumigate the workplace every morning.

When I turned up on my first day, Marie showed me up to newsdesk. I'd been really nervous, walking into the bright, clean reception – it was noisy with typewriters clacking, phones ringing and people talking, but Marie's warm smile put me at ease. She noticed that I was trembling – I'd had to walk up and down Bampton Street twice before I'd felt able to come in and introduce myself – and I'd said I could do with a smoke, and she'd joked that I wouldn't need to smoke my own when I got up to News Desk; that the air in there was more nicotine than oxygen.

She was right. The ceiling was – and still is – yellow with tar. Not a sort of off-cream – actually yellow. There's an advert on the telly – Superman saying don't smoke cigarettes – but what can you do when you grow up going to the sweet shop buying chocolate cigarettes with your pocket money, and when every adult you come into contact with is doing it? Also, I love it when I get a new packet of Panama. There's something soft and light about the burgundy box, and I love the crisp sound when you pop up the top and break the gold paper that keeps them fresh. It's comforting to have something to twiddle in your hand when you're on the phone to someone who won't stop talking, and it's a good excuse to take a break – you can have a coffee at your desk, but you're allowed outside for a cigarette break, even though you can smoke at your desk anyway. The cigarette break is like a human right, like going to the loo.

But my cigars are a thousand times worse than Lambert and Butler, apparently. Still, I like them, and I'm not going to stop smoking them. They're part of my self-image – my mates in Winchester used to say I had a 'Hemingway complex', and smoking cigars and drinking Scotch and soda is part of that, but, obviously, you can't drink Scotch at work. Unless you're the editor. And these thoughts bring the image of Geoff Kerslake's bottle of spirits, lying by the tree.

Geoff Kerslake is haunting me. Not literally, but I can't stop thinking that there is more to his suicide than alcoholism and breaking up with his wife, which has become the accepted conclusion. I contacted the ex-Mrs Kerslake to see if she wanted to give her version of events, but all I got from her was that although it was sad that Geoff had died, her life had been a whole lot better without him in it, and she was giving the insurance payments, along with the pension she was legally entitled to (when it came through), to their children who needed the money more than her – as Mrs Barton (she was already engaged to the man she'd been seeing behind his back) she'd never want for anything again, and in any case, she couldn't stand Geoff and thought that the world was a better place without him in it.

A cool breeze blows in through the open windows, and feeling a little chilled, I leave my desk, fill the kettle, and put two heaped spoonfuls of Maxwell House in the stripy mug someone had got from collecting tokens at a petrol station. I could really do with being given free crockery and glasses; I could really do with a car of my own. I'd call it Claryannabel, after Thomas the Tank Engine's coaches. As I stir my coffee, I try to work out how much I can save from how many pay cheques to be able to afford the second-hand yellow Metro City I saw in the paper last week.

The phone on my desk rings, startling me out of my reverie, and I dart across the room to answer it, slopping hot coffee over my hand in the process. Plonking the mug on the desk, and shaking the liquid from my right hand, I snatch up the receiver with my left. All calls came through the switchboard, so I answer with "Good morning, newsdesk?"

The crackling noise of a mouthpiece being covered with someone's hand comes down the line, so I wait a moment before repeating my greeting. Someone – I think a woman – starts to speak, then there's a sharp intake of breath and mumbling from the background. A chill runs through me. "Hello? This is Simon Hulme, chief reporter. Can I help you?"

There was no response, so on autopilot I asked, "Are you okay? Do you need help?"

More shuffling and crackling, and the woman said, "Umm, something's happened but …"

Then the line goes dead.

I press the button that the handset rests on a few times, in the hopes I can re-establish the connection, but it's to no avail. I sit at my desk and try to think, but I'm shivering, so I get up and close all the windows. I considered calling the police, but what would I tell them? That someone had called, there had been a kerfuffle at the end of the line, and then they'd hung up? Tracing calls was something for MI5, wasn't it?

"Ah, our illustrious chief reporter has done so much work this morning that he's on a coffee break already!" Derek Locke, the editor ,sweeps out of his smoky office at the far end of the room, like an overweight Dracula emerging from the Carpathian mist. He makes me jump, which makes him laugh, so he stalks over and slaps me on the back. "No cause for alarm, Shirley, no cause for alarm!" I smile, silently cursing myself for not having even put a sheet of paper in my typewriter. "Interesting call, was it?" he asks, pushing his thick NHS spectacles back up his nose. Derek has what he calls 'oily skin', but it's more than that. Everything about him is greasy, from his thinning steel grey hair to the sweat patches that are already soaking through his pale blue C&A shirt. It's like he hauls himself out of a deep fat fryer every morning, and I can feel the faintly smelling heat radiating off him. It makes me shudder.

My gut instinct is to tell him it was a wrong number, but if he heard the ring, he probably heard my half of the conversation, and if he catches me lying to him, he'll never trust me again. I mentally berate myself for my paranoia.

"Yes, it was odd, actually," I admit. "A woman wanted to tell me something, but then there was a kerfuffle, and she was cut off. I was wondering if I should call the police ...". I let the sentence hang, so Derek can bask in my evident reverence for his opinion; and bask he does.

Puffing out his chest and rocking back and forth on his toes like a cartoon police officer, he says, "Hmm. Sounds like a domestic to me. Bitter wives wanting to get one over on their husbands – it happens all the time. I'd let it go if I were you. If things are serious, she'll call 999, not newsdesk!" He pauses. "Your coffee's getting a skin on it. You can bring one into me when you make another. And if you could try to speak to Tom Forde about the brewery closure again today, it would be greatly appreciated. The blue-collars of Eskwich deserve to know where they stand." And with that, he skulks back into his office, closing the door behind him.

There hasn't been a fly disaster for a couple weeks, but Lee catches me on my way out of the office this evening and asks me to come for a pint in the Moon. Much as I like him, I'm really not in the mood. All I want to do is get home and relax with a plate of fish and chips and a cup of tea in front of the telly. I've got my routine of walking, bus, train, walking, and as long as there are no leaves on the line, my journey home each night is pretty painless. 'Going for a quick pint', however, means having to stay in the pub for at least three, a long, cold wait at the bus station, and the stress of missing the train back to Swansbourne. Everyone else could just stumble home in ten minutes. However, I haven't been able to shake the woman's call – or Derek's reaction – from my mind all day, and Lee seems to know everyone in Devon. He's also one of the few people I … no, he's probably the *only* person I trust. I sigh and acquiesce, pushing down my worries about getting home. My stomach cramps in protest.

I know I'm going to have to find a place in Eskwich if I'm going to continue working on the Gazette. It's not just for ease of travel, either. It's becoming ever more apparent that a local journalist does better than an outsider coming in. Mickey, Trish and Lee are Eskwich born and bred, which means they've been to school with most of the people who are making news in the area. People like them, trust them, and are infinitely more inclined to tell them about upcoming events, or little issues with the council. Heather and I don't have those connections, although Heather has the advantage of being an attractive woman, while I'm just a posh ginger bloke in a hat. But the hat and the coat are as much a part of me as the cigars and the battered paperback of *The Sun Also Rises* that I keep in my holdall. And part of me is defiant – I shouldn't have to change myself to try to fit in, just to keep what is almost certainly a dead-end job. The only way Derek Locke is going to leave the building is in a box.

Lee and I make our way over the road, through the market precinct and the car park and in through the muddy brown double doors of the Half Moon. As the name of the pub suggests, the bar area constitutes a slivered half of the elliptical building which acts like border control between the market and the high street. On each side of the pub, a narrow, covered alley leads onto Fore Street – the main shopping area, with Tesco, Boots, Woolworths and WHSmith, the cinema and just off to the right, and down Phoenix Lane, the bus station. The town hall marks the end point, and from there you drop down to the River Esk, cross the bridge and are in Westesk, which is kind of a mini second part of town where you can find a newsagents, the funeral directors, a butchers, a bakers and the bike shop. If you turn left when you come out of the alley, you get to a fork in the road. Up the hill and left again is Bampton Street where the Gazette office is, or down Gold Street, which other than the department store, Eastmonds, and the dingy but massive shop that sells quite literally everything under the sun, Buy and Save (or 'Buy and Scav', if you're local), bijou independent shops take you down to the road bridge over the River Esk, which runs under the road and out the other side, where, for some reason clearly only known to the locals, it is then known as the river Loman.

Beyond this is the path that used to be a railway line, and then come the residential areas. Normal rules don't apply in the countryside.

Anyway, the windows of the Half Moon wrap around the bar, giving you a view of everything that's going on in the market, and at this time on a late spring evening, that means quite a lot. The traders who hold stalls in the pannier building are beginning to pack up, making last-minute sales of fruit and veg, cheap clothing and second-hand goods to the workers coming out of their offices and shops. Some people are hurrying to the bus stop – I would usually be among them – some are wandering about deciding which pub to fall into. Now that the shops are shut and the waitresses are bringing in the plastic chairs and tables of the market cafe, the car parks are emptying, and the parking area on the right-hand side of the pub has become an impatient line of traffic as people manoeuvre their vehicles around the market traders' vans and stacks of cardboard boxes. A group of teenagers, still in their Eskwich School uniforms, are loitering about by the picnic benches outside the pub, and I watch as one of their friends – a girl with Cyndi Lauper hair, her school shirt untucked from her tight, black skirt, saunters over to them waving a packet of B&H, and they all cheer. One of them produces a box of matches, and I watch them pretending they all know how to smoke because they've been doing it since they were 11, and smile nostalgically as one of the lads tries and fails to suppress a cough.

"Are you going to try a pint this evening, Si, or is it whiskey and soda again?"

I smile. "Always a whiskey and soda, please, Lee," I reply. Ordinarily, he'd chuckle, walk off to the bar and come back about fifteen minutes later with our drinks because he'd inevitably get chatting to someone, but tonight, he raises his eyebrows and gives me a tight smile.

"I can't even interest you in a Foxy Forde's?" I must have pulled a face because he laughs and says "Fair enough, boy, fair enough! Just trying support the boys at the brewery, that's all."

There's nothing malicious in it, but I take the hint. If Tom Forde's beer can't compete with Whitbread's, there'll be nothing to stop the takeover, and a load of late-middle-aged men who've never worked anywhere else will join the youngsters at the Job Centre, and what hope will they have? I'm about to call Lee back and tell him I'll try a pint of Foxy's and have the whiskey as a chaser, but the moment's passed, and anyway, just the thought of seeing the stuff run out of the pump like a frothy urine infection turns my stomach. Maybe Charlotte and Maggie Thatcher are right: if you don't have a popular enough product, that's your lookout. It's just business. Survival of the fittest, like anything else. I shake the thought away, remembering the footage of that policeman battering a striking Welsh miner on the news last night. These are human beings with families to support. Where are the jobs going to come from? I glance out of the window. The girl with the Cyndi Lauper hair is kissing one of the lads. Most of the others have wandered off, but one girl – presumably Cyndi's best mate – is scratching something into the table with the pointy end of the compass I presume she uses in maths. A lad who's just stumbled out of the bar whistles at her and she turns round. He's holding a half-empty pint of beer and a small glass of white wine. He looks older than me. He says something, and they wander off round the side of the pub and out of sight.

Lee's still chatting to the barmaid, so I light a cigar and look absently around the pub. A few groups of office workers, a couple of couples, and the odd person sitting glumly in front of several empty glasses. And a girl with long dark, curly hair, sitting on her own in the corner by the door to the toilets. She's staring at me.

Recognising the girl from somewhere, I smile politely and look away before I blush. I look at Lee, who's now got his back to me and is in deep conversation with the landlady, Mandy. I gaze wistfully at my drink, standing by itself on a green beer mat, and will Lee to finish his conversation and bring it over to me. His pint is halfway down already – he'll be needing a new one before I've even taken a sip of my whiskey. Leaving my cigar in the little metal ashtray, and my coat next to it on the circular table, I decide to go to the toilet. If Lee isn't back by the time I've come out, I'll just go and get it before Mandy thinks it's been abandoned and pours it away. The trouble with going to the loo is that I have to walk past the girl, and when I do so, she's still looking at me, a faint smile playing about her lips. She must have noticed me blush.

The mirror in the toilets of the Half Moon is unusually large, and unsurprisingly cracked. I pull my Stetson back down over my auburn curls. 'Auburn curls' – that's what my mum used to call them to make me feel better about myself at school when this kid in my class was bullying me. She said I should be proud of them; be proud to be different. It was a noble and just sentiment, but far easier said than done. She didn't have to cope with the teasing, the laughing, the comments, the fact that no girl would look twice at me. And here I am in Devon, of all places, still an outsider. It's bad enough being the posh bloke in this pub, without having to be the ginger one as well. I've not even made it to the door when I feel the hat spring back up. Sighing, I tug at it again, step through the door, and head straight for the bar, keeping my eyes fixed on it, pretending the girl with the dark hair isn't there.

Mickey and some of the other guys on newsdesk are here now, slumped in the comfortable armchairs around the big table by the window. As I reach the bar, I'm cringing at the loudness of their voices, and the fact that they're discussing the stories of the day in the middle of the second biggest pub in town. I squeeze in beside Lee, who shoots me a quick look of apology and something else, grab my drink, and down it. Then, trying to listen in on Lee's conversation, I prop my elbows on the sticky bar, wave a fiver at the teenaged bartender and sigh again, my every instinct screaming at me not to look around to see if the girl is still looking at me.

There's a touch on my arm. "Excuse me."

"Oh, I'm sorry!" I move out of the girl's way on autopilot.

"Oh, no, don't worry – I'm not in the queue!" It's the girl with the dark hair. She's standing very close to me, and, nice as it is, I'm wishing there's room at the bar for her to be at arm's length. She's smiling. We both know I'm blushing. But then, so is she. "It's just … well, I thought I recognised you," she says.

"You recognise me?" I don't know why I'm surprised. We both know I stick out like a sore thumb.

"Umm … yes," she says. "You're the guy from the train. I see you every morning." A pause. "It's your hat."

The hand that isn't holding the fiver shoots up to touch my hat. I almost take it off, but then I remember my hair, so I reach out and try to swig from my empty glass instead. The girl laughs, and so do I, even though I'm dying inside.

"I said, *same again, mate?*" A stick-thin, pizza-faced lad behind the bar – he's more than likely Mandy's son – is leering at me. I nod, and he whips the note out of my hand. "Anything for the lady?" he slings over his shoulder.

This is ridiculous. "This is ridiculous," I say, turning to the girl with a genuine, but slightly apologetic smile. "I'm Simon, I'm not from round here, I feel really out of place, but I'd like to buy you a drink. If you'd like one, of course. Would that be okay?"

The girl – Lucie, *with an I E* – holds her Chardonnay carefully by the stalk of the glass – a mannerism that brings me unwanted memories of Charlotte – and waits for me to lead her over to the table, where my cigar is waiting patiently for me. I can't resist raising my eyebrows and smirking at Mickey and the others, who are staring at me in disbelief. Steve, the YTS lad is there, a can of Coke strategically placed in front of him. His jaw nearly drops all the way to the grubby blue carpet.

"Thanks," Lucie repeats, sipping her wine. She's sitting on the stool opposite me, and it's not until she crosses her legs that I notice she's in the ripped denim hot pants I saw her in when my train carriage came to a halt outside her window all those weeks ago. In spite of the flirty posture, she seems nervous. She spins her glass round and round on the beer mat.

Before I've thought about it, I'm saying, "I'd offer you a cigarette, but I only smoke cigars." She stops the spinning and smiles, bashfully. "I mean, you're welcome to have one, if you like!" I add, thrusting the packet in front of her.

Lucie laughs. "Thanks, but I don't smoke," she says. "My mum died of cancer."

"Oh, God!" I say, looking in horror from the burgundy packet on the table to the smouldering Panama between my thumb and forefinger.

"Oh, I'm sorry! I didn't mean you shouldn't either! No, don't put it out!" She reaches across and pushes the hand that's holding the cigar away from the ashtray. Her touch makes me shiver. Her skin is very soft and very cold, and her vermillion nail varnish is chipped.

"Oh my goodness, you're freezing! Here, put my coat on." It's still on the table, so I slide it over to her. To my surprise, she actually does so, pulling it tightly against her body so it covers her bare legs. Her hands are lost in the sleeves, and she pushes one back so she can pick up her glass.

"Thanks." A shy smile. An awkward silence. She spins her glass again. "You said you're not from round here?"

"No, I'm from Winchester, originally," I reply, hesitantly.

I don't want her to think I'm posh, or condescending, or rich, or – well, I just don't want her to think badly of me. Instinct makes me go for honesty over my habitual vagueness. I'm painfully aware that the pause is too long, and as my mind scrabbles around for words to elaborate on that, Lucie says, "Wow! Winchester! I'd love to go there – it's supposed to be really nice! Posh, isn't it?" Her gaze flits between my eyes. "What on earth are you doing here?!"

I'm blushing. Again. "It's a long story," I begin, cringing at the cliché. She gives her drink a resigned smile which I catch, so I blurt out, "No! Really! It is a long story! My girlfriend got pregnant by another man – my best mate, actually – and I couldn't bear it, so I got a job on the *Swansbourne Gazette,* moved down there, and then one day, Derek – sorry, Mr Locke – he's the editor on the *Eskwich Gazette* – called and said he'd pay me more to work here, but I like my flat in Swansbourne – you know, it's by the sea – so I thought I'd get the train in every day, but I didn't realise that Eskwich Junction isn't actually in Eskwich …"

"So you're spending half your day travelling to and from work," Lucie finishes.

"Yes. That's about the size of it." I feel like an utter amateur. No wonder Charlotte chose Dave over me. Yet something's telling me I haven't blown this. I take a long drink and look at Lucie. Her hair is so long that it falls onto the table when she leans forward, which she does now, reaching for what's left of her wine. I picture Charlotte, with her light brown hair, sprayed into its chiffon, and her shoulder pads and stilettos. Lucie is naturally the prettiest girl I've ever seen. I ask her what she's doing in a pub on her own, then cringe at myself. Lucie just laughs.

"I'm looking after my nephew," she said. "Oh! He's not here now! I just pop in here on my way home. My family's from Eskwich originally, but I moved to Exeter, and my brother's out at Willand, you know, where Eskwich Junction is. He's got a 2-year-old, but he works all day, and his wife's just had a miscarriage so she's in hospital. I'm not working at the moment, so I drive in before Tony goes to work and look after Harley – that's my nephew – and then go home when he comes back. I thought it would only be for a couple of days, but Anna – Tony's wife – is in a pretty bad way in hospital." Lucie lowers her voice. "It's her head, you know? She can't stop crying. They think she's having a breakdown."

"Oh." I don't know whether to touch her outstretched hand in sympathy, and as I dither, I'm acutely aware of another awkward pause. "Oh. Oh no. I'm sorry to hear that." The words stumble out of my mouth, and I touch her hand. Her cold fingers give mine the subtlest of squeezes, and I can't help but break out in a smile.

"Oh, thanks," Lucie smiles back, "but don't be – it's not your fault!" She slowly pulls her hand out of mine and reaches for her empty glass, then blushes. My smile's fading, because something's telling me she's telling me something more than just her life story. She continues, staring at her glass, "Anyway, Harley's a bit of a handful – takes after his dad, I suppose! – so I come in here for a quick drink with my friend before I go home." I'm looking around for the friend, and Lucie nods in the direction of one of the couples I noticed when I came in. "She's over there," she says, raising her eyebrows, "having a deep and meaningful with her ex-boyfriend." We both laugh – they're snogging each other's faces off. "Look, it's a nice evening and it's stuffy in here – do you want to sit outside?"

"Well, this is a fine lads' night out, isn't it, Si?" Steve's skinny frame casts a line of shadow over the table. He smirks at me, so I glare back. I'm just about to say something about it being his bedtime, and that I came out for a drink with Lee, and not all the rest of them, when Lucie slips out of my coat and stands up.

"Oh, I'm sorry!" she says, cheeks ablaze. "I didn't mean to ruin your evening! I thought … I ought to be getting off now, anyway."

I scrabble to my feet, nearly knocking over my stool. "No! You haven't! Please, stay!" I beg her, but Lucie presses my coat into my hands, and is halfway to the double doors before I can get to her. She pulls one of the doors open, glances back at me and says, "It was lovely to meet you, Simon. Bye." And then she's gone.

"You fucking bastard!" I hiss at Steve, but he just shakes his head and stalks back to his mates, laughing. I dash across the room, and out through the doors and down the steps, but I'm too late – Lucie is out of sight. Rush hour has past, the market traders have packed up, and the stream of cars is no more. As I stand there on the steps, looking left and right, scanning the scene for her, a faded red Ford Fiesta speeds out of the bottom car park, heading out of the market and into town. A bloke is driving and there's a blonde girl in the passenger seat. Through the back window, I see a mass of tangled, dark, curly hair.

I walk dejectedly back inside the pub, shoot a hateful look at Steve, who's sprawled in an armchair, laughing with Mickey. The Coke remains untouched on their table, and Steve is now openly swigging a pint of something fizzy and amber. "She's waaay out of your league, Shirl," he slurs, grinning. "Poor maid couldn't get out of the door fast enough!" Mickey cracks up, and Steve joins in, slopping his pint over his trousers. My cheeks burn, and I wish the ground would swallow me up. But all I can do is go back to my table and finish my cigar. There's still ages before the next bus.

I hold my Zippo to the stub of cigar and puff on it as it catches alight. "If you've got another one of those, I could do with one, boy," says Lee, plonking a fresh pint and a fresh whiskey and soda in front of me. "It's a double," he says, nodding at my drink. "Sorry I've been so long."

"Thanks." I take a gulp, feel the burn in my throat, and immediately feel better.

"What was all that about?" Lee says, glancing over at Steve.

"Oh, something and nothing," I reply.

"He'll get his just deserts one day, don't you fret, boy." Lee lights his cigar with one of those transparent, rainbow-coloured lighters you can buy from behind the bar.

"So, what was all *that* about?" I throw his question back at him.

Lee draws sharply on the cigar, and clearly wishes he hadn't, because his eyes start streaming. We both chuckle a bit, and he drains his glass.

"*That* was something I think you're going to find very interesting," he replies. "Very sad, but *very* interesting.

"You remember when you got called out to the suicide back along?"

"Geoff Kerslake? Yes, of course. That's not a sight I'm going to forget in a hurry; *and* there was something odd about it. In fact, I got a weird phone call this morning, and I was hoping to pick your brains about it." Lee smiles knowingly, and nods. I can feel my eyes watering now – I know he's going to confirm my suspicions.

"I was at school with Geoff – yeah, yeah, I know what you're going to say: small town, everyone was at school with everyone else. But I was in the same year, and we used to play football over the rec together. He was really good – he joined Eskwich Spartans in the end; played for Esky Town a few times until he got injured."

"What happened to him?"

"Oh, you know, a crunching tackle. The guy broke his leg pretty badly and it never really healed properly. It would ache a lot, and Geoff just lost confidence and packed it in. Anyway, we both left school early; he got a job with British Rail, I went into photography, got the Gazette job, and never looked back." Lee smiles nostalgically, nods at my already empty glass and says, "Fancy another one, boy?"

In for a penny, in for a pound. I reply, "Yes, please, but let me get these." I thrust a fiver into his hand. "In any case, there's a while before the last bus." I'm careful with my tone: I don't want him to feel bad for having held me up. Not that he has – I wouldn't have spoken to Lucie if he hadn't been chatting to Mandy.

Lee sighs. "Sorry for deserting you, boy." Another sigh. "And in any case, you need to hear this. How about you stay for a few more and I drop you back?" He grins. Swansbourne is nearly an hour away from Eskwich. It's hardly dropping me back.

"But you've had a couple already – are you going to be okay to drive?"

"Ha! This isn't the big metrop, boy, and I didn't learn to drive last week! I'll be fine. We'll go through the back lanes if you like, just to be careful." And he's up and off to the bar again. *Five and then drive,* that's the phrase they use. It's a different world down here. And I know I'm going to get in the car and let him drive me home, and I know I'm not going to tip off the police. Lee's a good guy. Funny how good and bad is always relative. He quickly returns with our drinks and tells me that Mandy's going to bring some chips over.

"So, in recent years," he continues like there's been no hiatus, "I've only seen Geoff in the street to say hello to. One of those things where you both say it's been too long and you must meet up soon, and you never do. Sad, really, because now he's dead." Lee pauses, tilts his pint to the ceiling in a kind of toast, and sips.

"And then they found him swinging by the railway line. Suicide, obviously, probably to do with his break-up, they said."

"Actually, Lee, who found him? The police never said …"

"Ah, well, that's the thing. I'd not seen Mandy since the funeral, and we never got to have a proper chat there, so I thought I'd catch her while she had five minutes this evening. Turns out, she had a lot to tell me – and not just about the takeover at Tom Forde's."

It's a bit of an non sequitur, but I let Lee stop to take a swig of his beer. He's leaning right over the table now, and I find myself doing the same, so we must look like Smith and Jones. Except this isn't funny. Not at all.

"Well, everyone knew that Geoff and his wife had split up, and it was no surprise, because their marriage had been on the rocks for years. The thing was, we all thought it was because Sue was such a battleaxe. Did you ever meet her – Sue Kerslake?"

"I never met, Geoff, Lee!"

"Nasty piece of work, she was. Well, still is, probably. Anyway, it turns out that Sue had caught Geoff having his end away with Mandy's sister, Cheryl. Apparently, Cheryl only told Mandy this because she felt bad about everyone slagging off Sue. Even though it turns out Sue was having an affair with John Barton! You know what it's like, when word gets round in a small town."

"I'm beginning to, yeah." Talk about a tangled web.

"Anyway, Mandy's just told me that last night, Cheryl turned up here after last orders, three sheets to the wind, crying and in a terrible state. So Mandy locked up and took her upstairs (she lives in the flat above, did you know that? Something to do with insurance), made her a cup of tea and just listened to her while she blubbed.

"Cheryl said that Geoff hadn't topped himself because he split up with Sue, or because he felt guilty for cheating on her. He topped himself because of this girl called Anna having a miscarriage."

"What?"

"Yeah. Apparently, this girl, Anna, and her husband – Tony, I think – live out near Poultry Packers …"

"They live near the abattoir?!"

"Yeah. Big house, lots of land, cheap as chips. Thing was, you know the railway line runs right behind it …"

"What, their house, or the abattoir?"

"Both."

"Well, yeah, I guess it must do because the station's out there, isn't it? Oh, and they used to do a lot of meat trade with people in London back in the day, didn't they?"

"Yep. Anyway, Geoff's a train driver, right?" I nodded. "Was, sorry, I meant was. Now, apparently, Sue went a bit bonkers after she found out about the affair, you know, women's stuff, crying all the time. So she jacked in her job. Stayed in bed a lot. So Geoff had to work more hours to make up for the shortfall." Lee pauses for a moment, thoughtful. "I suppose with him out at work more, she was free to see John. Funny old world, isn't it?" We both swig our drinks, and Mandy comes over with our chips. Lee shakes a thick layer of salt over them, stuffs one into his mouth, and continues. "So, Geoff started driving the track-cleaning train on the odd evening and weekend …"

"Track-clearing train?"

"Yeah. They have to run weedkiller down the tracks every so often to keep the lines clear … you get it? And that was fine. He was still seeing Cheryl on the side, even though he'd told Sue it was over, and he used to meet her out there after work. Sometimes he'd sneak her on the train with him. Well, Cheryl had been going on at him to leave Sue and marry *her,* and at the same time, both his sons had lost their jobs. One of them was out at South Crofty – and you know what's been going on there with the strikes and that – the other was running a pub out at Cadeleigh, but what with the recession, he couldn't keep it going, so it's shut, but he's still got to pay the mortgage and the tax, and he can't sell because no one's buying. Both of the sons have got young families. Bloody terrible situation. That Maggie Thatcher's got a lot to answer for.

"Anyway, one evening Geoff's off to drive the track-clearer, and his boss is there with this guy in a suit. They tell him he's got to change the chemical tank – swap it for something else. Obviously, Geoff asks why, all suspicious, like, and the boss man says that he's got to do as he's told – if he doesn't, he loses his job; if he does, he gets a big payout that he's got to keep under the radar. What choice does Geoff have? He needs the money, needs to help his boys, needs to keep his job. And it's only weedkiller, so what does it matter?"

I can see where this is going. My eyes are watering. I *knew* there was something more to all this!

"Well, it turns out that Geoff knows Anna. She's Cheryl's second cousin, or something. Lovely girl. Works as a dinner lady at Willand School. She was pregnant, too. And shortly after he's taken the track-clearer down the line, laden with this new weedkiller, Anna loses the baby. He told Cheryl it was powerful stuff, that new chemical. He's driven down that line for decades, and he's never seen the plants die like they did after he put the new stuff on it. Apparently, it was killing the trees down the side of the line, and everything. He'd known the stuff had been dodgy – they wouldn't have threatened him and paid him off for nothing. And with everything else going on, he hung himself, poor bastard."

"Oh my God! Has Cheryl told the police? We need to tell someone …"

"Oh, yeah! She was the one who found him – she'd come out to surprise him, and maybe have it off in the old railway sheds like they used to – she had to run to Poultry Packers to get someone to call an ambulance, and when the police turned up, she went down to the station with them and told them everything. They didn't want to know, she said. Told her it's a coincidence, that Geoff had manic depression and a guilty conscience. She's tried to get hold of people from BR, but she can never get through to anyone. And when she went *back* to the police station, a top brass *told* her that Geoff topped himself. I mean, that's what she *said* – the maid's made more than one mountain from a molehill -"

I sit here, staring at him. "It must have been Cheryl on the phone this morning." Lee scrunches his face up over the rim of his pint.

"Possibly, boy. But it could have been kids mucking around in a phone box." He puts his glass down and surveys me. "It could be something, it could be nothing. I don't want to try to teach you how to suck eggs, but when you're reporting, you need to report what's there. Don't get caught up seeing what you want to see."

I nod, but a shiver runs down my spine. I know I'm on to something. I have to find Lucie. I saw her from the train, opening her bedroom curtains in that terraced house that backs onto the railway line near St Thomas' station. I just need to find the street … and then what? Park up and wait for her to come past? Knock on all the doors? I need to find her, so that's what I'll do. Resurrect Agent Orange.

The only negative thing I have to say about my flat is that it doesn't have a washing machine. I can't complain about it, because, as I said before, I have the sea view for hardly anything. Flats are a lot more expensive in Eskwich – I check the ads every week, on the off chance something good turns up. But not having a washing machine means that I have to save up all my dirty laundry and take it down to the laundrette every week. It's only a ten-minute walk, but when it's raining and I've got a bulging bin liner slung over my back like I'm some kind of weird Father Christmas, it's, well, I could really do without it. It's just something else to factor in, some other restraint on my freedom. But it could be worse: the laundrette is next door to the White Hart, so I'm not confined to the long, low slat benches, and if it's raining, I go in for a whiskey and soda.

The White Hart is a tiny little pub, with a crescent moon, mahogany bar. It does locally brewed real ales (I have yet to learn what a fake ale is) and ciders on pump, and the floor-to-ceiling wooden shelving unit behind it is literally packed with bottles, many of which I don't recognise. All around the top of it is a strip of coloured, stained-glass squares, and although it all looks chaotic, there's something really homely and cosy about it. There's a swirly pattern red carpet throughout, which is sticky in places, and throws back the odours of the night before, and there's a dartboard and a jukebox, and then out in the back room, there's a pool table and a bowling alley. It's a real old-fashioned English boozer, and it's run by a couple of lesbians. The fact that they're lesbians is neither here nor there to me, but apparently, they got a bit of stick when they first took over. The result is, though, that everyone's welcome in there, and it's one of the few places I've found since moving down to Devon where I don't feel singled out for being posh. Or ginger. I can sit in the corner with my whiskey and read my book, and people will say hi when they walk past, but I never feel intimidated or uncomfortable for being alone. And sometimes, if they're not busy, Jackie, one of the landladies – the other one's called Rosemary – will ask me if I fancy a cheese toastie. There are pictures on all the walls (mostly hunting scenes, unfortunately, but who am I to judge?), and above the table I usually sit at is a massive one of – would you believe – a white hart. It's in an ornate, gilded frame, and looks like it's been painted with oils. I kind of want to stand up and touch it because it looks so tactile. But I don't. And next to it, a couple of feet away from my chair (I sit facing the dart board), is the jukebox. It's one of the big, free-standing things, where you see the record being picked out and the needle placed on it; it's not one of those ones that hang on the wall, with just the track listings in discoloured plastic sheeting. Unless someone puts money in it, it'll pretty much always be playing Rush, Iron Maiden or Kate Bush.

I'm there trying to feel the texture of the painting with my eyes one evening, when I notice this massive spider creep out from behind the frame. I mean, it is *massive.* It looks lethal: long, pointy black body, jet black legs about the width of the metal in a pipe cleaner. Its posture I can only describe as 'hateful'. It looks like it could, would and wants to kill everything. It's quiet in the pub, and as I stare at the spider in morbid fascination, it scuttles over its web and in behind the jukebox. I haven't noticed the web before – the wall being covered in that off-white, woodchip wallpaper – and it isn't like a normal spider's web. It looks soft and kind of flows down from the spider's lair behind the picture frame to the jukebox, like a mohair blanket.

I scan the ceiling, the corners of the room and the other picture frames for more, but everywhere else is polished to a shine. Standing up, I move closer to get a better look at the web. It's really thick, and, like I said, soft. I can't work out if the softness is because motes of dust have become caught in it, or whether it's just the texture of the spider's silk. I tentatively poke at it with my finger. The spider shoots out from behind the jukebox, making me scream.

Jackie and Rosemary erupt into laugher as I jump back, knocking into the table and spilling my drink. "Beryl, meet Simon; Simon, this is Beryl!" Jackie calls over the bar.

"What the … ?! 'Beryl'?! Firstly, what kind of name is that for a spider, and secondly, you named a spider?!"

"Yeah! Isn't she beautiful?" Rosemary says, coming over to where I stand. She picks my hat up off the floor and hands it to me.

"Thanks. But I can think of other adjectives," I reply. "So, you know she's – I'm presuming she's a 'she' – there, and you're not going to evict her with a duster and a rolled-up newspaper, then?"

"Simon!" Jackie mock-scolds. "Everyone's welcome here; you know that!" She laughs. "Anyway, Beryl's not doing any harm. And she keeps the flies under control when we've got the doors open in the summer. She's really good at her job; and she looks the part." The image of Lee and I ushering the swarm out of the darkroom pops into my head, making me smile. Maybe I should hire Beryl for him.

"What's so funny?" asks Rosemary, grinning.

"Oh, nothing," I reply. "She looks like she wants us all dead, that's all!"

"If she was fat and squishy and bright pink, the flies wouldn't go anywhere near her, and she'd probably get eaten by a kid thinking she was a piece of candyfloss!"

"Fair point. But I think I'll switch tables when I come in next."

"Why? What do you think she's going to do?"

"I don't know – crawl on my hat and run into my ears or something!" I shudder.

"Wow, Simon!" says Jackie. "Why on earth do you think she'd want to run into your ear?!"

"I don't know! Spiders are just creepy, that's all."

"Creepier than the guy who sits alone in the corner in a hat and coat no matter what the weather, peering over the top of the same book, watching people?"

"Oh no! Do people think I'm creepy?!" I feel my face flush. I'm shocked. Mortified.

"Shit, sorry, Simon! 'Creepy' was the wrong word. But people do wonder why you left the Gazette, and why you're always on your own. This is a small town, you know."

"Well, I got headhunted! I work on the *Esky Gazette*, now. I did put a bit in the paper when I was leaving, thanking everyone for … well … for talking to a stranger, I suppose."

Jackie raises her eyebrows. "A handful of words lost somewhere in the middle of the paper. A new guy in town, who's not a tourist, doesn't seem to have any friends, works on the paper for a bit, and then drops out of the public eye, but can always been found at the same time on the same day in the same pub at the same table wearing the same clothes. Old Scamper reckons you're a spy!"

"Bloody hell! Did you set him straight?" Scamper is an ancient ex-military guy, who dresses like a tramp, smells like a tramp, and sits in the White Hart from eleven in the morning till last orders, drinking real ale, from his own special toby jug. He's got a million stories to tell, although no one can understand what he says, and everyone loves him. I'd say he was a pillar of the community, except he doesn't fit the stereotype. In fact, he's pretty much the antithesis of the stereotype. But he's loved, and Swansbourne wouldn't be Swansbourne without him.

"Nope," Jackie says, grinning.

"To be fair, you do kind of look like a spy, Simon. Like a secret agent. Oh my God, is that why you carry the same book about all the time? Because it's not really a book – it's a disguised box for a gun?!"

"Jesus, Rosy, calm down!" Jackie's laughing though.

I'm unsure as to how to react. I've had another drink while we've been talking, and I let it go to my head. "Actually, when I was at school, they used to call me Agent Orange!" I dissolve into giggles, wondering why I just told them that, but they're laughing too.

"'Agent Orange'," Rosemary echoes. "Oh my God, we should let this rumour grow! Can you imagine?!"

I laugh, but everything is becoming a bit unreal. I'm sweating. The panic is rising, and I have to get out of here. My laundry will be nowhere near done, but I tell them it is, and leave.

The irony is, they're not far off the truth. I do feel like a secret agent, because all I can think about is Geoff Kerslake and the family who live in the house next door to the abattoir, and I'm sneakily looking into it while pretending to be writing about the impending brewery closure, and doing press releases about school barn dances.

I'm getting nowhere with BR, nowhere with Devon County Council, nowhere with anyone. The police don't seem to care, and neither does Derek. He ran the story once, putting it in between some ads on page twenty-eight, despite the fact that the nationals got hold of it and ran it on the front page. When I confronted him about it, he said that the nationals just wanted some other story to take the pressure off Maggie and the unemployment rates. While that may be true, something's telling me there's more to it than that. So, after I've got in early and hammered away on my typewriter for an hour and a bit, I decide to go to the source. Lucie told me not to go, that her brother, Tony, had told her to tell me to stay out of it, that it didn't matter, that his wife's miscarriage was just one of those things. Neither of us bought that – a total 180 – but the fear in her eyes was enough to make me hesitate for this long. No more. It's my duty to find out what happened, my duty to report it. If I'm honest with myself, though, my motives aren't entirely altruistic. I don't want some big-shot yuppie working on the *News of the World* to get all the credit for *my* story. It's sad, but it's true.

I hadn't realised the line to and from Eskwich Junction ran so close to the abattoir, which is more evidence – if any were needed – that I am *not from round here* (they pronounce here, *y'err*). Once upon a time, this line was a hive of activity with countless trains coming out of Poultry Packers with fresh meat speeding their way to London. I stop Trish's car half on, half off the pavement on the edge of Lloyd Maunder Road. It's the first place to park that I've come to and I'm not risking losing it. I cut the engine and check my coat pockets for my notebook, pen and press ID, and am suddenly aware of a God-awful stink. I check under my seat for rotting vegetables that might have fallen out of my carrier bags last week, and then I check the bottom of my shoes in case I've stepped in something. I get out of the car, and the stench nearly knocks me over. There's a low hum which must be emanating from the factory, and that's when it hits me – the smell is coming from the abattoir. I remember what officer Al said to me when I'd been called out to see Geoff Kerslake's body that day. Caged birds, bird poo, dead birds, dying birds, cut up bits of birds, bird … waste, blood and feathers. My stomach churns, but I shrug my arms into my coat sleeves and grab my hat from the passenger seat. Slamming the car door, I stride off in the direction of the factory checkpoint, where I can see a beefy bloke has already clocked me.

"Oi!" I spin round to see an even beefier bloke in a high-vis jacket marching towards me. "Oi!" He shouts again, "You can't park here, *mate*!" He stresses the word 'mate' so hard that it's clear he means the opposite.

"What do you mean, I can't park here? I'm not on double-yellows, and anyway, there're cars parked all along this stretch of road!"

"Oh, I'm sorry mate," the man says, stepping so close that he looms over me even though I'm six foot, "maybe I didn't make myself clear. Maybe I stressed the wrong word. What I meant to say was, *You* can't park here, mate. Now, get in your bloody Batmobile or whatever it's supposed to be, and fuck off."

Claryannabel is my pride and joy, even though she's not even mine. She's Trish's immaculate and beautiful Triumph Herald, and she's an exquisite shade of burgundy. I fell in love with her the first time I drove her, which, funnily enough, was out to here, and I've driven her enough times now to bestow the name I was going to call my own car, upon her. I'd hardly call her a Batmobile, but I can see where the guy is coming from. Trish let me borrow her yet again, because I said I needed to chase up a lead about old Tom Forde's brewery (the imminent closure of which Derek has elected to keep a running page-two story for the last month), and that the guy I needed to speak to wanted to meet me outside Eskwich. I had to push down the guilt I felt about lying to Trish, but I was out of options. I have to know what's going on out here.

"What do you mean, *I* have to fuck off? It's still a free country, as far as I know!" I take a step to the right, and try to shove past him, but he's too strong, and grabs me by the shoulder. Just as I'm about to threaten him with an assault charge, he pushes me back and flicks my lapel. The plastic covering of my press lanyard dinks with the force of his meaty fingernail.

And that's all the evidence I need to know that my instincts are right, and something big *is* being covered up. A grin spreads across my face and I feel … well, I feel *triumphant*!

The big man reddens. "Listen, *mate*," he says, "unless you want me to call the police, I suggest you get off this land – it's private property, and you're trespassing!"

I can't help but smirk when he says 'get off this land' in his broad Devon accent, but this situation is more annoying than humorous, so I step back, retorting, "No it isn't! This is a public road, and I have as much right to park here as anyone else!" Something occurs to me, and I search his jacket and the navy-blue polo shirt under it for some kind of ID. There is none. "And who are you to tell me what to do, anyway?!"

The man is clearly not used to being argued with, and he's flummoxed. For a moment, I think he's going to hit me, but he chews his lip and says quietly, "Look. If you want to speak to somebody, you'll have to make an appointment." He glances over his shoulder, presumably to the guy in the checkpoint.

"I've been trying to do that all morning, but I can't get through to anyone! Look, *mate*, we're both just trying to do our jobs here. I'm not one of those animal rights nutters trying to bust into the factory – my friend lives over there," I wave my arm in the general direction of Lucie's brother's house, "and suddenly everything in their garden is dead, and his wife's lost their baby. I just want to know what's going on out here, so the police can put a stop to it before anyone else dies. I mean, I like a roast chicken on a Sunday as much as anyone else, and if something nasty's got into the air and my mate's home, then it sure as hell will have got into this factory as well. And you know as well as I do that Lloyd Maunder don't want to be sued for something that isn't their fault." I'm well aware that I'm making a lot of generalisations and assumptions here, but it's clear I'm going to have to appeal to this guy's better nature if I'm going to get anywhere.

The man turns back to the checkpoint again and pulls a walkie-talkie out of his trouser pocket. Walking a short distance off, he lowers his voice and speaks into it. Adrenalin shoots through me, and I consider sprinting off down the road while the man's back is turned, but I think I'm getting through to him and I don't want to blow this, so I get out my notebook, lean against Claryannabel's driver's door, and jot a few notes. When I look up, the security bloke is staring at me.

"Sorry, mate," he says a bit sheepishly, "but I've just been informed by my colleague that the council want this road closed. It's a no-can-do, I'm afraid."

From behind him, I can see another big guy in a high-vis jacket striding towards us. The first guy must have heard his footsteps, because he straightens up and regains his composure like a schoolboy in a playground dispute who's big brother has come to stick up for him with fists instead of words.

The new guy is clutching a *Road Closed* sign in his saveloy fingers and drops it in the road just in front of my car. He leers at me, and his colleague says, "The road's closed. Now fuck off." Out of options, I do.

The phones stop ringing and the chorus of fingers hammering on typewriter keys decreases, sometimes by one, sometimes by a couple, until there is only one person on the newsdesk still typing – me. With the lights on in the office, everything looks black outside, and the clock on top of the pannier market has struck six times. I know that

Derek will be either itching to get off home, or itching to open his bottom drawer. Much as I'd like a Glenfiddich with him, I know he'll never offer me one. I sometimes wonder why he wanted me here. I'm getting tired, and my mind's wandering. My fingers slow on the keys, and Derek stalks out of his office through a fog of cigarette smoke.

"Right, Simon," he says, "it's just you and me now! I'm going to have one last coffee before I lock up. Would you like one?"

"No, thank you," I reply, taking the hint that he wants me out of here. "I'm just about finished."

"And what, may I ask, are you working on so diligently? You realise it's after six o'clock?"

I rip the sheet of paper out of my typewriter. "Oh, umm, the takeover at the brewery," I stammer. Lying doesn't come easily to me. "I thought I could do a local take on a national issue with it. You know, how Maggie's planning to privatise everything to encourage competition and make a load of money, yet all these small, independent companies are being bought up by big franchises like Whitbread's, and people are losing their lifelong jobs left, right and centre. Did you know inflation got up to 21.8 per cent? …"

"I think you'll find that the name of our Prime Minister is Margaret Thatcher, not 'Maggie'," Derek cuts in, "and that if the Labour Party hadn't let the country get into such a state in the 70s, the Conservatives wouldn't be having to take such aggressive measures now. And in any case, old Tom Forde will be making a pretty penny out of this takeover, so any job losses ultimately rest at his door."

Trying not to show my frustration and anger, I place the sheet of paper, my notebook and my packet of Panama into my holdall, and shrug on my coat. "Well, a lot of people are worried about their jobs, and I have to explore both sides of a story. That's what journalists do, isn't it?" I say, hoping this will appease him. It doesn't work.

"Hmm," Derek says, standing right in front of me like a shiny wrecking ball, "but those who are lucky enough to be in employment would do well to try to keep it, don't you think?"

Each time my morning train approaches St David's, I look to Lucie's window, in spite of the fact that every day for the last week, the blue curtains have been drawn. I haven't found the courage to get off the train and make my way to Beaufort Street. I bought a map of Exeter from the newsagents just down the road from the Gazette offices, and I've memorised the route. I've even counted the houses from her window to the end of the terrace, so I can easily find hers. All I have to do is get off the train when it stops at St Thomas'.

It's Saturday morning, and the tide is out, so I watch the birds on the mudflats as my train speeds up along the estuary. I almost didn't make it out of my flat today, I was so shaky. I don't think the whiskey and sodas I'm having in the evening are helping, either. Yes, sleep comes quicker, but my stomach protests in the mornings, and all I want to do is curl up in bed, pull the covers over my head, and cry. What I do instead is get up, get washed, put David Bowie on, smoke a Panama out of the window and watch the sea. The sea is always there, and there are always people going places on trains. I feel like Major Tom.

Well aware that I need to control my thoughts, today, I let myself slide into self-pity. I had all these grand plans, but my best mate betrayed me. I said goodbye to Winchester and all I knew, and made the brave decision to start my life again somewhere else; for a while, I did well. I turned the *Swansbourne Gazette* around – everyone said I did. Then I was headhunted! I was that good at being a reporter, that powerful people got wind of me, and poached me for their own paper. With all this experience, I could go back to Winchester, or go for a job on a national. All I need to do is break a big story. And I have a big story. I just need to stick with it, do my own digging, go to Trish rather than Derek, because I know she'll back me up. Or do I? I didn't even really know my best mate. And now I have no friends at all, just acquaintances and colleagues. No girlfriend. I don't understand what happened with Lucie in the Half Moon that night, but she clearly doesn't want me in her life anymore. And my boss has threatened me with unemployment. Despite my best efforts, I'm being thwarted at every turn. My train passes through St Thomas', and the blue curtains punch me in the heart again. All I want to do is stay on the train, and let it take me far away. No one would miss me. I could just disappear.

As soon as I step off the train, it starts raining. I pull my coat around me, holding it tight with my holdall in one hand pressed against my body. My other hand keeps my hat from flying off, and I hurry out of the station willing my connecting bus to be on time. It's not, of course, and the rain has run down the sleeve of my jacket from where I've been trying to hold my Stetson in place. The sky is a darkening, thick white-grey, the wind has picked up, blowing dead leaves, litter and discarded tickets around my feet. I'm thoroughly wet and miserable, and once the bus arrives, I can't even get some joy from the view of the valley, because the windows have steamed up and are streaked with mud. Tears prick my eyes, and I wonder what the hell I'm doing here.

I can hear the kettle boiling before I open the office door. Trish greets me with a jolly smile, which I try, and fail, to return.

"Oh, my goodness! Are you okay, Simon?" she asks, pausing with a spoon in her hand.

After everything, the fact that she calls me by my actual name is what makes the tears fall. I turn away, apologising. I must look like a right idiot. I hope to God Mickey isn't in yet, because if he sees this, my life won't be worth living. I feel Trish's warm hand, heavy on my shoulder, and I pull away, wiping the tears off with my hands, and then wiping my wet hands on my wet trousers. Trish moves back to the 'facilities', saying, "You go down to the loo; I'll put a coffee on for you. There's not much on today, and Mickey's not coming in because the pitch is waterlogged so they've cancelled the match …"

"The pitch is waterlogged? It's only been raining for half an hour!"

"This is Eskwich, Simon. Wettest place on earth! It's been raining all night," Trish says, turning to me with both thumbs up and an exaggerated grin. It makes me chuckle as I leave the room.

The morning passes quickly, and although Trish has been very kind, I decide not to confide in her about the story I'm secretly working on. I manage to pull myself together and concentrate on my work, even though it feels like we're shoehorning stories out of non-events.

"Do you ever feel like we're shoehorning stories out of non-events?" I've said it without thinking.

Trish laughs. "We've got to fill a paper every week!"

"I know, but other than the brewery thing, which doesn't seem to be happening or not happening, there's really not much going on."

"If Tom Forde's gets taken over, it'll have serious ramifications for Eskwich, Simon. It's big news."

"Yes, but we keep writing about it, keep getting quotes from anxious workers, keep getting fobbed off by Mr Forde and Whitbread's … I mean, it's like we're making a story out nothing! Can't we just shelve it until something actually happens?"

Trish pushes the empty press release tray back into its holder. "Derek's the editor, Simon. Ours is not to question why!"

I'm annoyed by this, and blurt out, "But it *is*, Trish! That's the point! We're journalists! We're supposed to get to the heart of things, find out the truth, tell the public! That's the whole point of having a free press! It's why I got into journalism, anyway." Something occurs to me.

"If Derek doesn't like me questioning things, why doesn't he just get rid of me, and get Larry to be chief reporter?! Why did he bring me here in the first place?!"

Trish is still and silent for a moment. Then she meets my eyes. "Prestige," she says. "And money. You turned the *Swansbourne Gazette* around. It was losing money, and the Were Group were about to shut it down and amalgamate it with all the other 'local rags' into one newspaper covering the whole of Teignbridge and Torbay. Money talks, though. They had to increase the print run by stupid-percent. Derek wanted that for the *Eskwich Gazette*."

"So, we were about to be taken over as well?"

"No! No, nothing's been said about that, but it's always a possibility … look at Tom Forde's – takeovers are happening all over the place!"

"In spite of Maggie's mantra about competition and privatisation bringing prosperity."

Trish shrugs. "Also, did you know that you are the only member of staff who holds a degree?"

"No. No, I didn't. I thought Heather had one."

"Nope. She's got straight As, one of them being in English, but she doesn't have a degree. Derek's encouraging her. He wants more professional staff on the Gazette. It looks good."

"Looks good to whom?"

"The people who matter."

I'm still reeling as I stand on platform one, waiting for my train home. I smoke a cigar in one go, and drop its butt into a puddle. A ropy-looking pigeon pecks at it, so I crumble up the custard cream I took from the jar at work for my lunch, and sprinkle it in front of the bird. It pecks greedily, and I feel like I've done my good deed for the day. A flock of pigeons appears from nowhere, each one hell-bent on stealing some biscuit, but before they can land, my train pulls in, scaring them back into the heavy sky.

I find an empty seat and light another Panama. There are surprisingly few passengers in this carriage. I suppose the weather made them stay at home. Something occurs to me: I'm not just the only member of Gazette staff to hold a degree – I'm also the only member of staff who's not from round here. I don't have the contacts the others have. Maybe Derek thought he could get me in and mould me into the chief reporter he wanted. Maybe he thought that not having friends and family here would mean I wouldn't notice what's really going on. I shudder, and my eyes prick again. We're pulling out of St David's.

I wait until we're running smoothly, then get out of my seat. I can't sit down – I'm full of energy. I leave the carriage, intending to stand by the door on the left and breathe in the estuary and then the sea air once we're out of the city, but someone's piled a load of luggage there, so I have to stand on the right. I pull the window down. At least I won't get the smell of the sewage works or the abattoir on this side. We rush through St Thomas. And there she is, in her window. I lean out of the window, waving desperately. She sees me, waves back, also desperate. "Stay there!" I yell, "I'll come straight back!"

I can only hope that she heard me.

I stay by the door, and at Starcross, I throw it open and dash out into the rain. The wind, blowing off the sea, is really strong, so I take my hat off and run with it, ignoring the view, which, in any case, is murky as hell, and dash over the bridge onto the opposite platform. The rail service on this coastal route is really good – it has to be: it's the only way into Cornwall from South Devon – so I know I won't have long to wait. I just have to hope that the next train passing through actually stops at St Thomas.

Starcross is a kind of a non-entity of a place. I can't imagine why anyone would choose to live here. A few houses, a yacht club, a couple of pubs, a corner shop and the Atmospheric Railway Inn. The town reminds me of a Little Chef – a stop-off on the way to somewhere else. Oh, there's also the mental hospital and the veterinary lab. I did a story on the lab when I was on the *Swansbourne Gazette* and the place had just opened. It was lauded as somewhere that would bring jobs to the area – it was going to be good for the local economy. However, the only vacancies that weren't for university graduates were for a couple of secretaries and some cleaners, and as the lab isn't actually in Starcross, but in a field quite a way out that happens to have an EX6 postcode, it hasn't done anything for Starcross at all. And the only reason I found out about the mental hospital is because I had to walk to the lab from the bus stop, and I passed a golf course and a field full of geese, beyond which was a low brick wall where loads of strange-looking men sat, waving at me. White-coat workplaces are best kept away from the general population, I suppose.

Starcross Station is weird, too. Two thin platforms, one only separated from the expansive Esk estuary by a four-foot-high iron fence and a sheer drop, and an ugly-by-virtue-of-being-cheap-and-functional bridge that connects the two platforms, with an extension that reaches out onto a small jetty for the birdwatching ferry. The tide is now fully in, and private sailing and fishing boats are being tossed about by the wind-whipped waves. The rain is torrential. Then comes an announcement, the bodyless voice almost completely lost on the wind. Some poor soul has thrown themselves in front of the London train as it sped through Teignmouth. There'll be no north-bound trains for the rest of the day.

Thwarted again. If, by some miracle, Lucie had heard me, she'll think I've let her down again. I could go for the bus, but that means going right into Exeter city centre, and then having to make my way all the way down to St Thomas on foot. It will take ages. I may as well cross the bridge again and catch the next train home. Utterly dejected, I trudge back towards the estuary. I could throw myself in, but I can swim, and I guess the survival instinct would just kick in. I could wait for the next HST to London and throw myself in front of that. No one would see that coming. I imagine the editors jumping for joy: *Hold the front page! Two jumpers on the same line in one day!*

I see the headlights of the Penzance train, yellow and blurred by the rain. It's slowing down. Not today, then, Simon. Back home for fish and chips, and a hot bath. The train screeches to a stop. I trot along the platform and open the nearest door, but it's stiff, and my Stetson flies out of my hand. I curse, and chase it down the platform, shouting to the conductor to hold the train for a moment. How it's stayed so low to the ground, I don't know, and I'm able to stamp on the brim to stop it. I reach down to pick it up, soaked through and muddy, and someone calls my name. I spin round. It's Lucie. We run to each other and embrace, and I don't realise how clichéd it must look until the guard calls, "If you two are getting a room at the Atmospheric, can I let the train go?"

"No!" I shout. "We're getting on, we're getting on! Thank you. I'm so sorry!" And we apologise to everyone we pass in the carriage until we find two seats together, and fall into them. I turn to Lucie, whose face is streaming with rain, her hair frizzy with it, and sticking to her cheeks, and without thinking about it, I kiss her.

It isn't until we step off the train and into the wild weather, that I realise there's nowhere to go unless Lucie wants fish and chips in the greasy cafe opposite the seafront and the station. The one below my flat. She laughs when I tell her as much, and we walk there, arm in arm and wet through, while Lucie hums *Oh, I do like to be beside the seaside.*

Lucie squeezes into a booth by the window, and I fold myself into the chair opposite her, actually looking forward to my chips and mushy peas. We crack open our cans of Coke. We did the reconciliation and small talk on the journey, and we know we've both got more pressing things to discuss. Swansbourne in autumn is pretty much devoid of tourists, and it seems that the inclement weather has kept most of the locals at home, so other than a few stragglers who were waiting for the replacement bus service, the cafe is ours. Lucie sighs.

"You know I said when we bumped into each other the first time, that I was babysitting my nephew?"

"Yes. Your brother doesn't get home until late, and his wife miscarried and is in hospital."

Lucie smiles her pleasure at my remembering, but the smile quickly fades to a frown as she continues, "Well, my brother, Tony, actually tried to get hold of you – the Gazette – a while ago. He thinks what happened to Anna – you know, his wife – is because of something they sprayed on the railway line. Sorry, I'm not explaining myself very well! Their house backs onto the line, and Tony said he saw some smoke or something in the air wafting over their fence after the weedkilling train came through one day, and the next thing he knew, all the vegetables in his back garden were dying. He's got a massive vegetable patch – he grows everything – it's one of the reasons they bought the house so near to the abattoir, you know, big house, big garden going cheap. They ummed and ahhed for ages about it, because of the smell. If the wind's blowing the wrong way, Anna can't hang the washing out! But they wanted a big family, with loads of room for the kids to play, and we all love railways, so they just went for it. Anyway, Tony tried to contact British Rail, but no one there will talk to him, and the council won't talk to him, so he thought he'd go to the press, but then he got scared because they closed the road, and there were all these men in suits wandering around – one of them even came to his house saying that there'd been an incident at Poultry Packers, but it was all in hand and not to worry – that the relevant parties had been informed and there was no need to talk to anyone about it – and what with Anna being so ill, and him having to work and see to the kids, he never called, but now all his vegetables are dead, and so's the lawn and even the big beech tree in the field has lost all its leaves when the ones the other side of the factory haven't, and then I said I'd met you, so I'm talking to you instead." She paused. "My brother's scared, Simon. There's something weird going on."

I stare at Lucie, my brain whirring. I'm speaking before thinking, again, "And they're talking about closing Eskwich Junction altogether, aren't they?"

"Yep. How did you know that?" Lucie seems surprised.

"Well, I've always liked railways, actually. Particularly steam locomotives. My grandad was a fireman. But …". We're interrupted by the waitress who arrives with our meals, and then another couple, with a baby, dash into the cafe to escape the rain, and sit in the booth behind me. I lean close to Lucie and whisper, "There *is* something going on, which is why I was so desperate to talk to you …". Her face falls, so I correct myself. "That *and* the fact that I really like you, Lucie. We'll talk when these people have gone, okay?"

Smiling and nodding, Lucie carries on, only slightly louder than would have been natural. "So, your grandfather was a fireman! As in the man who shovels the coal into the firebox?"

"Yes. His main port of call – if you'll excuse the pun – was Southampton Docks."

"Wow! I would have loved to have seen that, back in the heydays. Isn't Southampton Docks the place where the E2 worked? You know, the …"

"The original Thomas the Tank Engine!" We blurt out simultaneously.

I'm so happy – this is the first time I've been able to talk to a girl about railways without feeling like a bore. People who love trains have somehow got pigeonholed into sad, lonely blokes who stand at the end of platforms in the rain. There's so much more to it than that. Especially with steam locomotives – they're a marvel of engineering. And there's something exciting about being near railways. A feeling of uncertainty, like the world is your oyster and you could go anywhere and meet anyone. Freedom.

"And that's why you've got a house that backs onto a railway line!"

Lucie laughs and pushes a chip through a blob of tomato sauce. "No, that was just serendipity. It was my aunt's house. When she died, I took it on. I wanted to get out of Eskwich, you see. You know, make a life for myself … I know it's only sixteen miles up the road, but I saw an opportunity, so I took it."

"In the true spirit of the 80s," I mutter.

Lucie tenses. "You say that like it's a bad thing."

"No! No, that's not what I meant. I've been at work this morning – obviously – and I've been talking politics with a colleague. To be honest, Lucie, it's got more to do with your brother and his wife than you'd think."

The baby in the booth behind me starts to cry. Lucie watches the mother take it into the cafe toilets, presumably to change its nappy. We eat our meal in silence for a while, but the baby won't be comforted. The mother returns from the toilets, bouncing her child up and down in her arms. "Take him outside, Lin," the dad hisses, embarrassed, and Lin does, but the driving rain is blowing at the cafe as if it were falling horizontally, so the woman comes back in.

"We're going to have to go back to the hotel, Nick," she says. "Sorry," she murmurs to Lucie and me.

Lucie smiles and shakes her head slightly. "It's fine," she says. "My nephew used to be inconsolable sometimes, when he was little. I don't think I managed to drink a cup of tea while it was hot for about a year!"

The couple leave their own teas to cool on the table, and Nick buys a couple of bags of crisps on their way out.

"It looks like hard work, having a little one," I comment.

"It's harder when you're expecting to have one, and it suddenly dies," Lucie returns.

I'm quiet for a moment. "I honestly can't imagine, Lucie. It must be … devastating." I let the sentence hang, but I have to move the conversation on. I have to get to the bottom of this. "So. The weedkiller …"

"Yes. They have these special weedkilling trains that go out every so often, when the line's quiet – mostly overnight – to keep the tracks clear. Not many people know about them, but why would they, I suppose. Anyway, the train goes quite slowly, spraying weedkiller out of a cannister behind the engine." I know all this, but I don't interrupt.

"And you think that the weedkiller – what? Got into the vegetables and made Anna lose the baby?"

"I'm sure of it."

"I really need to talk to your brother, Lucie. I mean, if track-clearing happens all the time, why would it suddenly affect people?" Lucie's silent, staring at me. I've asked a leading question because I don't want to put words in her mouth. I don't doubt what Mandy told Lee, about what Cheryl said to her, but there's a lot of he-said-she-said in that, and I'm going to need proof …

"He thinks maybe they got the dilution wrong. Or maybe they were using different stuff." She pauses, her eyes watering. "He told me that he was out in the garden one evening, putting slug pellets down, and he heard this train come past pretty slow – apparently, the track-clearers never go over sixty miles an hour – and then all this mist, or water vapour, or something started wafting over the back fence."

"Bloody hell, Lucie. If this is true, then …"

"Then it's negligence."

"Or attempted manslaughter, or something."

"Heads are going to roll."

"Exactly. And the day after Tony contacts the council about it, the man in the suit comes round out of the blue and explains it all away."

If I'm honest with myself, I was hoping Lucie would stay with me that night. But after her revelations, there was no way I could try to be romantic. Tony and Anna had been trying for a baby for years, she'd said. No wonder Anna is in bits in hospital. She must be having a nervous breakdown.

The trains are running again, after the incident earlier today. How sad, when someone's life and death becomes an *incident*. Lucie leaves to go back to Exeter on the last train. I wait with her, holding her hand. It's still raining and windy as hell, so we stand at the top of the stairs rather than on the actual platform, where we have a little shelter. I tell her to get a taxi from the station to her house, but she just laughs because it's no more than a minute's walk. I'm worried about her. If people are getting bricks through their windows, maybe someone's watching Lucie. And what if someone has seen her with me, and knows I'm a journalist? I shiver. But I can't keep quiet and do nothing – if there's been foul play, then someone needs to be held accountable; if what happened was an accident – and I doubt that very much – then the truth should be brought to light for Anna and Tony's sakes. And poor Geoff Kerslake's.

It's so natural to hug Lucie before she boards the train, and we kiss very briefly. The carriage is pretty much empty, so she takes a seat right next to the window where

I'm standing. We smile at each other, and the train pulls out, leaving me alone on the platform under the orange glow of the streetlights. It occurs to me that I've fallen in love with her. I don't remember it being like this with Charlotte. But that might just be psychosomatic, and there's far too much going on to be distracted by a girl. I decide to walk along the sea wall to burn off some nervous energy.

Exiting the station, I turn left and pass under the low middle arch of the railway bridge. A few pigeons are still bustling around between the metal understructure, and I wonder if they have second clutches. It is funny that you never see a baby pigeon. There must be millions of them every year. Maybe we do see them, but they grow quickly, and we mistake them for adults. I resist the urge to coo under the bridge and test it for echoes. Despite the seriousness of the events that I'm dealing with, I'm excited, and a bit giddy. I must calm myself down. A few feet further on, the stream that runs in a straight line through the centre of Swansbourne – The Water, as the locals call it – meets the ocean, so I stand by the low brick wall, and watch the waves. In the daytime, the ducks splash around on the grey pebbles that make up a miniscule estuary type of area, and gulls strut about, and bob on the surf. It's too late for them to be out and about now. I glance back up The

Water, but I can't see any black swans, either. With the exception of a few teenage stragglers, everyone's asleep, or in a pub. I make myself breathe deeply. I need to think.

I need some sort of proof before I approach Derek with the story. In fact, I should have the entire story finished. I have a nagging feeling that it's Trish I ought to approach. I wonder when Derek will next be off on holiday. I'll have to check the office calendar on Monday. In the meantime, I need to have a plan of action.

If Anna and Tony had got an official visit that was tantamount to a threat for speaking to BR and the council – albeit via the switchboard operators and not managers – and if 'Poultry Packers' don't want me sniffing round either, what can I do? I need to get proof that there is something dodgy in the soil in Tony's garden. Which means I need to get into Tony's garden, and take a soil sample. Maybe there'll still be a chemical residue in it. If there ever was a dodgy chemical in it. I can't allow myself to presume a crime has been committed. This might just be small-town gossip spread because of a small-town family feud, mixing with my paranoia. I used to trust Charlotte. I trusted Dave since playschool and look where that got me. For a moment, I'm lost, swept away by a tide of grief, and depression. Can you trust anyone? Hell, at the moment, I can't trust my own instincts! But that might just be a result of having been betrayed.

I feel the familiar light-headedness coming on. My palms are clammy. I'll walk it off. I'd like to walk along the sea wall, but as there's no barrier, and it's dark, I retrace my steps and go along Marine Parade instead. When I've reached the end of the road, I'll stand on the railway bridge by Kennaway Tunnel for a bit and go home.

A soil sample seems sensible. After that, I need to find a scientist, or a chemist who could analyse it for me. Ha! The lab out at Starcross! I'd been out there to do a story when it opened! I need to go through my old notebooks and try to find the name of the woman I'd spoken to. Then, I need to hope like hell that she'll help me.

My flat being above a chip shop in the hub of the town, I have to enter through a small wooden door at the back of the building. Its blue paint is scuffed and faded, and it opens onto a narrow, half-turn staircase that's illuminated by a small window and two naked light bulbs. There are two doors on the top landing: one leading up onto the flat roof, the other being my front door.

The armchair by the window is mine, but the rest of the flat is furnished by the Bartons – the family who own and run the chippy, and have their fingers in the pies of most of Devon's lucrative businesses – and was all made of teak veneer, I think from MFI. A thought strikes me. Barton! Geoff Kerslake's wife is now engaged to a Barton. She's right: she'll need no outside income if she marries into that family!

I make straight for the chest of drawers in my bedroom – three wide, deep drawers, the bottom of which is stuffed full of my notebooks. My filing system is meticulous, so I have no trouble locating the flip-over reporter's notebook from last winter which contains my notes about the opening of a chemical research laboratory in some fields just outside Starcross.

It was a state-of the-art centre: all crisp, white, antiseptic decor, automatic doors, and the reception desk held a big PC monitor and keyboard. I spoke to a woman named Eleanor, who was head of research for veterinary medicine, and she told me they would be developing medication and vaccines, primarily researching into various common canine and feline diseases. She'd said it was a historic moment for the West Country, and would take the pressure off the centre near Bristol, while being more accessible for those living in Cornwall. Eleanor herself had degrees in biochemistry, and forensic pathology, and we'd hit it off immediately.

True, her work is primarily to do with animals, but surely she can test for a poison in some soil? She's the best chance I have. The only chance. I just hope she still works there. And in the meantime, I have to work out how I'm going to get a soil sample when I'm not allowed anywhere near Tony and Anna's place. And if people are being watched, no doubt the phone lines will be bugged, and if the phone lines are bugged, then the house probably will be, too. Or am I getting carried away? The one thing I can be sure of, though, is that I'll only get one shot at getting a sample. If someone found what I'm hoping to do, they could stop it or sabotage it, and they'd certainly make sure I'd never get the chance again. I have the urge to speak to Lucie, but I don't think I should.

I make a coffee and sit in my armchair, looking out over the railway line to the darkening sea. In summer, when the schools have broken up, the beaches and cafes are crammed with tourists, holidaymakers, and locals out enjoying the evening sunshine, or waiting on the sea wall to see the sun set. There's a buzz about the town, and the little primary-coloured light bulbs that have been permanently strung down the route of The Water and are lit up in the evening, make sense. The cafe below my flat is infinitely busier, too – people, like me, sit with fish and chips on the seafront when they finish work, and teenagers hang around the arcade, smoking, and swigging from plastic bottles of cheap cider in the park. Mums are out with babies and toddlers on the beach till bedtime. And most evenings, there are drunken people falling out of the pubs and making their ways to the station, singing.

As soon as the kids go back to school, though, out-of-season-syndrome sets in. It's the curse of the seaside town. The crazy golf closes, most of the ice cream and souvenir shops close, the cafes shut early. The buzz in the town cools along with the weather, and as the days darken, the string of coloured lights along the water is incongruous, mocking. The arcade still blares out its music and its over-bright lights are gaudy against a slate-grey, rainy sky. Teenagers who'd had holiday work are no longer needed, so they hang around the arcade, playing on the two pence machines, or just smoking, out of the rain. In the mornings, mothers with young children in pushchairs hang around in groups, putting their children on the Thomas the Tank ride that looks like it's been there since the Victorian times. I watch them on my days off, as they drift into the cafe below me for a cuppa and a warm-up, and I wonder if Charlotte's doing similar in Winchester. I wonder if she and Dave are still together. I wonder – I hope – he's making a better dad than I would have.

Over the road, on the corner of Marine Parade, I can just make out a couple sitting on the wall of the Marine Tavern. There'll be no one in the beer garden in this weather, and inside it's probably dead, too. They must be having a very private conversation, otherwise they'd head inside, surely. Pushing up the sash window, I lean out, smelling the seaside and chip shop on the air, and I can hear laughter coming from up the road. I could go over and have a drink and a smoke at the Tavern. If I sat by the window, I could watch the trains. I could chat to the bar staff; make some friends. Or I could go and see Jackie and Rosemary at the White Hart. It's not laundry day, but it doesn't matter – they'd be glad to see me – they're always welcoming – and we could have a chat, and I wouldn't feel alone. Maybe I should ask about joining the darts team or something. Or I could invite Lucie down again. We can't play crazy golf, but we could get some chips and go for a drink. Like a proper date. I could try to win her a Minnie Mouse in the arcade. I watched an old couple sitting in the bus shelter with their shopping bags and trolley. They were just watching things come and go, life pass by, like me. I might be alone when I reach their age. Panic rises in me. On the near side of the bus shelter stands a phone box. I grab a couple of 20ps, jog down the stairs and out the door, and dash over to it, my head bent against the rain.

Inside, it smells of piss and ashtrays. I dial Lucie's number. I'm so relieved when she picks up that she asks me what's wrong. I tell her I've been out walking along the coast and have got so cold I can hardly move my mouth. She laughs, dispelling some of the irrational fear that's pulsing through me, until the laugh turns into a coughing fit. She's in her pyjamas, dosed up on Lemsip – there's no way she's going out into the rain and the cold to get on a grubby train to Swansbourne. Not tonight. I'm so disappointed, I could cry. I want to go to hers, snuggle up with her, keep her warm, make her some soup. She's calls me sweet, but says she's going to get an early night – she's just going to finish the chapter she's reading. I ask her which book, and she tells me, *High-Rise* by J G Ballard. The chapter she's on is called *Critical Mass*, she says. She likes the sound of it. If she's well enough to babysit Harley tomorrow, she'll meet me in the Half Moon after work.

I struggle getting out of my flat, and I struggle getting into the Gazette offices. I *can't* walk round the block again. I have to keep it together. *It's okay, I'm meeting Lucie later,* I chant under my breath as I get off the bus. I keep it up all the way up Bampton Street, and only stop when I put my hand on the blue side door.

I force myself straight up the stairs, and when I get into the newdesk office, I open a window and go straight to the facilities. I have to keep moving. Derek's door is closed, but I can tell he's in there because of the light shining under his door. Trish arrives as soon as I light up a cigar, so I make her a coffee, and we talk about our plans for the day.

The office door is thrown open, banging against a filing cabinet, making us all jump. Mickey stands in the doorway with a face like thunder, like some kind of cowboy bursting through a saloon door. He doesn't hold pistols, thank goodness, but his fists are clenched. This is going to be a bad day. Derek's called him on his day off because Heather's called in sick. "I bet it's just bloody women's troubles," Mickey grumbles. "And Derek better be paying me double for this – I'm the only one of you lot who works weekends!"

"Reeeaaally?" Trish says, her eyebrows raised.

"Well, you're a bloody manager!" Mickey spits back. "I should bloody well hope you're working on the weekends, the size of your wage packet!" He storms over to the facilities, and dumps two heaped spoons of Maxwell House into Heather's mug. Heather doesn't like coffee. It's such a childish act. I look at Trish, Trish looks at me. A laugh bubbles up in me, so I try to cover it with a cough, which sounds so fake, Trish actually snorts. Mickey doesn't notice though – the cheap Woolworth's kettle boiled as loud as a pneumatic drill.

He and Steve spend the whole day smoking, decimating the box of Family Circle biscuits, and moaning. Workwise, Steve manages to find a mountain of paper to photocopy, and Mickey has a long look at the press releases. I'm busy on the phone, being passed through the ranks of personnel at Whitbread's, getting nowhere, so at about one o'clock, I walk down to Forde's Brewery to speak with Tom face to face. If I'm there, he'll have a hard job avoiding me.

It's a longer walk than I'd anticipated. I've never been down through Westesk South before, and when I get to the Prince Regent – the pub on the corner – I realise I haven't had any lunch, and consider dropping in for a drink. I decide against it, however, and it's a good job I do, because when I make it down to the bottom of Howden Road and into the reception area of Forde's, a group of men in expensive suits are doing a taste test and slapping me on the back like an old friend. Old Tom gets me involved in it too! I play along – he's in a good mood and, softened by his own beer, I might get some truth out of him.

I'm not a lover of beer, and the thick, warm, real ales turn my stomach more than anything. Unfortunately for me, real ales are what Forde's Brewery does. As the local reporter, in spite of the fact that I'm supposed to remain impartial and simply report, I have to support local business – the memory of what Lee had said in the Half Moon is now a constant in my thoughts – so I take the pint glass offered to me and force down a sip of the liquid. It feels viscous going down my throat. I hope I'd managed to turn my grimace into a smile.

I understand Lee's point of view to an extent: we depended on the locals for stories, we depended on them to buy the newspapers. And then, for Lee and Mickey and the guys, the people in the stories are old school friends, kids they've seen grow up, in some cases, family. The politics of it all – especially in a small community – is complex. The problem I have with it all is that I believe in a free press, which means an impartial press. Forde's is struggling, their workforce ageing, and I know that many kids are leaving Eskwich School wanting out of a dead-end town for bright lights and big cities. The Whitbread's takeover might actually be good for the town. It'll bring in some new blood, if nothing else, and God knows Eskwich needs it – its reputation for inbreeding is unsurpassed.

Eskwich, like most of the country, is suffering under Thatcher. Companies are going under all over the place. There are rumours that Global Elastic is going to be the next. Which is why Poultry Packers is, literally, a lifesaver to some. Though not for the chickens, but you can't worry about them when you have a family to feed. I wonder if, at some point, people will start growing their own veg and living off the land – but I guess that was what Tony and Anna had had in mind. Like that sitcom, *The Good Life*. And now, rumour has it that the national firm, Whitbread's is looking to take over Forde's. I suppose old Tom Forde is wanting to retire now, and I don't blame him, but I wonder if the *And Sons* have lost interest in the trade and are just looking to make a fast buck and bugger off to the Costa del Sol, like half the rest of the world. And if they do, will Whitbread's keep the current staff on, or will they replace them all with guys from 'Up North' who will do the job for less money? Some of the old boys who work here have never worked anywhere else. The implications for the town are massive. Thinking this, as I look at the men in suits, white-haired Tom, and the nervous faces of the girls on reception, behind their typewriters, I have to concede that Derek is right, and this is newsworthy, but I have the nagging feeling that it's only because he wants me to drop whatever is happening out at Willand. And, as I said to Trish the other day, other than circumspection, nothing is even happening at the brewery. It might be paranoia, or my imagination getting the better of me, but it feels like this is a smokescreen.

I spend the afternoon at the brewery, sampling beer – which goes straight to my head – and while I'm able to talk to a few of the staff, old Tom, the current Forde of Forde's and Sons – is monopolising me, and basically giving me the guided tour he'd give his bank manager. These bureaucrats are so self-serving. Don't they know they're completely transparent?! I can answer my own question – yes, they probably do, but I'm not exactly pushing him to get at the truth. I feel a strange loyalty to him, and to his reputation, and the drink isn't helping. I try to absorb what he's saying and not saying, and make a mental note to speak with Lee, and maybe even Mandy in the Half Moon. There are two sides to every story, as they say. At least.

Climbing up the stairs to the office is a struggle: the alcohol has hit me, so I head straight for the facilities and get a coffee. I make it stronger than I usually would, so it covers any beery smell on my breath as well as sharpens me up. I'm not used to drinking very much anyway, let alone drinking in the middle of the day. There's only an hour before we knock off, and I'm glad when Trish, who's *mmm hmmm*ing down the phone, nods me in the direction of the press releases.

I pick up the whole in tray, plonk it down on my desk and spark up a Panama, which just exacerbates my light-headedness. I flip through the scrappy bits of paper for an easy job to end the day, and find it. Old Terry White's been on the phone to Nick Beer, who's got the desk opposite me, for half an hour about the veg competition he runs every year for the fete, and as Terry speaks so slowly, Nick's managed to jot the conversation verbatim, which makes me laugh. Still, at least it means I won't have to ring him back. I can almost hear his broad Devon accent, and I have to suppress another laugh. I shove a piece of paper into the typewriter and am just about to start listing the people who'll be there, and the fact that the glory is worth more than the prize, when Derek wafts through. I needn't have bothered with the coffee – he stinks of whiskey. He looks a bit harassed.

"Oh, um, Simon. I see you're going through the press releases, there. Find an easy one for Steve, could you – he deserves a byline, having been here nearly two months."

Nia, 2022.

"I've never seen your mum angry before."

Matt and I are walking into town. We've got to the roundabout by Damon's Hill, and we cross over and mooch down the gently sloping hairpin-turn walkway rather than going straight down the steps. There's something about standing at the top of a long flight of concrete steps that makes me want to hurl myself down them. It's like when

I'm on a plane and I find I've got the emergency door seat: I spend the whole flight thinking that at any moment I'm going to open the door, and hundreds of strangers will be sucked into the sky at 30,000 feet.

Matt hasn't said a word since we left his mum's house. It was weird. Everything seemed fine, and we were all around the kitchen table eating freshly baked brownies with Danny, and as soon as Matt mentioned the woods at his dad's, Misty blanched and almost fell off her chair. She shrugged it off, laughing, saying she got an electric shock off her mohair jumper, but we could all see she was shaken. So Matt asked again. "Well, why do you think I didn't want you running off into the woods, Matthew?" It was a rhetorical question, and Matt had the sense to keep quiet. "Because I didn't want you getting lost, or getting stuck up a tree, or falling out of a tree, or getting your foot caught in a snare – you know your dad still shoots pheasants; he probably hunts rabbits and … honestly, I wouldn't put it past him not to have a go at eating anything with a pulse."

Danny's nodding, probably thinking of his little girl, Gwen. It makes sense to me, too, until Matt says, "But you never used to mind me and Nia climbing trees down the railway walk!"

It's true. When we were kids, Mum and Misty actively encouraged us to go out and play – especially down the railway walk. The railway walk is what we called the path that, back in the heyday of steam engines, had been one of the main lines out of Eskwich, to Bolham, and beyond. When they closed all the stations in Eskwich – sometime in the 60s, I think – they took up the tracks, leaving a walkway between the trees a lovely, pretty path, lined with a stream, and speckled with lovely, old, soot-stained, red-brick railway bridges that Matt and I used to stand under and shout because they made brilliant echoes. And I have no idea how they made them. How do you make an arched bridge entirely from solid bricks? I love railways for lots of reasons, one of which is that they're a miracle of engineering. Anyway, the railway walk was out in nature, and we made camps and tree houses, and swung across streams on ropes tied to branches. Nowadays, the town side of it had become a main road, and the bit behind Blundell's Road and beyond has housing estates encroaching on it. It's sad, really, but things change. Mobile phones and the internet didn't exist back then.

Misty pushed back her chair so it scraped the floor noisily, picked up the plate of brownies and started to pick them off and put them in a plastic sandwich box. "Me and your dad didn't get on, Matthew, you know that. It was a long time ago …"

"Yeah, but the way you used to say it," Matt cut in, "it was like you were scared or something …"

"Matthew, for God's sake, would you just leave it! It was a long time ago! I can't remember! It doesn't matter any more!" Misty tried to soften her voice towards the end. She'd turned her back on us and was washing the few cups on the worktop.

"Mum …"

"Matthew! Just bloody leave it, okay?! I don't want to talk about your bloody dad!"

Danny was sitting there with his mouth open, staring at us. He popped the end of his brownie in, flashed his eyebrows and left the room.

I stared at Matt, who was frozen, glaring at his mum's back. I touched his arm, but he shrugged me off and walked out of the kitchen and out of the house. And now, here we are, walking into town for no apparent reason.

"Everyone thinks my mum was so hard done by, by my dad. Poor little Misty, left to raise a child on her own!

Poor little Matty with a daddy who was embarrassed to acknowledge him! But he paid for our house, all our bills, everything. And Mum just used to get in these rages and slag him off! It wasn't his fault he didn't love her!"

"Matt! Jesus!"

"I mean, what was he supposed to do? Stick with her in misery his whole life?! Dad's a worker; all Mum ever did was get herself pregnant so she could leech off him her whole life! Fuck!"

Matt pulls his vape out of his pocket and inhales deeply. In all the years I've known him, I've never seen him angry like this. It's scary.

"Matt," I say, quietly, "why have you never told me any of this before? I mean, I thought you hated your dad because he just chucked money at your mum, I …"

We're at the bottom of the hill now, at the pedestrian crossing that stands where a railway station once did. It's started drizzling, and the lights and wipers of the passing cars are automatically coming on. Matt's staring straight ahead in a cloud of smoke that smells pink, if that makes any sense, and there's no obvious break in the stream of traffic, so I press the button.

"Seriously?! You're seriously wondering why I've never spoken to you about my life? Ever?" Matt laughs, hatefully. He's facing me now, eyes narrow, mouth set like stone. Looking at him, I can't think of what to say. I can feel tears prick my eyes. "Little Miss Fucked-Up wonders why I've never been able to get a word in edgeways! It's always been about *you*, Lavinia! *You* and *your* absent father! We were both raised by single mums, Nia! Except you had the advantage of your father never being able to fuck up or fail you. Your dad's a myth and a legend; mine is the old, rich fucker who ran the paper and got a young girl pregnant!"

"Matt!"

His face softens for a moment. "Jesus, Nia. You have no idea." He glances away when my tears start falling. "Look, I can't talk to you right now, okay? I'll message you, or something, later." And with that, the traffic stops, and he crosses the road. I shake my head at the questioning driver who tuts and accelerates away, and watch Matt disappear round the corner.

The drizzle becomes rain as I make my way back up the winding path, back up Canal Hill, back onto the tow path. I watch the raindrops hitting the canal, making waves on the still water. A moorhen cuts in front of me, sprinting to the bullrushes on its incongruous legs; a group of mallards quack hopefully at me, and a mute swan glides past us all with regal distain.

The barge cafe isn't open, as usual. It floats there, all ornate paintwork and inviting signs, and gives you hope, but when you get up close, the serving hatch is closed and the lights are off. I have no idea how they make their money. Maybe they don't – maybe that's why it's always shut. Unless they're waiting for the school holidays, so they can pay the bills with ice cream sales. I'm jobless right now. Maybe I could take it over. Sighing, I decide not to walk any further, and I go down the steps by the children's play area and into the car park.

I parked Annie-bel – my blue Nissan Juke – under a tree to keep the sun off. All that's happened is that the sun went in, and a bunch of pigeons or seagulls or something perched in the tree and shat all over the roof and down the windscreen. I laugh, because it just about sums up my day. If Matt was here, he'd say something really useful like *it's good luck if a bird shits on you,* but he isn't here, and Mum isn't here, and Dad was never here. I know exactly what I'm going to do: head back to Exeter, get the train down to

Exmouth, and swim as hard as I can. They say that saltwater is the cure for everything.

The weather turns for the worse as the train follows its route along the River Esk and its estuary. Wind hits the carriage hard, and 'hits' is the right word, because it sounds like it's punching the windows. I feel the occasional jerk, and it's almost like I'm on a roller coaster. The sky gets darker and moodier, with big black cumulous clouds, sheet-like slate-grey ones, and the odd wispy white ones that remind me of breaking waves. The light is a menacing golden-grey, and the trees and bushes we pass are hyper-illuminated against the steely skies.

Eventually standing on the raindrop-pocked sand, I'm not surprised to find that the sea is crashing; spray whipped off the tops of the breakers is becoming a mist on the horizon. It's exhilarating, and I already feel more alive. There's hardly anyone about, and I want to strip off and run into the waves naked – a sort of baptism – but the tides along this stretch of beach are dangerous at the best of times, and there are no lifeguards on duty. Part of me doesn't care. Maybe this is what happened to my dad – he got sick and tired of being sick and tired, and in an attempt at renewal he walked into the water until he could no longer touch the bottom, and then he just swam and swam until he drowned, or he swam and swam until he made it to Swansbourne, was delirious with hypothermia, and assumed a new identity in hospital. Or maybe he just got sick of my mum and ran away when she said she was pregnant, like Matt's dad did, except he wasn't kind enough to pay maintenance. My dad might have been an absolute selfish wanker, for all I knew. At least Matt knew his dad. At least he could have it all out with both his mum and his dad, if he had the balls. No chance of that with me and my parents, unless I did a Ouija board, or went to a seance. Or maybe I just left it too late.

Staring at the coastline in front of me – Swansbourne Warren, Swansbourne, the parson and the clerk, Teignmouth … what was next? Paignton? Torquay? Was it Berry Head? Always the recurring, unanswered questions. Maybe I was never going to know what happened to my dad, and I should just give it up and get on with my life.

I walk into the wind, pulling the hood of my cagoul as far over my forehead as it will go. I have to hold onto it to keep it in place. Sand has piled up on the promenade, and the wind picks up grains and whirls them round, stinging my hand and face. I keep as close to the ocean as I can without getting my feet wet. There's nothing like a beach walk for blowing the cobwebs away. It's always helped me put things in perspective.

I need to think logically. What do I know about my dad? Only what my mum told me. Which is weird, because if Misty was her best friend – or the closest thing she had to one – then why has she never spoken about him? She's never even made that comment everyone makes when they see someone's offspring: *oh, you look just like your dad/mum/sister/brother.* Maybe she never knew him. Maybe I'm the result of a one-night stand. Or maybe she found it difficult to talk about, like she did with Matt earlier. Why would she get upset about some comment she made about a wood thirty-odd years ago? The imaginable possibilities make me shiver.

It's tempting to pass all this off as me being paranoid, or having some kind of midlife crisis, but my gut is telling me that there's something wrong about all this. I spent my teenage years running away, my twenties lost in work. A gull mews sharply, and I glance up to see it hanging in the wind. It's close enough for me to see its wings automatically adjusting to the wind, to keep it where it wants to be. I can't tell if it's having fun, or if it's looking for stray chips.

I remember the photo Mum showed me. A tall, thin, pale man, with a shock of red hair. 'Red'! It was orange. Like mine. He hid his under a hat; I cover mine in dark brown dye and eyebrow pencil. But it's always there. My hairdresser says the dye washes me out, makes me look deathly pale. 'Agent Orange', they called him. An investigative journalist. Maybe I need to take a leaf out of his book and do some investigating of my own.

So, what do I know from Mum? They were obviously in love – I can see that in the look she has – had – in her eyes when she spoke about him. They used to go to the beach a lot. He liked trains. But if she loved him that much, why does she keep her photo hidden behind another one, in that album? Why not have a photo of him on the mantlepiece, or in her purse or something?

I'm almost at the lifeboat station now. I should get off the beach and get a coffee from Fortes. And go to the loo. At this time of year, the little hut halfway up to Orcombe Point is closed.

There's a little semi-circular bench with a little semi-circular roof just to the side of the cafe which faces the sea, so I sit there with my oat milk latte and watch the crashing waves, the gulls hanging like kites, the few dog walkers, the clouds scudding across the sky. It brightens up for a moment, and the colours are glorious. The sunlight is coming down like laser beams, and weather like this almost has me believing in a god. Almost.

Mum never decorated the house, even when pine furniture was considered dated and you could buy tables in Ikea for like eight quid. Even when I was earning proper money and said I'd have the place done up for her if she wasn't going to sell. I'd thought she was just old and stuck in her ways, but now I'm thinking she might have been doing that thing grieving parents do – keeping their kids' bedrooms exactly as they were the day they lost their child. Or maybe she was hoping he'd come back – Mum's equivalent of tying a yellow ribbon round the old oak tree, proving she still loved him. She still loved him.

I saw she had black, bruise-like patches appearing on her fingers, and I knew something was wrong. I told her to go to the doctors, but she didn't. She never liked going to the doctors, even though if there was ever anything wrong with me, she was straight on the phone booking an appointment. She put those spots down to old age, and I chose to do the same. I didn't look it up on the internet. I still haven't, so maybe it wasn't a sign of terminal cancer. But it gave me the gut feeling that something was wrong with her.

But what could I do? I lived miles away. We had the odd coffee, the odd catch-up, a couple of phone calls a week. She said she was fine. She saw my Uncle Tony and Aunty Anna a lot. It seemed like she was always out there, at their house in the sticks, next door to the abattoir. She used to look after my cousin, Harley, before he moved out, when Uncle Tony was at work, and Anna was having one of her 'bad days'. Harley isn't Anna's son – he's Uncle Tony's, from a previous relationship. Apparently they tried for a child of their own for ages, but when Anna finally got pregnant, she had a miscarriage. It broke her. Broke Uncle Tony, too, so Mum did the childcare and the accounts for his business, and then when Harley left, Mum looked after Anna.

To be honest, when I heard Mum had died, I'd expected to be asked to fill her role: look after Anna, do Uncle Tony's accounts until he retired, go out there and keep them company. But it turned out, I burned all those bridges with my behaviour when I was a teenager. Anna says I put my mum *through hell,* running away, getting drunk in the park, doing drugs, after all Mum had been through. Those were her words: *after everything your mum's been through.* If I hadn't already planned to leave Devon as soon as I had a car, that would have been enough to do it. *After everything your mum's been through.* What about what she put me through, not giving me any indication if he'd been unwell, if they'd had a row, if the thought of being a father scared him away. Nothing. Except for showing me the photo and telling me he liked trains and the beach at Exmouth. Or was it any beach? She just used to shut me down! I'd ask her something, and she'd get cross. *I don't know what's happened, Nia! Sometimes people go missing and are never seen again. Like that man from that band you used to listen to all the time.*

A shiver wracks my body, and it isn't because my coffee has gone cold. There must have been articles in the papers about my dad going missing. And aren't newspaper archives online now? I down the rest of my coffee, cross the road and chuck the cardboard cup in the recycling bin and stride off to the train station. I need to get home.

There's a loud, rhythmical buzzing. I reach my hand out in the darkness and grab my phone, intending to snooze the alarm and go back to sleep for five minutes. Flipping open the case, I curse myself for not cancelling the alarms, now I'm on compassionate leave. It's still dark, but streetlight filters in from the window. I wonder what time it is. But instead of the digital clock and the snooze and alarm off button, my phone displays Matt's name and the red and green buttons to accept the call or not.

"Matt? What's up? What time is it?"

"I'm so sorry, Nia."

"Matt? Are you drunk? Where are you?"

"I'm on third bridge."

"Third bridge? What?"

"I'm on third bridge, Nia. You know, like you go to Exmouth on the train when you're feeling like shit. I go to third bridge."

I can hear a train whoosh past, and it sounds really close to him. I jolt upright in bed and flick the bedside light on. "Matt, I'm worried about you. Tell me where you are, and I'll come and get you." I swing my legs out of bed and grab my jeans from yesterday. "Matt, are you crying?"

"I'm sorry, Nia! I'm so sorry!"

I'm pulling my jeans on and stuffing the T-shirt I use as a nightdress into them. It's faded black, years and years old. On the front in big capital letters, it says *BABY I'M BORED.* "Sorry for what?! Seriously, don't worry about earlier! I've been wrapped up in myself, Matt – I'm the one who should be sorry!"

"No, Nia, you don't understand. Look, I have to go now. Go back to sleep. I shouldn't have rung." He hangs up.

As I run downstairs, I realise I don't have any socks on, but think, I haven't got time to go back up and put them on. I need to get to Matt, but then I realise I can't get to Matt because I don't know where third bridge is. Should I call the police? I need to think. *Calm down, Nia.*

I switch the kettle on and go back upstairs for some socks and a jumper. A jumper. My blood freezes as I realise this is what Matt could be planning. Third bridge. It definitely can't be in Exmouth, because the line ends there. He said it was his equivalent of me going to Exmouth when

I'm feeling bad. So where did he used to go? Maybe it was with his dad; somewhere they used to go together. But I thought – until yesterday – that Matt hated his dad. Maybe he didn't. Maybe his dad did used to take him places, on the quiet. I mean, Misty always said it was like his dad was ashamed of him, and the little affair he had with a girl half his age – that's why he paid for their living expenses, but never wanted anything to do with them. Or maybe it was just Misty who Derek didn't want to have anything to do with. Maybe he loved his son, but thought the affair might harm his reputation. Yes, there must be something in this, because Misty always told Matt never to play in the woods at his dad's house!

I get Google maps up on my phone and start looking for railway bridges near Eskwich, then abandon it and call Danny. I hope he hasn't changed his number. He picks up on the second ring.

"Kerry! What's wrong?"

"Sorry, Dan, it's not Kerry. It's me, Nia."

"Nia! What the bloody hell are you calling me for at half four in the morning?! I thought something had happened to Gwen!"

"Oh, God, sorry, Danny. No. It's Matt. He just called me, and he sounds pissed and in a terrible state. He says he's out at 'third bridge', but I haven't got a bloody clue where that is …"

I can hear a low rumbling and the occasional bang of metal on metal.

"Third bridge is out near Willand – not far from Poultry Packers. There are five of them, pretty close together. I'm at work, but I can come out …"

"No, Danny, that's fine, I'll find him. I'm just getting in my car now. I'll call you later."

"Okay …"

Danny's about to say something else, when I hear someone shout, "Oi! Put your phone away, Dan, unless you're ordering a Domino's!" He hangs up, and a train rattles past on the viaduct above me.

Poultry Packers. It's the abattoir in Willand. It only does chickens. When the wind's blowing west, the village stinks: a fatty, pooey kind of smell. When I was little and we were driving through Willand, I asked Mum what the smell was, and she said it was the 'Sellotape factory'. It was really kind of her, but I remember going out to Verbeer

Manor clubbing one Saturday (Verbeer Manor had been a nightclub just outside Willand, since Mum was a teenager, but I think it closed down before I was 20) and someone said, "God, it bloody stinks here!" or something along those lines, so I said, "Yeah, it's the Sellotape factory. It stinks round here when the prevailing wind is blowing!" And, obviously, everyone laughed at me.

I've never been a fan of driving at night, especially when it's raining. The light seems to bounce of all the droplets and it's really disorienting. I've got the satnav up on my phone, in the drinks holder bit, so having to continually glance down at that doesn't help either. I go through Cullompton, keep on the main road, and I'm surprised to see that they haven't taken the Verbeer Manor signs down. Maybe it's reopened. On the roundabout, there's a sign to Diggerland, but I think that closed down during Covid. It's dead out here. At least Exeter has a pulse; it's faint, but it's there.

Suddenly, the satnav tells me to turn off left, and I do so. The road narrows and I have to slow from sixty to about twenty. There are a few houses on my right, and a field on the left that has sheep and chickens in. I wonder if the chickens know that there's a death camp for their kind a quarter of a mile away. Maybe they can smell it. I stamp on the brakes as the road bends left again and we go over a railway bridge that is only just wide enough for my car. There was a fluorescent, red-bordered sign on it, but I didn't catch the name of the bridge. It couldn't be the one Matt is on, though, because you can only just get a car over it – there's nowhere to stand and make a phone call. Unless he's in a hedge. Unless he's already jumped.

I drive into a patch of long grass, cut the engine, and run back to the bridge. There's a bit of light from the houses and the streetlights along the main road, but I flip on the torch on my phone and scan the land around the bridge. It's all fenced and hedged off, so I can't get down to the line, but I pull myself as far over the top of the bridge as I can, both sides, and scan the line. Nothing. Something horrible occurs to me, and I check Devon Live, the local news, on my phone. Nothing about the Plymouth train being delayed by a suicide. But then, I heard the train go past as I was leaving Exeter – if anything had happened it wouldn't have got there, let alone carried on with its journey. And Matt had said *third* bridge. Whatever direction you count from, this can't be the third.

Letting the relief I now feel turn into hope, I get back into my car, wheel-spin it out of the grassy verge, and head on up the road. It's just a country lane – one car width wide, woodland either side. I can't go very fast even if I'd wanted to, but the road seems to go on and on. Eventually, there are floodlights – the lights from the factory. There's a lit-up parking area in front of a very tall wooden fence, a winding lane disappearing off to my left, and a railway bridge on my right. This must be the one! But where's Matt's car? He can't have walked all this way, and it's a bloody weird place to get a taxi to, unless you work for 2 Sisters. That's Poultry Packers' real name. I guess it's now run by two sisters. The thought nauseates me.

As soon as I open my car door, the warm, sickly, horror-inducing smell hits me. The wind isn't even blowing now. Maybe it's always smelt out here when you're near enough to the factory. I shiver, imagining what it must be like inside, and the familiar tears start to well. Factory farming is the main reason I've gone vegan, and for some reason, it upsets me more when I think about birds. *Free as a bird,* the saying goes, the connotation being that there is nothing on earth as free as a bird. Yet the one natural light these birds see is what reaches them in their crates as they're driven miles from their farms to their death. Just the journey must be terrifying for them. I can't bear it. Every cell of my body urges me to get out of here immediately. But I have to find Matt. The brick walls of this bridge are much lower than those of the previous one, and because of the light from the factory, I've got a clear view of the track below. No sign of Matt. I can see another bridge a couple of hundred yards ahead. It seems to lead into the factory. I cross the bridge I'm on, scanning the fields and hedges until I come to the top of the road, where I'm surprised to find houses. Like, proper houses where people actually live. A terrace. There are cars in the driveways, the gardens are mainly neat and sport flowers in pots, or fuchsia bushes, and in one there are a couple of kids' bikes dumped on the grass. On the other side of the road is a massive car park – the car park belonging to the factory. It's an immense complex. I walk on and come to a mini roundabout. There's a kind of gatekeeper's building next to a barrier that can be raised, presumably once you've shown your ID. Why a does place like this need so much security? I mean, who on earth would want to be let in, unless you work in an office? Or desperately need a job? I presume that because of the nature of the work, it must pay pretty well. But then, it takes all sorts. I once worked in a supermarket with someone who had wanted to be a butcher, and had ended up running the meat department. And there are certainly more meat eaters in the Western world than vegans or veggies. Maybe I'm one of the weird ones. Looking under the barrier arm, I can see that the road into the main body of the factory is indeed over a railway bridge. How weird! But Matt can't have gone in there. Movement in the gatekeeper's building catches my eye.

A tall, burly bloke in a high-vis jacket strides out of the door towards me. "Can I help you, Miss?" he shouts, in a way that can only be interpreted as *what the fuck do you think you're doing here?* He's holding a walkie-talkie in one hand, and what I presume is a taser or something in the other.

"Sorry, I'm looking for my friend," I say, as meekly and as charmingly as I can manage.

"At five in the morning?! What do you take me for?! Go and 'look for her' somewhere else," he barks, "or I'll have to call the police."

"No, I really am looking for someone," I insist, because it's so obvious that he doesn't believe me. "A boy – well, a man, actually – in his thirties; slim, dark hair, possibly drunk …?"

"I ain't seen no one," the man says, "and I'm not supposed to see no one at this time of the morning, and if I do, nine times out of ten, I call the police. Now jog on and have your little affair in a hotel or something."

"Sorry," I say, sheepishly, embarrassed, and I continue down the road until I reach the main road, and when I look left, what looms above me, but another railway bridge! That's three bridges I've seen. Danny had said there were five in quick succession. But there couldn't be another one in this direction – not until you got past Eskwich Parkway, at Sampford Peverell. Why they chose to call the station 'Eskwich Parkway' is beyond me. It's about seven miles away from the town.

I hurry back to my car, hoping the security guy won't notice me. He can't have, because I make it back without incident. Now that I have a landmark, I check Google maps. I find the line, and, yes, there are five bridges in quick succession. I can see the one over the main road, and the one leading into the factory, the one where I've parked my car, another one, and another one. The last one is the one I'd driven over – the one by the houses, not far off the main road. So where's the other? I must have driven past it.

Very slowly, I retrace my route. I find myself back on Dean Hill Drive, by those free-range chickens. The lucky ones. I drive back, and notice a little road off to the right, so I drive up it only to find it's fenced off like a maximum-security prison, and is full of mobile homes and bricked-up caravans. I have no choice to reverse back, but when I put the car in reverse, the parking sensors go off. My eyes flick up to the rear-view mirror. Three big men stand directly behind me, their features reddened by my brake lights. I gasp, flooded with fear. One of them puts his hand on my back windscreen, the other two stalk up either side of my car. I hit the automatic lock button, and fumble around for my phone. The man on my left taps on my window with a brick, smiling malignantly.

"I'll call the police!" I shout, holding up my phone so he can see it. My voice wavers, and my hand's shaking.

"It's us who should be calling the police, lovey," the man comments, still smiling, "you're the one who's trespassing."

"I'm sorry, I'm just looking for my friend, that's all," I counter, trying to sound cheery and light. "I don't know this road and went the wrong way. I'm sorry." I try a smile.

"OI!"

The three men whip round, and I'm beyond relieved to see the silhouette of Matt, striding up to them.

"She's with me, so leave her the fuck alone!"

"Ooh, all right, lad, all right!" says the one who'd knocked on my window. "We don't get many people round here at this time in the morning, and when we do, they're usually trying to move us on by chucking Molotovs and the like. Why d'you think we've had to put this fucking fence up?"

"All right," Matt says, glancing at me through the windscreen. "Well, there's clearly been a misunderstanding by both parties here, so why don't you let my girlfriend get off your land, and we'll call it quits?"

"Fine by me, boy," the guy says, and he moves out of the way with a sweeping gesture of his arms that suggests he's letting royalty through. "Nice to see you, lovey," he says, leering at me, "you take care, now." And they stand aside, and I reverse as carefully as I can with still-shaking hands, back onto the lane. Matt pulls at the passenger side door, but it's locked, so I press the button and let him in. I immediately press it again to lock us in, and Matt laughs, and pats my knee. He stinks of alcohol. I drive back to the parking space by the factory, cut the engine, and turn to face him.

"I am not your fucking girlfriend!" I yell. Then we lean over and hug.

"Right, are you going to tell me what all this is about, or what?" I can't help it – I'm angry with Matt. I spend the best part of an hour thinking he's going to top himself, driving round country lanes in the middle of the night, getting ambushed by weird men, and then suddenly Matt's there to be my knight in shining armour. It's almost like it's been orchestrated. And he hasn't said anything.

"Did you set this up?"

"What?"

"Did you set this up? So you could come and rescue me and then I'd have to love you forever? Is that what this is?"

For a moment, Matt looks horrified, but it snaps into anger in a nanosecond. "No, I did not fucking 'set this up'! Do you really think I've got nothing better to think about than … than being with you?! You'd like that, wouldn't you? If all else fails, at least you've got me to fall back on. Fuck's sake!" He opens the door and hauls himself out of my car. "You are the most self-obsessed bitch I've ever met, Lavinia!" He slams the door and marches back in the direction of the gypsy camp.

Right, that's it! I get out of the car, slam my own door, and start off into the darkness after him, pressing the key fob to lock the car as I shove the keys into my back pocket. "Matt!" I shout. Fucking hell, I've left my phone in the car, and |I can barely see a thing. "Matthew!" This far along the lane, the light from the factory is gone, and I can't see where the road goes. The only reason I know that I'm off track is that my feet are wet, the ground is uneven, and I'm slipping. I stumble and put my hands out in front of me and immediately wish I hadn't because I get stung by some nettles. They're tall – taller than waist height. They're on my left, and rubbing my hand, I sidestep to the right hoping my feet will find tarmac, but the ground to the right is lower, and I fall. "Matthew!" Rainwater soaks right through my jeans, and my hand is wet, too, but I can't tell if it's blood, water or mud. Getting to my feet, I wipe my hand on my jeans and carry on. I'm scared about the men, and all I want to do is turn back and head for the light, but

I've come this far. Something's going on with Matt, and I want to know what it is. I might not fancy him, but I do care about him – he's my … not 'oldest' friend, because that's not what I mean … he's been my friend longer than anyone else. I suppose he's my best friend. But it seems my mum was right: men and women can't ever just be friends, because men always have this sexual subtext to everything they do. Why can't they get over themselves?! Maybe it's nature. That song from the 90s pops into my head – we're just mammals. But I don't feel that need that everyone else seems to have. I just want to get things done.

And I want to get this done. "Matthew Saunders! For fuck's sake, stop messing around and tell me what's going on! I drove out here in the middle of the night because I thought you were going to do something stupid, and now I'm covered in mud, and I haven't even got my phone! You're pissed and upset, and I want to help you!" I sigh, wishing I hadn't said about not having my phone. Then I add, "You're my best friend, Matt. Please. Let me help."

I've been creeping forwards as I've been shouting, and I find myself in the undergrowth again, this time being scratched by brambles. I jolt away from the pain, and bash into something hard and cold. And metal. A car bonnet.

It's got to be Matt's car, and it seems to be parked ninety degrees to the road, like he's backed into a parking space. I feel my way towards the back of the car, with long, wet grass brushing against me, and then I see him. He's about fifty yards ahead, and I can see him in silhouette because he's looking at his phone. I march towards him. Bang! Straight into a metal gate. Matt laughs. I laugh.

"I wish I'd got that on video!" The light changes over his face and body, and then his flash goes off.

"You little shit!" I say, still laughing. "You'd better delete that right now!"

Matt walks towards me using his phone like a torch. He's smiling. When he gets near me, I can see that I've walked into a metal cow gate that blocks a narrow road that looks like a bridge. "Third bridge," I say, nodding.

"Yep. You'll have to climb over – the mechanism's all rusty and I can't move it. Careful – it's wet."

"Yeah, thanks for that!"

I drop down next to him, and he holds my hand and leads me to the middle of the bridge. Its walls are low, and with the gap in the trees, I can make out the railway line.

"So, this is your Exmouth-by-train."

"Yep."

"Want to tell me why?"

"I suppose so, now you're here." Matt rests his elbows on the bridge, and I mirror him, cupping my face in my hand. I feel the damp from old brickwork soak through my jumper, set off by the warmth of Matt's body, so close to mine. He's silent.

"I thought you were going to top yourself," I say to the double sets of rails, glinting in the faint light from the factory.

"I'm sorry."

"So; what's going on?" I keep my head still, but my eyes flick towards Matt. He swallows.

"I don't know. It's like I've always had this gut feeling that something wasn't quite right with my life, but I've only just realised it now. I'm … well, I'm *lost,* if that doesn't sound too wanky." A quick, ironic smile.

I laugh, watching a spot of light in the middle distance get bigger. "Sounds like a midlife crisis to me." Then, "Woah!" A passenger train passes beneath us so fast that it almost takes my breath away.

Matt turns to me, suddenly relaxed and laughing. "Seriously?! You've never stood on a bridge when an HST's gone underneath?"

"No!"

"Exhilarating, isn't it?"

"Yeah. 'Exhilarating'. That's the word I was searching for!" I retort, my voice dripping with sarcasm.

"You should try it on the bridge by Kennaway Tunnel in Swansbourne when a steam train's going through! It's brilliant! If you stand in the middle, you get smoke so thick it almost chokes you!"

"Whatever floats your boat."

"More like, 'whatever keeps you on the rails'. I thought you liked trains."

We're standing side-on to the bridge now, facing each other. When I put my hand in my back pocket – just because it feels like its dangling weirdly and I'm conscious of it – Matt does the same without realising. I'm finding it hard to concentrate. He's waiting for a response.

"Well, yeah," I say, moving my head about a bit like the awkward pause has been due to me considering my reply. "I like travelling on them. And I used to like playing with them; you know, like we did when we were little. And I do like living by a railway line. It's nice hearing them go by in the night and that. You're never really alone if you can hear a train."

"But you don't like being by the smoke and the actual workings of them?" It's a loaded question. I know I'm in the realms of metaphor, but I'm not sure what he's trying to say.

Matt raises his eyebrows because I haven't replied. What can I say? "No. I guess not."

He turns back to face down the line. "My dad used to bring me out here when I was a kid. He had mates who worked on the railway – one of them was a train driver. Dad told me he let him ride in the cab once!" He pauses, smiling at nothing. "I was so jealous – Dad promised he'd get his mate to let me do it too, one day. But tomorrow never comes. You know."

I look at Matt's profile in the half-light. I'm not sure what the time is, but the sky's more grey-blue than black.

"I'm the product of a one-nighter, you know that?"

I nod, not that Matt's looking at me.

"Mum's twenty-odd years younger than Dad. She used to work on reception at the Gazette, back in the day. She used to be a model, too, on the sly. She did make-up, mainly."

"Yeah, I remember that photo she used to have on your mantlepiece, with that rainbow eyeshadow."

"Yeah. Well. She also appeared in *Playboy*."

"*Playboy*?!" That's news to me.

"Yeah. It paid well, and she said it was fun. Well, Dad … came across her in a magazine once. If you'll forgive the pun."

"Pervert." The word's out of my mouth before I can stop myself.

"Fucking hell! This is just what I'm talking about! Name me one person you knew when we were growing up who hadn't looked at a porno? You can't, can you? You used to look at the ones Danny's big brother had stashed under his bed! And what's wrong with it?! Sex is part of human nature!"

"Yes ... well, not all humans, by the way ... and it's exploitation!"

"Is it? Mum knew what she was doing. She said, if people were prepared to pay megabucks to see a pair of tits, then it's easy money! Supply and demand. Anyway, Dad saw her in a magazine, mentioned it to her at the staff Christmas party, they got drunk, he said he had connections in America. Then she was pregnant."

"And that was the end of her modelling career." Men are all the same.

"No! Being pregnant didn't stop her having pretty eyes! She still did make-up!" Matt pauses. He's angry at my responses, and he's trying to tell me something important. I feel like I'm failing him. "But, anyway, she told Dad she was pregnant, my nan told her she ought to get married, Dad wasn't having a bar of that, Nan threatened to tell everyone he'd got a 16-year-old up the duff, so Dad fired Mum, but said he'd pay for everything if she just kept her mouth shut. And for all her morals, Nan was fine with that.

"Mum was heartbroken, obviously, because he'd promised her the world. It was the 80s – they were living the consumer dream; it was cut-throat, take what you want and as long as you have what you want, nothing else matters. You know? And, as she saw it, it was her mum who'd fucked it all up for her. So she changed her name to her modelling name – Misty – and moved away.

"But Dad didn't desert me. Obviously, he paid for everything, but he used to take me out every other weekend. And then sometimes of an evening, he'd take me trainspotting. We used to come here. He gave me this little book with all the numbers of the locomotives in, and when I'd been out with him, I'd come home, go up to my room, and underline the ones I'd seen, with a ruler. And he had a model railway in a shed out at his place. It was really cool – he'd bought this old signal from somewhere, so he had that outside the shed, and when we were inside, he'd let me switch it to 'stop'. I loved it, because you had to pull this massive lever like you get in an old-fashioned signal box."

Matt laughs at his nostalgia.

"So that's why you always knew which engine was which! You never said!"

"No. It was our secret. Dad was big on secrets. I mean, Mum knew, obviously, but, yeah. I had to keep it under wraps so we could stay in the house, Nan said."

"Bloody hell, Matt! That's a lot to put on a little kid!"

"Yeah. Well. Fear's a great motivator, isn't it?"

I'm chilled to the bone now, but I don't want to ruin the moment. If we sat in Matt's car, it would still be freezing. Dawn's breaking – well, as much as it does on a November day – and I can see the outline of an approaching locomotive as well as its headlight.

"So, go on then, trainspotter-extraordinaire, what's that?" It's a bizarre-looking thing, coming towards us. It's got an engine on the front and the back, and these weird metal cylinders in the middle.

"What? The engines, or the actual train?"

"Both."

"They're Class 66 locos, and the whole thing is the weedkilling train."

"The weedkilling train?"

"Bloody hell, Nia! I thought you were supposed to be intelligent! If they didn't spray weedkiller up the lines every now and then, they wouldn't be able to run trains along them!"

"Seriously? I thought just the trains going up and down would do that."

"Really? Look at the bare bits."

I look at the railway line as if for the first time. The rails, the sleepers, the raised bit for the ballast, the perfectly clear sunken two feet on either side, and the wall of brambles. I know that Network Rail come and strim the foliage back from time to time, but, yeah, now I think of it, you'd have at least dandelions and grasses all over the clear area, if they didn't kill the roots.

I shiver. Matt notices. "Well, I'm pretty much sober now," he says. "Do you want to go home?"

"Are you sure you're all right to drive?" Matt shrugs. "Well, I need a wee. Do you want to hang around until Esky 'Spoons opens? We could get a fry-up. Then you could come back to mine for a bit. If you want."

So, that's what we do. And it's not until he's left mine that I realise he never told me what he was sorry about.

Simon, 1984.

I have to go through the Cofton Lab switchboard. There's white noise, punctuated with clicks, and just when I think the receptionist is going to tell me that Dr Powell is unavailable, Eleanor answers.

I'm in the office, and in spite of the heavy clattering of typewriters, I lean forward so I'm crunched over my desk with the receiver pressed as close to my cheek as I can comfortably get it. I shouldn't be making this call here, I know that, but the alternative is doing it from the phone box on the corner by the bus shelter, where the world and his wife can see me, and the very fact that I'm calling from a public phone will suggest that I'm doing something dodgy. From here, when I announce myself as Simon Hulme from the *Eskwich Gazette*, if they check the number they'll know I'm legitimate. I'm doing the right thing.

"H! Hi! It's Eleanor! How are you? What are you up to these days? And why are you ringing me at work?"

In as low a tone as I can feasibly speak, and with as relaxed a posture as I can muster, I ask her if she is able to check for a specific chemical in a sample of soil.

"Oh, I'm so glad you're well and everything is working out for you. I'm also very well, thank you for asking." She's being sarcastic. Sarcastic with a sharp edge. I've hurt her.

"Sorry. Sorry, El. Sorry. I … It's … How are you?"

"You've missed the moment again, Simon."

"I …"

She cuts me off. "Theoretically, I could analyse a soil sample. But that's not really what we do here, Simon."

"I know. But – and please don't take this the wrong way – you're the only person I know with the skills to do this."

"There are other labs in the UK, Simon."

"But you're the only person I can trust."

"Go on."

I lean back in my chair and nod a few times so that if any of my colleagues are watching me, it'll look like someone's talking to me. I surreptitiously scan the room. Everyone is either on the phone, hammering away, or making coffee. Steve appears engrossed in his photocopying, and the door to Derek's office is closed. It must be whiskey time.

"Can I tell you something off the record?"

"Yes, of course," Eleanor says, lowering her own voice. I hear her cover the mouthpiece and speak to someone else who's in the room. A door clicks shut. "Okay."

I sigh. This is hard. Once I've told her, I can't untell her, and if my suspicions are unfounded, I've … well, I don't want to think about the repercussions.

"Simon? Are you still there?"

"Yes, excuse me, Eleanor, it's just a bit of a sensitive matter. Is there any chance we could meet so I could explain things in private?" I tap a cigar out of a fresh packet, more for appearance's sake than needing a smoke. However, I do need a smoke.

"Not really, Simon," she says, a little curtly. "I'm very busy, and I'm travelling to London for a conference tomorrow afternoon. Can this wait?"

Well, that's made up my mind. I pop the Panama in my mouth and light it with my Zippo, holding the receiver between my jaw and my shoulder. Then I crunch over my desk again. "No. No, it can't. I have reason to believe that someone or some company sprayed an illegal chemical, or the wrong dilution of a chemical weedkiller, on a stretch of local railway line. As a result of this substance seeping into the soil, or into the air, a woman has been poisoned and has miscarried her baby. In addition, the woman lives in a house very close to an abattoir, and it's entirely possible that the chemical has got into the food chain."

I can hear her try to suppress a gasp. "What evidence do you have to support this?"

"Nothing concrete so far, but the husband of the woman said he saw some kind of mist floating up over his back fence when the usual weedkilling train went by – the miscarriage happened in an otherwise healthy pregnancy shortly afterwards. And there's the suicide of a train driver. And unexplained vandalism of properties of people who have looked into the matter."

The silence at the end of the line seems unending. "You do know how this sounds, Simon, don't you?"

"Yes."

"And this is the South-West. Major crime doesn't tend to happen here, but local gossip does."

I'm disappointed with Eleanor's response, then remember I was guilty of similar thinking not so long ago. "Yes. And I know it sounds like a conspiracy. But that doesn't mean there's nothing in it. In fact, if you were messing about with chemicals on purpose, it would make more sense to do it in the country where there are fewer people about, and, as you say, nothing ever happens. And if it was an accident, it was an accident, but if an unborn child has died as a result of it, and many more people may have ingested contaminated food, then we need to help them. And there needs to be an official investigation. All I'm asking you to do is take a sample of soil from the woman's back garden, and some from nearer the railway line, if I can get it, and run whatever tests you do to see what's in it. If it's normal, then at the very least it will have put my mind at rest, and I can let the woman know that her baby didn't die because she was poisoned. The hospital have diagnosed her with manic depression, or antenatal depression, or something."

Another long pause.

"Okay, Simon. Okay. I need to put my mind at rest too now. You realise this is coercion, don't you?"

I cringe. I hadn't thought of it like that.

"I'm so very sorry, Eleanor," I say softly. "That wasn't my intention. It's just that you're the only scientist I know – well, have met, in all honesty – and I'm certain there's something to this. I didn't know what else to do."

"You won't be the first person to do something wrong with the best of intentions, you know." She lets the sentence hang. Is she talking about the police and the miners? "But, yes. I will help you. And in return, you can take me out for dinner."

Nia, 2022.

When Matt's not working at the South Beach Café, he's volunteering at the West Somerset Railway. It's a heritage railway, run entirely by volunteers, as far as I can tell, and their base is the station at Bishop's Lydiard – a weird little place in Somerset, so it's one hell of a drive for Matt, now he's living in Exmouth.

He's been going out there for years. It started when Danny's dad took them all – Matt, Danny, Leon, and Crofty – on one of the railway's Steam Special events. Basically, they all got to ride on a steam train, have a chat with the driver and the other volunteers, and have a go running the model trains on the model railway, which took up the top floor of the railway museum. They met an older guy called Jason Mallett there, and by the time they were 18, they were running the model railway, bringing their own engines in and putting on a show for visitors. They'd show people round the museum and stuff like that, too, but mainly – from what I've gathered – it was the geeky boys having fun. It was serendipity that them having fun meant that the general public got a taste of the 'Golden Age of Steam'.

Then they started their YouTube channel. Danny had been a bit weird about having his name used online, because anyone watching could link him to his daughter, so he wanted them to go by false names. Matt said they spent ages trying to come up with decent names, but he hadn't wanted to go down the Thomas the Tank route, so eventually Jason had suggested they use British Railway shed codes. Apparently, back in the day, each major steam engine shed in the country had a code. Matt chose 72A –

Exmouth Junction shed, because he lives in Exmouth; Danny went for 9A – Longsight, because he's short-sighted (he finds this hilarious still); Crofty went for 26F – Patricroft, because his real name is Patrick Mycroft; Leon is 9G – Gorton, because his last name is Bennett, so it's like Gordon Bennett (which he still finds hilarious); and Jason is 71A because his family is from around Southampton way. Collectively, they're known as the Platform Five Boys, because they hang out on platforms, and there are five of them. Ugh.

Anyway, Matt's taken me out to Bishop's Lydiard with him a few times when I've been having bad days, or bored days, and, yeah, I see the attraction: massive, noisy, beautifully painted, majestic steam locomotives pulling up at a pretty platform that's still got all its Victorian features. I love the hissing of the steam when they start the engines up – the steam that comes out round the front wheels, not just out of the funnel. The smell of it! And if you get close enough, you can feel the heat from the boiler and the firebox. It's like you can see the pure power of the things, the mechanics of it. Yes, engines now are stronger, faster, etc., etc., but they're all sleek and antiseptic. All surface, no substance. Or maybe that's just me being nostalgic; after all, I love the old yellow and blue HSTs because they remind me of my childhood. How lovely it would be to find joy in the present moment! Anyway.

What I don't understand is why anyone would want to be indoors watching miniature versions of those magical engines going round and round and round a miniature, fake world with plastic sheep in the plastic fields, and plastic trees and plastic bridges. It's not like they even push the trains along or anything! You just press a button and then chat about the different models and gauges. But they all love it – hence the YouTube channel. They review new models, run their little engines, and sometimes do 'shunting missions' where they put loads of trucks all over the layout, draw straws for engines they've randomly placed on the tracks, and then see how many trucks they can shunt together. It's basically just a load of big kids messing about, but if they've got nearly a million subscribers, well, that speaks volumes about what I put value on. And, to be fair, the 'shunting missions' are fun to watch. The best part of it is that they're using the West Somerset Railway's model railway, so it's raising awareness and boosting the tourism.

The trouble with it is, the railway relies on coal, and that's kind of frowned upon these days, what with global warming and all that. But Matt says if they just opened up the coal mines, it would bring jobs, stop Britain importing coal from the rest of the world, and how much damage is a heritage railway really doing compared with all the cars and factories, and factory farming, and all the politicians and billionaires flying around in private jets, ad infinitum? And they've been cutting up swathes of countryside for HS2 which has been causing all kinds of havoc for 10 years, and it's still not finished. And then there's the view that we're all going to hell in a handbag anyway, so we may as well enjoy the time we've got. Unless this is the way it's supposed to be – our culture was meant to eat itself.

It's a week after I drove out to third bridge in the middle of the night. I haven't seen Matt since then because he's been working, and I've been sorting things out, going through Mum's house and stuff. At some point I'm going to have to find a job. Matt asked me if I wanted to work in the cafe, behind the bar, because in spite of the fact that the economy is totally messed up, post-Covid, they're having trouble recruiting seasonal staff. Any job's better than no job, especially the way things are with the 'cost of living' at the moment. He's right. I may well have to take him up on it, because my inheritance isn't going to last forever.

Anyway, Matt asked if I wanted to come out to the WSR with him, just for shits-and-giggles, and I thought, *why not?* So he picked me up at half seven, and here we are pulling up on the vast expanse of gravel that is the WSR car park. He's been chatty and bright and positive – normal Matt – all the way up, so I haven't had the heart to ask him what he was sorry for, when he said it the other day. There's a sign on the fence saying that we have to drive into the parking spaces that run along closest to the railway, and I'm just querying it in my head when it occurs to me that because most of the people who visit heritage railways are old, so maybe they have a tendency to reverse through the fence ... and then I mentally slap myself for being so judgemental.

"What are you laughing at?" Matt turns to me with an amused smile as he presses the stop button to turn the car off.

"Just that sign, that's all." I concentrate on taking my seatbelt off so I don't have to make eye contact.

"What? The one about having to have your bonnet towards the fence?"

"Yeah." I step out of the car. It's blowing a hooley, but at least the sun's out.

"Yeah, I wondered about that, too," Matt says conversationally. "I thought it might be so they could get your face on camera, or something, but I think it's so everyone's aware that cars will be reversing out, so fewer old people and little kids get knocked over."

That makes me laugh out loud. "Seriously?!" I manage to say. "If they were worried about that, then why wouldn't they make people reverse *in* so they could see what's in front of them?!"

"Oh yeah," he says, blushing a bit. "Then maybe it's so you don't get distracted parents and old people wondering where the beeping noise is coming from, and reversing through the fence!" And then we're both laughing. "Why don't you ask?" Matt says.

"Why don't *you* ask?! You work here!"

"Yeah, but then I'd look like a tit."

"And nobody would be surprised!"

"Fuck off." He gives me a dead arm, and we're laughing like we're kids again.

He guides me round the hairpin, sloping path, past the public toilets, and down into another, smaller car park, which I guess is for staff, and then up onto the platform. The volunteers take really good care of the station. All the planters are made from old railway sleepers and are full of bright flowers; the paint on the shutters and doors is immaculate; the old-fashioned advertising signs for cigarettes and Bovril and the like are all shiny; there's a second-hand book shop, a cafe, a ticket office … it's lovely. Matt leads me down to the end of the platform, where it slopes down level with the tracks – a crossing point designed to be used by railway staff only, but seeing as no trains are running today, and the WSR is not connected to working passenger and freight lines, anyone can use it, if they're careful – and we walk across the line. I like to look down the rails when we do this. I suppose it's not a million miles away from standing at the top of a flight of concrete steps and rolling forwards on the balls of your feet. Matt stops, and I bump into him. He's crouching down picking a load of marigolds that have somehow sprung up in the corner between a rail and a sleeper. Again. I'm about to say something about bees, when Matt straightens up and presents me with the bunch of marigolds. It makes me smile, in spite of myself.

I could take them from him, lean over and kiss him on the cheek, and then we could walk arm in arm into the museum and up the open stairs to the floor which holds the model railway, and his mates would all cheer, and they'd do a special video, maybe with Thomas the Tank Engine, and Rosie, who's his love interest, if you can have a love interest in a toddlers' TV show, and we'd all live happily ever after.

What I do is smile, take them from him, and say *we'll have to get these in some water and give them to the lady who runs the bookshop.* And I walk off over the rest of the rails and up on the sloping side of the opposite platform, looking straight ahead and smiling like it's the most natural thing in the world. In a couple of seconds, Matt has caught up with me and is chatting about how Danny's ex wanted Marigold for Gwen's middle name, but Danny had wanted Annie or Clarabel, so they'd settled on Rosie, and I'm glancing into his heartbroken eyes wondering if any of it is true. If there's some kind of afterlife, and Mum can see me, I know exactly what she'd be saying: *Matt's a good man, Nia, and he loves you. That's so rare in the world. Why can't you love him back? You'd both be so happy.*

Inside the museum is colder than out – they've only just opened up, and the heating hasn't kicked in yet – and smells of death. I have no idea what death actually smells like – the only dead person I've ever seen is Mum, and I was crying so much I couldn't have smelt Vicks – but death is the word that springs to mind. I suppose *history* or *old, dry paper* would be more accurate. It's a shame museums have to smell like this – I'm sure it's what puts people off going. It's almost like the smell is trying to say *you shouldn't be looking at this; this is over and gone; look forward, not back.*

"Oi, Oi!" That's Leon, aka 'Gordon'. He's standing on a stool fiddling about with a spotlight in the far corner of the room. He reminds me of Smithy in *Gavin and Stacey.* "Danny just said you were out at third bridge for the weedkiller the other day! I never saw your picture on Platform Five!"

'Platform Five' is what they call their internet forum-cum-Facebook-page. It's surprisingly popular. Well, it's surprising to me, at any rate. Trainspotters, or 'railway enthusiasts' as they're known these days, are a tiny minority of the population, I thought – a bunch of geeks enjoying a little counterculture. Turns out, there are thousands of them across the globe. But with – what are we on now? 7.2 billion? – people on earth, I guess that is a tiny minority. Anyway, there's a pause, so I blurt out, "He didn't get a decent shot, Leon. The light was bad."

"Ooh, out on a lonely bridge at six in the morning with our Matty, were you?" Leon chimes in, "Just passing by and happened to bump into him, I suppose ..."

"Yeah, leave it out, Leo," Matt says, the red disappearing from his cheeks as quick as it had arrived. We exchange an awkward glance, and I hide the marigolds behind my back, much too late.

"The light was bad at third bridge, was it?" Alan's beer gut appears round the corner of the 'signal box' before his face. Alan's run the museum since the year dot. "I caught it out at Whiteball and it was fine there." Again, Matt's cheeks flush, and I shoot a look at Danny, who busies himself polishing up his replica City of Truro.

"Yeah," Matt says, suddenly conversational, "Nia hadn't seen a weed killer before. She didn't even know they existed!"

"Well, how did you think they keep the weeds down?" Leon says in bafflement.

"We've been through that, thanks, Leo," Matt smiles.

"Oh yeah," Alan lollops over. He's on the waiting list for a hip replacement, but he makes it in every day. "The weed killer, the squirter and the nuclear train are my favourite ones to take! Take a look at these!"

Alan grabs his camera from the signal box, switches it on, and brings it close to us so we can all see the display screen. "That was yesterday at Cogload," he says, scrolling through loads of burst shots of the train we Matt and I saw the other day, backlit, the sun reflecting off its wet metal. Alan's still scrolling – I wonder how they managed in the days when you used to have reels of film.

"Nice shots, Al," Jason nods approvingly, handing him a soot-stained mug of builder's tea, and peering over his shoulder. "I like a bit of moody lighting!"

"Cheers, Jase," Al says, slurping from the cup. I shiver. I don't know any of them – well, other than Danny – well enough to ask for a coffee. "Ooh, and that's it again going through Whiteball," Alan continues, "and that's one I took of it round the back of 'Nam last week."

"Sorry? 'Round the back of 'Nam?' That looks like … well, it looks like that place I parked by the other day when I was looking for you, Matt." It'd be hard to confuse the two tracks down the middle with the curved sidings at the sides, with that flat bridge in the background. That's the abattoir bridge.

"Ah, so it wasn't a bumping into kind of thing then," teases Leon, "it was a deliberate rendezvous!"

"Grow up, Leo," Matt snaps. "Yeah, that's Esky Loop, where we were the other day," he says to me.

"Anyone else want a hot drink?" Jason calls.

"Yeah, we'll have a coffee, please, mate," Matt says, nodding in my direction. I smile, and Jason disappears.

"So why do you call it 'Nam then, Alan?"

"Ah, it was long before your time, lovey," he says, like I'm still in my twenties. "There's an old house behind Poultry Packers – you can't see it so well now they've built that industrial site up – that's known as 'Nam, coz back in the 80s someone sprayed Agent Orange on the line, and everything round it died, including a baby. Well, that was the rumour round here, anyway. It got into the papers and everything, but nothing ever came of it. Just some local journo inventing news to make a name for himself, it turned out. But the name stuck!"

Simon, 1984.

"So I have to go out to my grieving brother and sister-in-law's, act like everything's normal in front of them and Harley, make up a reason for going in the garden when it's chucking it down with rain, and somehow get a 'decent-sized' soil sample without anyone noticing, and then smuggle it out past a blockade?"

Lucie is doing her utmost to sound affronted, but there's a glint in her eye that tells me she's secretly going to enjoy the risk-taking.

"It would be much easier if I could just tell Tony and Anna. And they have a right to know what's going on."

We're walking over to the King's Arms, in Exeter. There's a band on tonight – a group of Esky lads who – for reasons best known to themselves – go by the name of Nashville Skyline. They've got a bit of a following, and, according to all sources, are exceptionally talented. Although I have the ulterior motive of asking Lucie to get me a soil sample that I can pass on to Eleanor to test, this counts as a date. In addition, I am staying at Lucie's house tonight, because we are – at her request – going to have a few drinks together and stay out until the pub closes. She says we both need to let off some steam, and that I'd never make the last train home, and she doesn't want me sleeping on a platform all night, not that I've never done it before. By the way she's squeezing my hand, and walking so close to me that bits of us are rubbing together, I'd say there was more than that, but I'm not going to count my chickens or make assumptions, and I'm certainly not going to take advantage of a girl who's had too much to drink, and, if I'm honest, I'm very nervous about the possibilities this evening holds, while simultaneously desperate to get this soil sample. Also, she's told me that she only has a single bed, and that I can kip on the settee. But I think that was just for appearances' sake.

All the same, I'm excited about this evening, and I'm enjoying being the man who's holding her hand, when every bloke we pass is staring goggle-eyed at her, in her denim mini skirt and fishnet tights. I just wish we weren't going to spend it in the King's Arms. It's a good music venue, by all accounts, and it supports local bands, but it's got one hell of a reputation. The police station a vehicle outside it every night there's live music, and even so, last week a bloke got glassed and nearly lost an eye. But it's Lucie's local, and she used to go there a lot when she was younger, and she knows that landlord, and we're virtually guaranteed a lock-in.

A train passes by slowly on the bridge above us, and squeals to a stop at St Thomas'. Lucie and I cross Cowick Street, dodging the traffic. We can hear a group of lads pile out of the train singing football songs. I expect they're heading for the King's Arms, too. Lucie spins round and grabs my other hand as we reach the kerb, and I laugh as we kind of dance down the street to the pub. She leads me up the steps and opens the arched wooden doors onto a wall of noise.

Nashville Skyline are incredible. Getting drunk on watered-down lager and lime is incredible. Seeing Lucie dancing right in front of the band until there's a massive crowd around her, is incredible. The fact that I am the man she's dancing with, laughing with, having a night out with, is incredible. And when the landlord rings the bell for last orders, Lucie says, "Shall we just go back to mine?"

I have never, ever been happier. Trish is the first of my colleagues to comment on the change in me. She says she's never seen my 'real' smile before (a phrase that's bittersweet to me). Larry and Mickey just laugh and make lewd comments about my getting my end away, finally;

popping my cherry. My first response is anger, but I push it down. In any case, they don't know me, and never will, and I don't have to be friends with them to work with them. They can think what they like.

And a couple of days later when I meet Lucie in the Half Moon after work, she says, "I got that sample for you," and she nods at her bag. A chill runs through me even though we're in a packed, over-warm pub. I nod, and we say no more about it.

The next morning I'm bashing out a quick press release about a school fete, killing time before something happens. My theory about the brewery takeover being a smokescreen for the Willand Incident, as I'm now calling it in my head, has proved to be a yet another product of my paranoia – we're expecting an announcement later today. The sound of a door creaking makes me glance up to see Derek wafting out of his office on his nicotine cloud. He reminds me of Jabba the Hutt in that bar scene in *Star Wars*.

"Simon," he says, smiling in a way that makes me feel a little ill, "how are things progressing at Tom Forde's?" He walks past my desk nonchalantly and flips the switch on the kettle. I'm forced to stop what I'm doing and follow his movements.

"Progressing?"

"Yes." Derek catches himself. "I mean, how are things developing, rather, with the takeover. Any news?"

I find this an odd question from someone who edits a newspaper. I find this an odd question from someone who still lives in the town they were born in.

"Well, the workers are expecting an announcement this afternoon. I've asked Tom to call me after he's spoken to his staff, but I expect I'll be inundated with people giving their two cents. In all honesty, I can't see that the news is going to be favourable to the brewery staff. As you pointed out the other day, people are losing their jobs left, right and centre. Money talks. And Tom is past retirement age."

"Yes, well, as Mrs Thatcher says, it's competition that will strengthen the economy. Time for a change in all areas, I think, don't you?" He stirs his coffee and heads back to his office, without asking anyone else if they'd like a drink. Come to think of it, I'm surprised he didn't just bellow for Trish or Steve to make him one and bring it to him, like he usually does. I have the foreboding that what I say next will have a significant bearing on my future. So I say nothing. I just smile.

I'm going through the press releases again, because I simply can't concentrate on anything. Eleanor met me outside the Marine Tavern the previous evening and drove me to the Smugglers Inn on the Teignmouth road. It's one of those halfway houses, so it picks up a lot of tourists and passersby, has very few regulars, and is a place neither Eleanor nor I had ever frequented. The idea was, we wouldn't be noticed. I bought her scampi and chips, and she took the soil sample. I knew that as I sat at my desk, smoking, she was in her lab finding out what – if anything – was in that soil. And that whatever was said at Tom Forde's today would hold next to no importance for me, compared with the next words I would hear from Eleanor.

When the phone rings, I nearly jump out of my chair. "Bloody hell, Si!" says Trish, "Anyone would think nothing ever happened in Esky!" I scramble for the receiver, feeling my face flush. I shoot a glance at Trish, and I hope she interprets it as a smile.

"Hello, newsdesk, Simon Hulme speaking." I flick my eyes towards Trish again, and see suspicion and concern in her face. Bloody hell.

"Simon, hi, it's Ellie."

Ellie? I pause, confused, and while I'm gathering myself the woman says, "Ellie. You know, the scientist you took out for dinner the other night?" Her tone is playful, thankfully. But, 'Ellie'? Oh no.

"Hi, Ellie! Sorry, it's been manic here today, and I'm expecting a call any second relating to a major story. Sorry."

"Oh." Eleanor sounds affronted. "What, a story more 'major' than …"

I lower my voice. I can't lose her. "No! No, nothing like as important, but it's one my editor has been making me cover all month, and ours is …"

"Still off the record?"

"Yes." I'm glancing around the room. Everyone's preoccupied. Except Trish. She's watching me. I try to relax my posture. I smile at her. She's not buying it. I hold her gaze, then nod. I'm going to have to tell her. Eleanor is talking.

"It won't be for much longer, Simon. What I found … well, it's serious. People could go to jail for this."

She doesn't elaborate. The silence is all-consuming. "Ellie? What did you find?"

"I couldn't believe the analysis at first, so I did the whole thing again, on the remainder of the soil. I always save some of the sample in case something goes wrong. So I tested it again. There's a potent chemical defoliant in the soil sample you gave me. 245-T."

She pauses to let the information sink in, but, other than the fact it's really important and really bad, I haven't got a clue what that means. "Ellie, I haven't got a clue what that means. Dumb it down, please, if you can."

"245-T is commonly known as Agent Orange. It's the incredibly effective defoliant the Americans sprayed over large areas of …"

"Vietnam, in the early '70s."

I place the receiver back in its cradle. I'm reeling. I need to tell Trish. I need to tell Derek. I need to tell the police! I light the stub of my cigar. I need to think, but the phone rings. It's about to kick off at Forde's and Sons. I grab my hat and coat.

"Simon, I'm going to need to know what's going on." Trish collars me in the stairwell as I'm dashing off to Tom Forde's.

"Yes. Yes, you do. Honestly, you won't believe this, Trish. But Tom Forde's making his announcement and they want the press there, so I'm going to have to speak with you later." I hop down a couple more stairs.

"If it's that important, Simon, you need to tell Derek, too."

"Yes, I know! I want to tell you both – I want to tell – *need* to tell – everyone! But I can't miss the announcement. Whichever way it goes, it's going to have a profound effect on the town, and this other thing has waited for several months, so one more day isn't going to hurt, and the staff at Forde's deserve to have their story covered properly."

Trish smiles and nods. "You're talking like a local," she says, then immediately corrects herself. "Well, you'll never talk like a local, but I think you're beginning to understand what it means to be chief reporter on a 'local rag'."

I cringe. She's obviously overheard me muttering to myself. I do that a lot. It's a nervous thing. Words just come out when I'm stressed. Like a soft version of Tourette's.

"Simon. Don't worry. You're good at this job. You were headhunted, remember? You can hide under that hat and cloak if you want to, but you have a way with people. And you're fair. Now stop acting all coy, and get yourself down to Tom Forde's! Here, take my car. Again!" She pulls her keys out of her bag and throws them down to me. I fluff the catch, and we both laugh. "And when you come back, there'll be a new box of biscuits and some Kenco – *I'm* stocking the 'facilities' today!"

The scene at Forde's is unbelievable. The road is packed with vehicles and people milling about – press, workers' families, the TV. And the police. There's a riot van parked off Howden Road. I only noticed it because I had to park on Curzon Crescent and jog over to the brewery.

There's no getting through the crowd, but suddenly there's a security guard on my arm, pulling me to the front, and into reception. It's packed. It seems that the entire brewery workforce is here. And that's as it should be. Tom Forde is standing halfway up a flight of stairs, so everyone can see him. He looks like a rabbit in the headlights. Behind him, leaning on the banister, are two of his sons. And at the bottom of the stairs, off to the side, flanked by two security guards, are three men in expensive suits. Old Tom is in jeans and a Forde and Sons Brewery polo shirt. He's dressed like his employees. This could either mean he's on their side and sticking by them, or that he wants to soften the blow – he's one of them, and this is as hard for him as it is for them.

"Hello, gentlemen. And ladies." He nods to the receptionists. Everyone falls silent. "Forde's Brewery – *your* brewery – is as much a part of this town as the rivers Esk and Loman." The tension becomes palpable as no one makes any response. Tom blanches, and his Adam's apple bobs up and down. "My sons and I, and my father before me, and his before him ..." Tom stumbles. There's an awkward pause as he tries to pick up the thread of the speech he's obviously rehearsed. Then he looks down at his shoes and shakes his head.

"Boys," he says, looking his workforce in the eyes, "this brewery has been in my family for generations. Some of you have worked here since you were teenagers. This decision has been agonising for me. I mean, it's broken my heart that I've had to think about it at all. But the world's changing …"

And that's it. A wall of men in dark blue polo shirts crashes over the stairs like a tsunami. Security guards brace themselves against the banisters, trying to force them back. Tom's sons are at his side, pulling him further up the stairs, but Tom shakes them off. He tries to raise his voice over the cacophony of voices. I pick up fragments of what he's saying, but I'm being pushed up against the factory walls, and I've dropped my pen …

"So sorry, boys … I'm old now …sons have … own lives to lead … market's changing … simply can't compete … change as good as a rest …"

The Whitbread's men are nowhere to be seen, and suddenly there are police everywhere. The glass around the reception desk smashes, a woman screams, men are shouting. I see the receptionist who spoke to me the other day fall to the floor, and I run to her, pushing people out of the way, trying to drag her out. I make for the doors, shielding the woman with my body. My hat's gone. There's a thick, wet sound, a muffled scream. I turn round on autopilot. A policeman has his baton raised. He brings it down on a worker's torso. I'm almost sick. This is a scene from the TV news. This cannot be happening.

We go through till midnight. The guys in Plymouth have to reset the whole paper. In the midst of it, Derek says he's just glad that they chose to make the announcement on a Monday and not a Friday. I can't believe all he's thinking about are the sales. But maybe that's how you need to think if you want to be an editor. Maybe that's how you need to think if you're going to survive in Thatcher's Britain. Still, it's undeniable that there's an atmosphere in the office. A buzz. Things are happening. Real, big news, happening. We have a 'real' news story at last. Someone's wheeled a TV into the office, and we catch snippets of Spotlight as we bustle by. A cameraman had been filming live down at the brewery – God knows how – and I watch myself, the terrified receptionist sheltering under my arm, pushing against the flow of bodies, away from the brewery buildings. Steve's watching it too. He looks over at me, his expression serious and earnest for once, and gives me a barely perceptible nod. He's young; he's shocked. I wonder how many of his family are now out of work. I wonder if any of them got hurt. Twenty-odd men were arrested. A couple more, and one policeman, had to be taken to hospital.

Society is dead? Not in Eskwich, it's not. Margaret Thatcher, all over the national news, claiming that competition will boost the economy. Maybe it will. But at what cost? How many families in this little town are now without an income? Repossessions, homelessness, unemployment, poverty, rioting, hatred. Yes, the new staff at Whitbread's will undoubtedly bring their families here, needing new homes to be built, more shops, more roads, more schools. Fresh blood in a town notorious for its inbreeding. But then will taxes increase to cope with the demand for Jobseekers' Allowance? Pitching one demographic against another. Divide and conquer. Or maybe Maggie's right, and it's more about survival of the fittest. Maybe a shake-up is what people need. Maybe it will lead some to better jobs. Maybe some will learn guitar while on the dole, and be happy. Maybe bored housewives will be forced to find work – a new path, independence. Maybe it will shake up stagnant relationships; break some up; lead to affairs. Maybe, in time, people will look back at the takeover of Forde's and think of it as the best thing that ever happened to the town. Then again, maybe there'll be suicides.

Suicides. Like Geoff Kerslake's.

Here I am, writing my big 'exclusive', and all I can see is the image of Geoff, swinging from that branch. When do I raise the issue? And who do I go to first – the police, or editorial? Or the *News of the World*? I could sell my story and make a lot of money. It would be some sort of compensation for Lucie and her family. And maybe I'd get headhunted again, maybe by a national? This could be the making of me. But if I did that, I'd be selling out both Geoff and Lucie. And Geoff only drove that train because they offered him money, and his family was suffering because of the Tories closing the mines. I'd also be selling out Anna and Tony and their unborn child. Cashing in on the misery of others. Then throw the fact that I'm a journalist into the mix. I got into this to expose truths, to make a difference. This story *has* to be told. The people who did this – the 'they' who made Geoff drive that train and press the button or whatever the mechanism is that releases the weedkiller – have to be brought to justice. Also, where the hell, in a backwater place like Devon, would anyone get their hands on a canister of Agent Orange?! The irony of the name of the chemical defoliant being the same as my old nickname isn't lost on me. I choose to interpret it as a sign.

I write my exclusive, and while it's being processed and printed for publication tomorrow morning, I make my way to the Half Moon. I'm hoping for a quiet, reflective drink, but when I enter the bar, I find that the whole of newsdesk are in there. In fact, it seems like the whole town is in there: all the tables are taken, it's sardines at the bar, and Mandy's yanking a cover over the pool table, so it can be used as tables, chairs or both.

A bitter laugh escapes me – it's Maggie's manifesto incarnate. Sudden mass unemployment has boosted Mandy's takings for a Monday night at least 200 per cent.

Squeezing my way through the throng back out into the market precinct, I see that all the outside tables are occupied, too. I pause, wondering whether I can face the Eskwich Inn, or whether I should just get on the bus and go home. But in Swansbourne, I'm literally miles away. I need to be here, where things are happening. It's as if Eskwich's turned into London – a metropolis with cultural change bubbling beneath the surface, not some backwater little place where nothing important ever happens. Then I hear her.

"Simon!"

Lucie runs over to me from out of the shadows. We embrace, openly.

"Simon! I have something *really* important to tell you!"

I catch her by the shoulders and look as deep into her eyes as I can without tearing my soul apart. "And I have something really important to tell you, too!" I lead her away from the pub and into the alley that runs between the market and the town centre. We must look like a couple of teenage lovers.

The alley is empty and dark, and would have been noiseless if the stream that trickles into Cogan's Well – a kind of ornamental drain built into the pavement – hadn't been engorged by the heavy rain.

Lucie opens her mouth, but I hush her. "Lucie. Your brother was right. I had the soil sample tested. You won't believe what's in it. Someone needs to be brought to justice, but I'm not sure how to go about it. And you deserve to know before I tell anyone else."

She cuts me off. "And *you* deserve to know something before *I* tell anyone else!" Her face is pale, but radiant, scared but excited. "I'm pregnant!"

The following Saturday morning, I'm at my typewriter before Trish arrives. I don't even bother with the 'facilities'. I just sit down, slam a piece of paper into the machine and hammer away. I have to get it down, then present it – I've decided this is the best way to approach Derek.

"Wow! You're keen!" Trish's voice makes me jump; I hate working with my back to the door. I twist my head around and meet her eyes.

"Yes. This is the important story I mentioned the other day, when Forde's broke …"

Trish tries to cut in, but, for once, I talk over her. "The best way to explain it is if I just write it down and let you read it."

"Ooh, I'm intrigued," she says in her habitual, jolly way. Then her tone changes. "Really. It's about bloody time. I don't like keeping secrets from the boss. Fancy a coffee to keep you going?"

"Please, Trish." I try a smile, and am relieved when she returns it warmly. Then it's back to work.

After about half an hour of intense typing, my fingers and wrists are painful, but I'm satisfied I've got the basics down. Trish has seen to all the press releases and answered all the calls. I've been aware of her eyes on me over the top of her typewriter, but she's said nothing. She's simply let me get on with it. When I finish, I lean back in my chair and reach for the stub of my cigar. I'm surprised to see that the glass ashtray is empty – I've been too engrossed even to light one.

I fumble in the pockets of my coat until I touch the familiar texture of a fresh packet. The burgundy cardboard is embossed with little dots – another charm of smoking Panama. I rip the gold paper off the top of the inside of the packet, select a cigar and light it. I puff enthusiastically, accidentally inhaling. The smoke makes me splutter, makes my eyes water, and goes straight to my head.

Trish laughs. All I can do is raise my eyebrows. She gets out of her seat and swishes over to me, in her long, pleated skirt. "May I?" She plucks the final piece of paper out of my typewriter and sweeps the rest from my 'out' tray.

Trish takes them over to her own desk and starts to read. I just sit there, smoking, watching her intently. At points, her eyes widen, but other than that, she remains impassive.

Eventually she looks up and asks, "And you've tried BR and the council, to no avail?" She knows I have – their total lack of comment or communication is written into my story.

"Yes."

"How many times?"

"Many. And I'm not the only one." I push down my irritation – she's only questioning me out of professionalism.

"A lot of this could be dismissed as hearsay, you know."

"Not with that soil sample."

"It would have to be verified."

"That's for the police to decide. This is a news story." I hold Trish's gaze.

"Indeed," she says, after a pause. She taps her pen, thoughtfully. "It would be nice if you could use your scientist's name."

"I'm sure they could be persuaded."

"'They'. Nice."

I shoot her a wry smile.

"Well. I'll arrange a meeting for Monday, so we can run it past Derek." She rises to her feet again.

"Where are you going?"

"To see if Lee's still in the building. If we send it to press on Monday, we'll need pictures." As she exits, she turns back and adds, "Good job, Simon."

I'm so happy, I could cry.

"*Page twenty-eight*?!" I slam this week's Gazette down on Derek's desk and say it again because I can't believe it. "*Page twenty-eight*?!" I push back the tears.

"Hmm." He doesn't even look up. He's rifling through some papers, his cigarette hanging from his bottom lip. "Do you like football, Simon?"

"What?"

"I asked you if you like football. You're shaking your head, and you've never shown an interest in Mickey's work, so I suppose not." He pauses, staring at me, taking a long suck on his cigarette. I watch the white paper become grey ash. Derek smokes it right down to the filter. Crushing the butt in his already crowded ashtray, his eyes meet mine again, and he continues.

"Sometimes, in a game of football, a player does something – a tackle, perhaps – that he interprets one way, and finds that the referee has interpreted it a different way. The referee will make a decision based on his interpretation of the player's action. Give him a yellow card, for example, or give the opposition a free kick. Or both. Occasionally, the player will be outraged by the referee's decision, loudly contesting it. The referee, as is his job, will attempt to calm the player down and explain his reasons. And that *his* decision is final.

"Because the referee's decision is always final, Simon. And if the player should push too far, then the referee is quite within his rights to give that player a red card, sending him off, and out of the game. Do you understand what I'm saying to you, Simon?"

I stare at my boss in disbelief.

"This isn't a game, Derek," I spit. I think this is the first time I've ever used his Christian name.

"Oh, I know it's not," he croons, getting to his feet. The editor leans over the table, the weight of his body supported by his fat fists. "It's far more important than that."

He glares at me. This is going nowhere. I'll tell the nationals. Derek Locke is not my keeper. I break the hostile eye contact, turn, and make for the office door.

"You can't accuse the authorities, Simon. It'll land you in trouble," he calls after me.

"I can and I will. And I have proof. I'll be the one to cause the trouble." With the briefest glance into his steely eyes, I exit, slamming the door.

I get off my train at St David's and walk as briskly as I ever have all the way along the river to Lucie's house. When I arrive on Beaufort Street, I'm flushed and tearful. I hammer on the glass of her front door.

The sound of her running down the hall precedes the growing, blurred shadow appearing in the glass. Her emotion is palpable behind the door. Lucie fumbles with the locks and tears it open.

"Simon!" I can see the dried salty rivulets down her cheeks. I stand on the pavement staring at her. I feel like I've failed her.

"Page twenty-eight?!"

She stands back from the door to allow me in, so I step over the threshold and wrap her in a hug, kicking the door closed with my foot. Speaking into her hair, I murmur, "I know. I can't believe it. I had it out with Derek, and I think I'm on the verge of losing my job."

"Simon! You shouldn't have! You can't!" She pulls back from me and her hand flies to her belly.

Covering her hand with my own, I say, "I know, I know, but a man's taken his own life. Tony and Anna have lost their baby," at which Lucie winces, "and who knows how many other people have been affected without knowing it. I mean, if it went over Tony's fence, then it must have got into the chickens arriving on the lorries, and the workers changing shifts ... into the factory through open windows ... it doesn't bear thinking about! I can't stand by and let this go!"

We're in the kitchen, now. Lucie is slumped in one of the pine kitchen chairs, elbows on the table, her hands taking the weight of her head. In true British fashion, I automatically put the kettle on to boil, and I lean with my back on the worktop, looking at her. Something occurs to me.

"Do you think Derek's trying to cover something up?" My eyes water.

Lucie smiles and shakes her head. "Why would he want to do that?! It's probably because of the Forde's thing. I mean, the riot was all over the news – the TV news, I mean – it's like ..."

"A local take on national events. Yeah, I understand that. And what's on the TV sells papers, I suppose. But Trish thought it was big. She really pushed for it to be front page, in the meeting. Maybe it's just because I'm personally affected by this one. It'll be interesting to see what the *News of the World make of it.*"

Lucie looks up and meets my gaze. "The *News of the World*?"

"Yeah. I made some calls before I came round."

The *News of the World* are interested enough to send one of their own reporters down to the 'patch' to investigate the story. I should be happy, but I'm internally seething, because if they run the story, I won't get the byline. I've got to try to get a rapport with their journalist and ensure he gives me a mention. I'm also sweating a bit because the guy they're sending down goes by the name of Dave White. It's a common name, I know that, but it's also my former best mate's name. It can't be him. He can't write for toffee.

We meet in the Half Moon, at the table near the toilets where Lucie was sitting that day. Simultaneously, it seems like years ago, but moments ago in my head. I arrive early, intending to look professional, perfectly at home in my surroundings, but also clearly … well … *better* than the natives of Eskwich. I don't like the sound of that, even in my head, but it's important. And true. And when I throw open the double doors of the Moon, Dave White, soon-to-be chief reporter of the *News of the World* is already there.

If I'd have pushed the doors open gently, like I usually do in case someone is standing behind them, I could have caught a glimpse and scurried back out. But I hadn't done that, and the sound of those double doors screeching and banging open, accompanied by the blast of cold air into the over-warm bar, results in the locals, and my former best mate, turning their heads to see me and my ego standing in the frame like a gunslinger in a Western. I want to disappear.

Dave is standing, smiling. He calls me over, cheerily, as if he hadn't cheated on me with my girlfriend; as if he hadn't had a baby with the girl I love. The girl I *loved*. I correct myself immediately, pushing down the knowledge that I'm lying to myself.

"Dave."

"Si, honestly, we can't –"

I cut him off. "We're here to talk about the story. That's all."

Dave smiles, sadly, shaking his head. "Okay, Si, if that's how you want it. But you better not run off in the middle of this one, without all the facts." He walks over to the bar. "Whiskey and soda?"

Warmed by the whiskey – not by the fact that I'm here with someone who knows me well enough to buy a round I'll actually enjoy – I tell Dave the story. From the scene with Geoff Kerslake behind the railway sheds, to Lucie and, finally, Ellie, I tell him everything. He listens, dispassionately.

Eventually, he says, "It's a story, Si. It might well be true – and if it is, it's awful for Tony and Anna – but without corroborated proof, it's just a story."

"But I've *got* proof, Dave! Ellie did the sample!"

Dave sighs. "Yes, she did, but there's no way we can prove that the Agent Orange came from the railway, and there's no way we can prove that there's some sort of conspiracy going on."

"What about Geoff Kerslake, though? What about what Cheryl said?!"

"It's he-said-she-said stuff, Si! Small-town gossip, all muddled up with the fact that everyone involved was either related or having an affair!"

"But a man died, Dave!"

"Yes. A man killed himself. Any truth and justice he was after died with him."

I open my mouth to say something, but there's nothing to say. He made up his mind when I sat down. He's never been my friend. He just uses me to get what he wants and humiliate me in the process.

A shadow falls over our table, and Mandy reaches out for our empty glasses, asking if she can get us the same again.

Dave asks for two coffees, and Mandy raises her eyebrows, shooting a glance at me. I don't respond, so she wanders off to get the drinks.

"Oh, bloody hell, Si. You look like a child who's about to have a tantrum."

I stand up, grabbing my hat. "Yeah, and you'd know all about that, wouldn't you, Dave?! Playing happy families with my girlfriend!"

Dave's standing, too. "Oh, here we go again! You make something out of nothing, Simon, every bloody time! Charlotte and me was a one-nighter. She came crying to me because you'd told her you were – and I quote – *never going to fall in love* with her. And if you'd stuck around instead of being a self-pitying idiot and running away and cutting all ties in a bloody temper, she'd have been able to tell you that *you* got her pregnant, not me, and that the day she found out, you'd told her you were never going to love her!"

"So, I'm a father?" I whisper.

"No! No, you're not a father, because once it was obvious that you were never going to come back, she asked me to take her to have an abortion. I had to bloody pay for it, too.

I can hardly keep still on the train on my way in to work the next day. I haven't slept – not properly, anyway. I stayed up drinking coffee and smoking all night, freezing cold in my chair by the open window. I wanted to hear the ocean smashing itself against the sea wall, but it was flat as a mill pond. As a weak dawn breaks, I'm woken from a doze by the smattering of rain on the glass, and on my hands. Heavy, flat, dark grey clouds cover the sky.

I wonder what Dave's done with my story. The newsagent in Swansbourne doesn't open until well after my train leaves, so I have no idea what the morning newspapers look like. When we slow down on the approach to Exeter St Thomas, I look out of the window and try to smile at Lucie, who's waving out of the small opening at the top of her bedroom window. She blows me a kiss, and then she's lost in the reflections.

Pushing down self-examination and allowing a mental fog to shroud my cognitive processes, I'm waiting by the bus doors when it pulls up in Eskwich, hands sweating, heart racing. I haven't bothered with my Walkman. No one's going to save me. As soon as the driver's opened the doors, I stumble out, mumbling a quiet *thanks, Drive'* over my shoulder. It's chucking it down with rain, so I suppose it doesn't look odd that I'm walking so quickly up into town that I'm almost jogging. Esk Valley News is only a couple of shops down from the Gazette offices, so I dash in out of the rain to look at their news-stand.

There's no sign of my story. The fog in my mind grows thicker. I pick up the *News of the World* with shaking hands, and fumble with the pages as I turn them. Somewhere towards the middle of today's edition, there's a page headed *Life's All White*. Dave's face grins up at me from the page and I feel sick. He has a column. He has a bloody column. It's mostly covered by his take on a story about the misdemeanours of a supermodel, and it's supposed to be funny in a let's-all-laugh-at-a-famous-person way, but it's horrible so I stop reading it. Squished into the remaining space down the right-hand side, there's a strip of stories that are no longer than three paragraphs each. One of them reads:

On the Wrong Track! *A country-bumpkin news hack tried to make trouble for British Rail yesterday, blaming the death of a train driver and an unrelated miscarriage on the service. Simple Simon Hulme, reporter on the local Devon rag that ran the story, got his knickers in a twist because of a series of steamy affairs, and suggested that the weedkiller used to keep the tracks clear on the local branch line near his home in Devon was swapped for the notorious chemical defoliant, Agent Orange, which poisoned the environment and led to the unfortunate deaths. The outlandish conspiracy theory* *angered BR, who deny the allegations, but what Simon said no less damages its reputation further. Maybe it is time for an industrial shake-up. And maybe Simon should put a piece of hay back in his mouth and take the next train out of town!*

Numb and broken, I go to the till. The proprietor, Bob, looks me up and down. I place the *News of the World* on the counter and force a smile. He raises his eyebrows.

"You made a bit of trouble for poor Sue Kerslake, the other day," he comments, scanning my face. I drop my eyes, fumbling for change in my pocket. "Her boys aren't happy, either, having all that dragged up for all to see."

I try to hand him the coins – it's the correct money – but he lets it fall onto my newspaper. "It might be all right in the city, but it's not all right round 'ere. You bear that in mind, boy." He snatches up the change, and I grab my newspaper and head out into the rain.

Adrenalin propels me up the office stairs, but as soon as I put my hand on the knob to let myself into newsdesk, the numbness is replaced by dread.

Trish is at her desk, quietly sipping a coffee. Other than that, the room is silent and empty. I hang up my coat and hat, and glance at her. I'm just about to speak when she shakes her head and nods in the direction of the closed door to Derek's office.

I sit at my desk for a second, visibly shaking, wondering whether to feed some paper into my typewriter, make a coffee, or light a cigar. I remember that I don't have any. Then the editor's office door opens. Derek's head emerges in its perpetual cloud of smoke.

"Mr Hulme. A word, please."

He partially closes the door behind him and disappears back inside. I glance at a tense Trish, and follow him.

The air in Derek's office is thick and yellow, but I can clearly see the row of national newspapers spread out across the polished mahogany of his desk. I can clearly see his livid, red face standing behind them, too.

"You may be our chief reporter, Mr Hulme, but I am still the editor. I ran your little conspiracy theory in our paper out of the goodness of my heart – NO! Let me finish! I ran your little conspiracy theory – because that's all it is, Simon, you do realise that, don't you? – and in return, you went behind my back and tried to sell it to the nationals.

Sensationalism sells, Simon. I know that you know that, and I presume you received some sort of payment from that scrap of an article in the *News of the World*. Luckily for you, I know the editor, and I was able to persuade him not to name our newspaper. But I didn't realise was that you were so short of money – NO! Let me finish! You are pushing your luck today, Simon, and I am this close," he holds his fat thumb and forefinger aloft, and they're barely touching, "this close, to terminating your contract. Now. I didn't realise you were in financial trouble, and I was going to offer you a raise – ah, ah ahh …" he waggles his finger at me as I open my mouth to retaliate, "and I was going to offer you a raise, because money is going to become even tighter now you have a little one on the way."

Derek Locke smiles malignantly at me. I stand there, rendered mute. How on earth does he know? He continues, "I understand that seeing a cadaver for the first time can be a shock, and I understand that you are young and ambitious – not to mention in love with a girl who has lost a baby nephew. So, if you allow me to make the big decisions – as I should, being the editor, and being your boss – and stick to doing what you are paid for – which, I have to say, you do extremely well as a rule, and which is why I'm reluctant to part company with you – I will happily allow you a ten per cent pay increase. Now, what do you say?"

After a beat, I stammer out, "It's not a conspiracy theory. Eleanor – Dr Eleanor Powell, head of research at the veterinary laboratory in Starcross – tested the soil sample. It was full of Agent Orange – she said so! And you know what that did to people in Vietnam …"

"Dr Powell, yes. Well, it seems that Dr Powell has been having health issues of her own, Simon, and has had to leave her employment due to a nervous breakdown."

I stand there, mouth agape. *Eleanor!* I'm scared.

"That amendment to your salary will appear in your pay cheque at the end of the month." He looks at me and his tone softens slightly. "Think of your own unborn child, Simon. That's what's important now."

Nia, 2022.

Redbank Court stands deep within a wood in the middle of rural Mid-Devon. It's been owned by the Locke family since it was constructed, sometime in the 1600s. Now, Derek and his wife, Vera, live there. Alone. And Derek's 'bastard' son, my best friend, Matt, is renting a two-bed terrace on Victoria Road, Exmouth, because he doesn't earn enough to be accepted for a mortgage. But, apparently, he *can* afford £800 pcm rent. This is the state of 'Great' Britain, right now. But I guess nothing much has changed since the 80s.

Anyway, Redbank. There's a small cottage in the grounds, which, historically, was the live-in accommodation of the estate's gardener. When he was younger, Matt thought that at some point his father would invite him to move into the cottage. It's funny how, even when all the evidence of your entire life is screaming at you that this is something that could never happen, how you, as a child, retain a certain faith in your parents. Later, when he could no longer fuel the delusion and hope, Matt's spoken to Derek a few times about the possibility of Derek and Vera moving into the cottage, which would be much easier to manage, so that they could hire out the court itself to residential groups, for conferences, team-building events, or even weddings. Vera actually had the gall to ask Matt who would manage such a venture. He turned the other cheek, as he does, but the slap stung. Derek just stood there and let her say it. My parents may be gone, but I think in a way that was worse.

And yet, when Vera starts going off her rocker, Matt's the first person he calls.

Matt's phone is connected up to his car, so I stay silent and listen to their conversation.

"Matthew."

"Hello, Dad."

"I was wondering if you could pop round sometime soon. Maybe this evening if you're not otherwise engaged."

Matt turns a bitter laugh into something between a cough and a snort.

"Why, Dad? Is your washing machine on the blink again? Or have I missed someone's birthday?"

There's no reply, but we hear a hissing sound, and a woman's voice, warbling in the background.

"It's Vera."

"What? Is she auditioning for *Britain's Got Talent*?"

"Don't be obtuse, Matthew. I'm worried. She's rambling."

Matt pauses before saying, "What do you mean, 'she's rambling'?"

There's a long pause, so laden with things unsaid that it speaks more than words. Derek is actually serious.

"She's running around saying the woods are haunted. In fact, she's running around shouting the woods are haunted. There's no one else I can call, Matthew. Please come round."

Without waiting for an answer, Derek hangs up.

"Well, that was weird!" Matt smiles at me briefly before his gaze fixes back on the road. He presses a button on his door, and his window goes down. Then he scrabbles around in the door pocket for his vape. Despite the window being open and the fact that we're pushing ninety on the M5, the car fills with strawberry-flavoured smoke. In seconds, it's as thick as the atmosphere. After Muse's *Compliance* finishes, the guy on Absolute Radio starts chatting about their 'make me a winner' competition, so I switch the radio off. My eyes are filling with water.

"Funny that your mum used to tell you not to play in the woods, and suddenly Vera's saying the woods are haunted," I murmur.

Matt inhales, leaving the vape in his hand as he puts it back on the steering wheel. He doesn't exhale until I'm wondering how he can hold that much smoke in his body.

"Sod the Platform Five Boys – they'll have to manage without me. I'm pulling off at Sampford. We're going to Redbank."

I've seen pictures of Redbank, but as I've never been there, I had no idea how far out it is. Once we get to Sampford Peverell, Matt turns sharply down a road opposite a bridge. I can't tell if it goes over a river or a railway line, the canal, or the river. We pass through a quiet residential street – mainly modernised cottages and farm buildings – and the road narrows almost imperceptibly until it's barely wider than Matt's car. The hedges are high, and it being such a dank day, I feel like we're being pulled through a tunnel. My stomach tightens with foreboding.

I glance at Matt, who's pale and expressionless, his eyes fixed on the meandering country lane. He seems lost in thought and doesn't notice I'm looking at him, but he could just be concentrating on his driving. Some people drive like nutters on these roads, thinking no one else is on them. Uploman comes and goes, the Redwood pub comes and goes, and I feel like we're falling away from civilisation. It's a cold day and Matt has the heater on high, but although I can hear it, and feel it blowing stiflingly warm air at me, I can't suppress a shiver.

The hedges are lower, and the surrounding countryside must look idyllic on a summer's day. Flocks of rooks tumble through the grey sky, and even though it's not yet autumn, it's raining leaves. The road is interminably long and winding. Sometimes I glimpse a river but I have no idea which it is. Pheasants run out in front of us, their panicked paths weaving so close to us that I keep jumping when they disappear from sight, bracing myself for the thick, wet bump of Matt hitting one. Finally, there's a sign for the court.

The sign is more like a noticeboard and has been hammered into the ground, right next to what is clearly an ancient yew. I bet it severed some roots going in. We turn off up a wide drive, and eventually the asphalt becomes gravel that crunches under Matt's tyres, and the road rises to the level of a steep grassy bank, and the austere, gothic court looms into view. Gargoyles; those pointy arches; lead-latticed windows; blood clot-red brickwork; turrets and towers. It looks as though it should be full of vampires.

Matt breaks the silence as I gasp. "Intimidating, isn't it?" But he's chuckling.

"You can say that again!" I breathe, relieved. "I'm not surprised the woods are haunted – Vincent Price would have had a field day!"

"Ha! Don't let it suck you in," Matt comments, meeting my eyes for a second as he reverses into a small parking space marked *reserved.* It's very close against the building, and I find myself pseudo-braking. "It looks gothic, but it's not."

"It must be! It's like 500 years old, or something!"

"Yeah, 500. Ish. It's imitation. No different to that estate up Moorhayes, where they modelled new-builds on Victorian farm cottages."

"Oh. That's disappointing."

"Par for the course, really," counters Matt, his shoes loud on the gravel. "People are always pretending to be something they're not."

I get out of the car and slam the door, wondering if I've missed something. A buzzard screams and I turn my head in the direction of the sound – high over the trees.

Matt looks up, too – herd mentality or mirroring, I'm not sure which. "Is it a raven?" he asks.

It makes me laugh. "No, just a buzzard," I tell him, astounded that he doesn't know.

"Oh," he says. "That's disappointing." We exchange smiles, but the moment lasts longer than it should, so I raise my eyebrows in a kind of 'Right, then, let's go, shall we?' way, and turn my body in the direction of the building. Matt takes the hint, and leads the way across the gravel drive up to what until two minutes ago I would have thought was a gothic-arched double-door.

I shoot a look at Matt, who shakes his head. "It's *supposed* to be intimidating, remember?" he says.

There's a shuffling sound, followed by the clunking of old keys in old locks, then a metal deadbolt being drawn back.

"It's just my dad," Matt hisses. "A sad old pervert with a dirty secret."

"Who used to take you trainspotting," I add, under my breath.

"Which obviously makes everything else he did fine!" Matt's fiery sarcasm burns me, and I automatically reach my hand out to touch his. Looking straight ahead, he whips his hand away. I can feel the heat coming off him, and I wish the ground would swallow me up.

One half of the massive door draws open, neglecting to creak. A little old man in a brown suit and checked shirt stands in the gap. His body looks helpless, but his eyes are hawk-like, and ice blue.

As I step over the threshold, I feel like I'm Jonathan Harker meeting Count Dracula. Mr Locke clocks my shudder and smiles. With nothing more than a nod of acknowledgement at myself and Matt, he walks off to the left, his footsteps in their formal heeled shoes ringing on the tiles.

Matt follows obediently and automatically. I hesitate, trying to take in the cavernous entrance hall. Shining black and white floor, a wide-based staircase that splits off in both directions opposite the door, flanked by a gargoyle, or an evil-looking griffin thing on each side. There's an immense chandelier above. Taxidermied heads on dark green walls. Ebony panelling. Not wanting to get lost in this place, for a multitude of reasons, I take in what I can in a glance and trot off after Matt.

We walk briskly along a wide corridor. There are large wooden doors at regular intervals down both sides, the dark green paint continuing above about a metre-high strip of panelling. The chequered tiles have ended, and we now tread on a narrow strip of vermillion carpet with a paisley kind of pattern that lies down the middle of creaking floorboards of dark wood. There are large oil paintings in ornate, gilt frames, and I catch myself looking at the eyes of the people, horses and dogs depicted, to see if they move. *Scooby Doo* pops into my head, and I suppress a laugh. This all feels unreal.

The very last door on the left is propped open with a familiar 1980's sausage dog draught excluder. A memory that's more than a flashback hits me, and I gasp. Mum had one like that in the house in Exeter. Our front door had a net curtain over it permanently, but when it got really cold, Mum would pull a very dark velvet one over it, and push the patchwork sausage dog against its base. I can see her doing it now – kicking the dog into place with her slippered foot. I watch her turn and head upstairs. Her skirt comes part-way down her calves, which are encased in nude tights. 'Nude'. That was the name of the colour. It was the 1980s. I scurry along the hall and kneel at the dog's side. I pat his tough little head and adjust one of his ears so they're both hanging down properly. I smile into his black, beady eye. I'm whispering something. I stroke his head and back. His left side – the side by the door – is already so cold it feels damp. "Nia." Matt's nudging me.

Feeling like I've been disturbed in the middle of something important, I sit down on a plush, flowery sofa. Matt sits next to me, but not so close that we touch. Derek seats himself in a leather armchair and lights a cigarette.

"Where's Vera?" Matt asks. It's more of a demand than a question.

"She's in bed, Matthew."

"Hang on a minute," Matt says, leaning forward, his voice rising, "You literally just phoned me up and insisted that I come round immediately because she's going mad, and – lo and behold – I arrive, like the bloody people-pleasing dick I am, and suddenly everything's fine!" Matt's standing up now, but one stare from Derek quells his defiance. He sits.

I know Matt feels powerless. I empathise with how he feels – controlled, emasculated … whatever. I sit stock-still and wait, willing Matt to punch his dad's lights out and swear never to see him again. But he doesn't. Derek allows the tension to grow with the silence. The beginnings of a pressure headache like the ones I sometimes get before a thunderstorm, stabs me behind the eyes.

"Vera had taken a tablet, and now she's sleeping." Fear seeps down my spine like an ice cube.

"However, this isn't – and can't be – a permanent go-to solution for her outbursts.

"As you've no doubt forgotten, it's mine and Vera's sixtieth wedding anniversary in a month. The dinner party has been arranged for weeks and cancelling is not an option. I cannot have my wife descending into madness in front of our friends and guests."

Eyes still fixed on the floor, Matt monotones, "So what do you want me to do?"

"I want you to tell her she has Alzheimer's."

"What?!" That's me and Matt, and we follow it up with insuppressibly incredulous laughter.

Derek's face doesn't change.

"Dad, if you think Vera has Alzheimer's, then you should speak with her and get her to see a doctor! There's all sorts of help out there! I'll look on the internet for you …"

"No. She won't go to the doctors. You need to tell her. Tell her about her outbursts. Tell her how she keeps forgetting things … leaving the taps running, calling you by the wrong name. That sort of thing."

"What? She's never called me by the wrong name …"

"Tell her about her outbursts, Matthew."

"But I've never seen her have an 'outburst'! And you've never mentioned her leaving the taps on and that!" Matt pauses. I shudder. "You haven't even tried to get her to a doctor, have you?!"

"And that's what I want you to do, Matthew. She's running around, spouting drivel that could have serious …" he searches for the right word "… implications. She must be told, and others must hear, that Vera has a degenerative memory disease. Then, if she has hysterics at the party – or anywhere else for that matter – there will be a valid reason for it, and no one will jump to silly conclusions."

Matt lifts his head and stares his father in the face. "No."

Derek smiles. "Matthew, there is no 'no'. I didn't phrase any of this as a question. Now be a good boy and do as you're told."

Matt stands, grabbing my arm and pulling me to my feet. I don't know what to say, or where to look. I feel … detached.

"No! None of it's true! It's psychological abuse …"

"Gaslighting," I murmur.

"Call it what you like – it's happening," Derek says, recrossing his legs and leaning back in his chair. He stretches his own arms along the chair's and flexes his fingers. "It's happening because I say it's happening. Now. Swear on your mother's life that you'll do as I say."

"No," Matt spits.

Derek titters. "I don't think you understood me, Matthew. I said, swear 'on your mother's life'."

I barely register the crunch of the gravel or the clunk of the car doors closing. I think Matt says something, but I can't be sure. I stare dead ahead as Matt drives me home. I notice his arm reach out and turn up the heater, but I'm not cold. I'm numb.

As we re-enter town, the streetlights and the headlights of oncoming vehicles catch the droplets and rivulets of rain, and it's almost as though a child has chucked a pot of glitter over the windscreen. I remember me and Matt making Christmas cards for our mums at school – when we'd finished, we'd always dunk our paintbrushes in the runny glue, squiggle over the whole picture and then throw glitter on it. Tiny fragments of shiny plastic that get everywhere and are only nice for a few seconds. Glitter is really bad for the environment, but no one knew that, back in the 80s. Or, rather, no one bothered to think about it back in the 80s. Why should we always have to be told? Can't we work things out? Maybe we don't care. Maybe we just don't think.

Aware suddenly that I'm thinking, I realise that I'm angry with Matt. Yes, I could have made a scene. I could have flatly refused and called the police. I can *still* call the police – I'm cradling the phone between my legs. Feeling impotent, my mouth goes for the anger. Anger and violence is always the easier option, I know that, but I need a release, and my reptilian brain takes over.

"Do you know why I will never be your girlfriend, Matt?" Not waiting for an answer, I continue, "It's because you have no fucking balls. You sit there, all 'yes, Daddy; no Daddy; please don't take my money, Daddy'. Screw him! And screw you, too! You're not stupid, Matt! You could get a proper job. You know, stop playing trains with your little friends and actually work for a living! Make your own money. You don't need him. You're not stupid. Well, not in an IQ way, at least. And as for your mum! Well, she needs to get up off her lazy ass and get a job, too. All she does is play the poor-hard-done-by. 'Oh, poor me! A nasty man got me pregnant, and I chose to have the child but I didn't bother with going down the proper channels and getting a legal agreement drawn up – No! I just took what was thrown at me and did as I was told. Poor little me!'"

I slap the dashboard with my phone, and in a sad and reckless parody of a driving test, Matt makes an emergency stop on Ashley Straight.

We screech to a stop. "Fuck off, Nia! It's you who's always doing the poor-hard-done-by bit! 'Poor me, my

daddy's not around. I'm so fucked-up. My life is so sad!'
Asking everyone, 'Did you know, I grew up without my
daddy? No? Well, I did, so feel sorry for me and forgive me
for all the fucked-up things I do, because it's not my fault.'
Nothing's ever your fault, is it, Nia? You're completely
powerless because you never knew your dad. Everything
that's wrong in your life, you can blame on not having a
daddy. Imagine if you knew your dad, and he was a
manipulative freak, like mine! I'm sick of all your bullshit,
Nia, and I'm sick of always picking up the pieces for you
and always being there for you. All you've ever done is use
me. You're no better than Derek!"

A car horn blaring from behind us prompts Matt to
start the car and drive off. We're both flushed and it's
suddenly very warm in the car. A loaded silence ensues.
Matt's driving too fast and is nearly in the back of the
Chelsea tractor in front before he realises and slows down
and drops back. That's so typical of Matt. Sensible and
polite. He's a matchstick, not a fire. The phrase 'damp
squib' pops into my head. It's why I've ignored or rebuffed
all his advances over the years. Not that he's actually made
a move on me. He's too nice a bloke to do that.

"Let me out at the Heron, Matt."

He sighs. "Come on, Nia. We're both upset. I'll drop you home and none of this will be as bad in the morning."

In spite of myself, I know he's right. There's no escape from this. And anyway, the buses around here are so unreliable these days, I know I'd end up having a drink at the Heron and calling a taxi. Basically, throwing the best part of fifty quid away. Cutting off my nose to spite my face. And the Heron's another thing that's pretending to be something it isn't – a beautiful thatched white cottage with well-kept gardens, right on the bank of the River Esk, where it flows under an ancient bridge that Simon & Garfunkel definitely didn't write *Bridge Over Troubled Waters* about, and is owned by the Marsdon chain, which means broken toilets, and that they've never heard of vegans – or if they have, they choose to ignore them – and the food's generally accepted to be crap and overpriced. It's a picturesque pretender. Ugh. I'm livid inside. I hate Matt almost as much as I hate myself.

"Fine."

We've crossed the bridge and rounded the sharp bend at the Bickleigh turn-off before I've managed to get the word out.

Simon, 1984.

The Willand Incident has been dismissed as a conspiracy theory. I've been put on sick leave – apparently, I'm of a nervous disposition, and am being treated in hospital for a nervous breakdown, brought on by the scenes I witnessed at the riot at Tom Forde's. I'm a talented, but very young man, at the start of his career, suffering from the pressures of the job, with the extra burden of worrying about how I'm going to support my wife and unborn child. When the national papers send their reporters down from London, British Rail and Mid Devon District Council are only too happy to talk to them. Tony and Anna are interviewed, and although they tell the reporters exactly what they had told me, just like that, the story goes away, and with it, my hopes of ever getting a job on Fleet Street, or on the TV.

Lucie and I are having a picnic of sorts out at Orcombe Point, in Exmouth. We'd got the train from St Thomas' at her suggestion. We needed some fresh air, she said; we both needed to go somewhere different, get a change of scenery.

When we got off the train in Exmouth, it had been bucketing with rain. Lucie put her umbrella up, and we used it both as a shield and as a battering ram against the elements. When we got to the seafront, we headed straight for the Deer Leap.

The pub was packed, and they had the wood fire burning, so everyone's wet clothes were steaming. I joked with Lucie that we'd gone back to Victorian times. When we ordered food, the barmaid said we'd have a half an hour wait at least, so we'd quickly drunk our drinks – whiskey and soda for me, half a Guinness for Lucie – and left. We got some packets of sandwiches, crisps and cans of Coke from the little cafe next to the chip shop – which didn't open till twelve – and walked along the sand as far as it went. It's still cold and windy, but the sky has cleared a little now, and is full of the whole spectrum of clouds, with streaks of bright blue in between. We eat with our backs to the sea wall, staring into the crashing waves. When sunbeams hit us, it's surprisingly warm. Neither of us has said anything for a while.

I break the silence. "Let's do this every Sunday."

My tone must have been overly bright, because Lucie snuggles into my shoulder as the bitter wind blasts us. "You did your best," she says, as I curl my arm tighter around her. "And nothing was never going to bring Tony and Anna's baby back."

"That's not the point, though. I feel like I'm earning blood money."

"You can't think of it like that. We need every penny we can get now. Have you given notice on your flat, yet?"

"Yep. We'll be living in sin very soon, don't worry!" I lift her to her feet and kiss the top of her head. We walk back along the beach. Lucie holds her sandals in her hand and splashes through the surf, her hair streaming out behind her. She's beautiful. I hold her close to me and kiss her. I can feel the little bump in her belly against me. The waves soak through my shoes, but I don't move.

On Monday morning I have to walk straight past the office, turn right onto William Street, go past the hospital, turn right again to go down Barrington Street, right again up Gold Street and right again past the Gazette offices three times before I feel strong enough to go inside. Even then, I go through reception, where Marie smiles at me. There's a rumour going round that she's a model, and she's been in

Playboy. Steve announced it to us the other day at the pub. He'd had a few, but he was adamant. He called her a slut, and said she'll shag anyone for a couple of glasses of Chardonnay. I could have thumped him.

"Welcome back, Si," she says as I walk through reception to the dark blue door on the far side. "Are you feeling better?"

"Much better, thank you, Marie." I try to shrug it off.

"Well, I've watched you walk past the office twice, so ..."

Oh no. I didn't think anyone would notice. There's no point denying the obvious. "Yeah. Just a bit shaken up ..."

"From everything that happened?"

"Yeah."

She smiles, sympathetically. "It's totally understandable."

Then I say the thing I have been told to say. "Thanks. I'm lucky to have a boss like Derek – he could have let me go."

Marie smiles, but her eyes are frowning and concerned. She glances behind her and then walks round from behind her desk. If I hadn't seen Lucie in the early stages of pregnancy, I wouldn't have noticed her swelling abdomen. She sees me looking.

"You've got sharp eyes, I'll give you that," she says, covering the bump with her hands. "Please don't say anything, Simon – I haven't told the dad yet. And to be honest, my friend had a miscarriage the other day, and it's got me a bit scared. I didn't plan on getting pregnant, but …". She does look pale, and I can see she's welling up.

"I won't tell anyone, Marie, you can rely on me. Take care of yourself, though." I smile and make to open the door that leads onto the stairs, but she catches my arm.

"Simon." She's scared. "I know what people are saying about me, but I'm not a slag. I …"

"Marie, don't. No one believes that. And you know what this town is like – one day you're big news, the next you're forgotten …"

"Simon, There's something else. I wouldn't have said anything, it's just that I wanted you to know that …

well, I wanted you to know that my friend – the one who lost her baby – she works at Poultry Packers."

I shake off the role I'm supposed to play and ascend the stairs with renewed purpose. I'm going to go straight into Derek's office and have it out with him. I can't sell out. This is serious. The police need to investigate. I need to get in touch with Eleanor. I need to make all this right, and if that means sticking to my guns and shouting about it, even if it does cost me my job, then I bloody well will.

I'm a flight from the top when the door to newsdesk crashes open. Mickey comes through it, backside first, carrying two heavy boxes.

"All right, Si!" he shouts when he catches sight of me. "You don't want to help me get these down to the cellar, do you?" It totally throws me, and I revert to type.

"Okay," I grab the top one. It's really heavy. "What's in it?"

"Dunno. Just some shit from Derek's office. He's having a clear out."

He must have seen the look on my face, because he says, "If you chuck it down the stairs, he'll know it was you!"

It's more than just his office Derek wants cleared. He says he's ordered some new filing cabinets, a new desk and some new swivel chairs for us – the Gazette is being done up. Steve calls out, "Can we get a new kettle, too? That white one takes years to boil!"

"And a tin of Fox's instead of Family Circle!" Mickey adds from behind me. Everyone laughs. I smile. Steve notices me.

"Oi, oi! It's Agent Orange!" Everyone turns round. I smile and look at the floor. I try to breathe deeply and relax, only to find that I've bitten my lip. There's a smattering of laughter, and Larry mutters audibly, "More like Randall McMurphy." Steve doesn't get the reference, and launches into a chorus of *nice one, Simon, nice one, son!* Until Derek glares at him, and he goes and busies himself at the photocopier.

The massive stacks of archived back-copies go into the cellar too, and Derek asks – and by *asks* I mean *tells* us

– to put all our piles of paper into a labelled box and take them down, so we can have clearer desks. When the new filing cabinets arrive, we go through everything and put the bits and pieces we still need in there. Derek's wife, who is into horticulture, is doing us up some plants to *dot around the office*. Apparently, it will lift our spirits.

The only thing that will lift my spirits is getting justice – for Tony and Anna, for Marie's friend, for Lucie, and also for me. The whole of newsdesk, with the exception of Trish, are now calling me Agent Orange. Mickey came and slapped me on the back, told me it was just banter, told me that I'm not the first and I wouldn't be the last to get the wrong end of the stick. He was very nice about it. He even said he admired my guts, going to the nationals, pushing the story forward. He said it would *blow over*. He told me I had to ride it out, and everything would be fine.

Eventually Heather announces that, as efficient as she is, it's impossible for her to answer three phones at the same time, and that although Steve has been with us a long time, he's still only the YTS boy and therefore shouldn't be left in charge of writing all the stories for this week's paper.

Steve looked daggers at Heather, which made me smile, and then Derek put us all back to work, and got Steve to do the rest of the lifting, which irked him even more. I decided to play along and bide my time. Wait until things had blown over.

At the weekend, I move in with Lucie. As my flat was furnished apart from my armchair, I only needed to rent a small van, and moved all my worldly possessions in one trip. I felt weird, leaving Swansbourne. I like the town, for all its twee *oh, I do like to be beside the seaside*ness, and I'll miss my sea view and the sharp cries of the gulls. At least I'll still be near a railway. More than that, though, I feel sad as I drive up the hill, past the Marine Garage and out of town, because Swansbourne is the first place I've lived alone. My flat was my little piece of independence, and in no time at all, it's gone, and I'm moving in with a girl, and soon I'll be a father. Yes, I love Lucie, but am I really ready to settle down and play happy families? It's a moot point – it's happening.

"Oh my God, you weren't joking when you said you didn't have a lot of stuff!" Lucie flings open the front door as soon as I pull up, half on, half off the pavement.

Beaufort Road comprises two lines of old Victorian terrace, separated by a narrow road. The residents park their cars on both sides, so it's effectively a one-way street. If I parked the van against the kerb, I'd block the road, but now there's not room to get a pram along the pavement. Oh well – this won't take long. Lucie and I lift my boxes of possessions into the house – she flatly refuses to not help, even though she's pregnant, so I make sure she carries the lighter ones – and return for the armchair.

"If you get in the van and push, I'll pull it," I tell her, so Lucie climbs into the back of the van. I have no intention of letting her bear any of the weight, so when the chair is on the edge, I kind of roll it to the ground. Lucie kind of waddles and flops out and makes to lift it from underneath, me one side, her the other. I protest with her so much that in the end one of our neighbours comes out and helps me carry it into the house. We dump it in the front room, near the window, and I let myself fall down into it and look at my new view of the red brick house opposite, through the net curtains. I take a deep breath and realise that I'm breathing too quickly. My palms are sweating. I look round at Lucie, who's watching me from the hallway.

"Are you okay?" she asks.

I spring up out of my chair and smile too widely. "Yes! Yeah, fine! Right, I'll take that box of clothes up to the bedroom then. Have you got space in your wardrobe, or shall I leave them in the box for now? We could go to MFI and get some new furniture once I've been paid – what do you think?" The words have all come out too quickly, I'm well aware of that, so I just have to keep moving, keep things moving, and then everything will be okay.

Lucie follows me up the narrow stairs. I walk straight into her room as I have done many times, but as soon as I step inside, I realise that although this room looks out onto the railway, we can't be a couple in here. It's the narrowest room in the world, containing only a single bed, and a dressing table that I remember knocking my knee on when I got out of the bed the last time I'd been here. I dump my box on the bed and turn to face Lucie.

I read fear in her face. Fear not of me, but of the fact that it's all too soon for her, too; fear that it won't work out; fear that she's about to be a mother; fear that she has the choice of making things work with me or doing it all alone. She masks it with a smile, as I masked mine with movement. Will we go on pretending everything is fine until it becomes fine?

I walk up to her and hold both her hands. "Lucie. I know. And I know that you know I feel the same, but neither of us can say anything because it would be awkward, but if this is going to have any chance at all of working, then we have to be honest with each other." She drops her eyes to the carpet, but I can tell she's trying not to laugh. "I'll go first. I'm scared. This has all happened so fucking fast. I'm ... it's ... well ..."

"Shall we go for a drink?"

"What about ..."

"Just leave it. It's not going anywhere. Why don't we just go out somewhere, get some food, have a dance, just be us? There's a band on at the King's again ..."

"Okay, but I wouldn't call a bag of pork scratchings and a pickled egg *food* exactly – although it is technically food – so why don't we go somewhere stupidly posh to eat, and then a few drinks at the King's on the way home? Because you can't really drink at the moment, so I could at least get you a tiramisu or something, as your treat ..."

Lucie's laughing. She nods and pulls me closer. "Yes. That sounds very fair and very fun."

"So where's the poshest place in Exeter to eat?"

"We could try the Royal Clarence. It's by the cathedral. We'll probably have to book though."

"Right. Where's the nearest phone booth? I'll get the operator to put me straight through. And when I've booked a table, I'm going to book us a taxi, too!"

We are very, very lucky, and manage to book a table. It's the receptionist who tells me that we are very, very lucky, and the tone of her voice makes me change my jeans to my one pair of smart trousers.

I'm sitting in my armchair looking out for the taxi when Lucie comes downstairs. Her long, crazy hair has been twisted up into a smooth chignon, and she's wearing a simple black shift dress and heels. Her bump is pronounced, but she looks elegant and beautiful. I barely take my eyes off her the whole journey.

The taxi driver takes us round the back of Cathedral Green and drops us right outside the Royal Clarence. It does appear to be a very classy hotel, and the doorman gestures us inside. Lucie walks directly towards him, but I pause to take in the sight of the cathedral, all lit up, surrounded by its expanse of lawns and ancient horse chestnut trees. There's a statue of someone who looks like a philosopher, which is also lit up, but I can't read the inscription. A crow glides down and perches on his head.

"Sir?" I spin round to see the man holding the glass door open, and Lucie waiting for me.

Apologising, I make my way through the tables in the courtyard at which couples are sharing bottles of wine and Champagne. There's a lot of laughter, and everything is very sparkly. Once the door is closed behind us, it's deliciously warm inside. Again, everything is glass and silver and gold, and I am very glad that I changed into my trousers. The doorman leads us to another man who is standing behind a kind of lectern. He catches himself staring at Lucie, so he quickly asks my name and checks it against his list. Then he smiles and leads us to our table, which is towards the back of the room. He pulls back the far chair and gestures Lucie to sit. I take the chair opposite, slightly miffed that my back is now to the view of the cathedral and the green. Then the man places menus in front of us and asks if he can get us any drinks. I smile politely and order sparkling water and just a small cab sav for me. I know Lucie would love a Guinness, but we're both thinking about the King's Arms later.

The waiter leaves us, and I reach out and take Lucie's hand across the circular table. Now I've done it, I have no idea what to say, so we both dissolve into hushed laughter, like a couple of naughty schoolchildren.

"Well, this is nice," Lucie giggles, and I snort with laughter and have to look away so I don't cause a scene, and that's when I notice Derek.

He's facing away from me, but I'd know the back of his greasy head anywhere.

"What?" Lucie whispers.

I nod in the direction of Derek and the three men he's sitting with, and she does her best to turn her head about one hundred degrees to the right without looking obvious. When she turns back to face me, her eyes are wide and wet.

"That's Derek!" she whispers.

"I know."

"And Superintendent Parker."

"What? Which one is he?"

"The tall one with the grey comb-over, sitting next to Derek."

"How do you know him?!"

"He's always in the paper – the Echo, I mean – he tends to be the one who does the interviews on TV. You know, the police statements. I thought you would have known that!"

"Well, yes, but I've only done a few court cases. I didn't recognise him from the back."

The men start laughing loudly, and a red-faced little man in an Armani suit grabs the nearest bottle of wine and starts sloshing what's left of it into their glasses. Derek makes a comment I can't hear, and red-face polishes off his glass of red in one swig and snorts before replying, "I wouldn't worry about that, Locky! They're all either foreigners or inbred anyway! What do you call the mutants again: Parks? NFEs?"

"NFEs?" That's the fourth man. He's built like a brick shithouse and must be well over six foot. "C'mon, y'all, help a man out, here!"

Almost crying with laughter, the superintendent replies, "NFE – Normal For Eskwich!"

The waiter arrives with our drinks, and once he's placed them on the table and taken out his notebook to take our order, the big American waves the empty bottle and shouts, "Hey! What does a man have to do to get a drink, over here?!"

The waiter looks at us, torn between politeness and the possibility of a massive tip. Lucie saves him. "It's okay, we haven't had time to decide what we want, yet." She smiles radiantly, and the waiter nods appreciatively and hurries over to their table, gathers up their empties and makes his way to the bar for another bottle. I have no idea what kind of wine it is that they're drinking, but it's certainly not the same red as I've been given.

"NFEs! Y'all are nuts, you know that don't ya?" There's a spattering of laughter, and the waiter returns with another bottle of wine. The man continues, "Well, are we gonna toast the deal, then? American-class sixty-sixes to replace your old, worn-out sixties! Bigger, better, faster …"

"Cheaper!" cuts in red-face, and everyone laughs.

Lucie and I stare at each other across the table, and when the waiter returns and asks for our order, I just say *the steak, please.* He asks how we'd like it cooked, then nods and moves off.

"The other day, M-, someone told me their friend who works at Poultry Packers had a miscarriage," I whisper to Lucie. "And they've got to be talking about … about … people who were born in Eskwich, haven't they? Something's going on, here!"

"Well, yes, but why do you think it has anything to do with what happened to Tony and Anna?"

"It's a gut feeling. I mean, it was the Americans who used Agent Orange on the Viet-Cong, wasn't it?"

"Well, yes, but they weren't the only people to use it. I mean, it's still used today, isn't it? Also, there are a fair few Americans in the world, you know! And anyway, he might be Canadian …"

"Fair point, but a *class sixty-six*? What the hell is that?"

"Simon. You – we – can't get involved with this any more. You tried your best, but the story died – for whatever reason! – and you've got a good job, which now pays decent money. People are going under all over the place. We have to look after each other – and our baby! You've just got let this go, and get on with things. Please. For me. For us."

We left the restaurant straight after dessert and went to the King's Arms, but it wasn't the carefree night we'd envisioned, and we were back at Lucie's – at *ours* – before the band had finished.

Lucie made a cup of tea, and we sat in the living room, curled up on the settee together until Lucie's head fell against my arm, and I knew she needed to go to bed.

"Look, you have the bed, I'll kip down here on the settee. I get paid next Friday, and we'll go and get a bed then – first thing on the list!" I'm helping Lucie up, guiding her up the stairs. "Shall I get you a glass of water?"

"Yes, please." She smiles, and I go back downstairs.

When I come back up with the water, Lucie isn't in the bedroom. "Lucie?" I gently push the bathroom door further ajar. "Lucie?" My heart's banging in my chest again, so I lean against the wall. *She must have gone downstairs when you were in the kitchen,* I tell myself, *she'll be up in a minute.* My hands are clammy. I call downstairs. "Lucie?"

"I'm in here!"

I follow the sound of her voice into what I'd presumed was the airing cupboard. It isn't an airing cupboard. It's a bigger room that looks out over the front of the house, and there is a double mattress complete with sheets and a quilt in the middle of the floor. Lucie has lit some candles, and her little ghetto blaster is playing Bowie's *Let's Dance*. Lucie's sitting cross-legged in the middle of the mattress. She spreads her arms with a flourish.

"Welcome to *our* room! I thought the back bedroom could be the nursery."

It's Monday morning again all too soon. Lucie's going to go to Tony's early, so she can drop me in to work. This is going to have to be the way we do things now – it's cheaper and it makes sense, but it irks me a little that it's her dropping me in and not the other way around. I know it's an old-fashioned view, but there's something ingrained in me that says it's the man who drives the car and looks after his family. But there's no way I can afford a car now – I can't even afford to get insured on Lucie's Fiesta.

And although it is so much quicker and easier driving down the valley road to Eskwich and being dropped off right outside the office door, and although I get to spend all that extra time with Lucie, I miss my old commute.

I miss being out in the sea air in the early morning; hearing the crashing of the waves and seeing the fairy lights that run along The Water blowing precariously in the wind; or on a summer's day, the lapping of the surf against the sea wall, and the sun peering around Red Rock and making a glimmering path over the waves. I miss saying *hi* to the other passengers who wait for the same train as me, day in, day out. And the journey up to Exeter: will the harbour at Cockwood be full as we pass over it, or will it be a stagnant, slimy mire, punctuated with dilapidated little boats? Will the world and his wife be out walking their dogs along the towpath, or will it be just the odd hardcore cyclist? On dark winter mornings, watching the white and red beams of headlights keep pace with the train on the A369, the light getting caught in raindrops on the window. The busyness of St David's station, where loads of people get on or off to continue up to Eskwich or not; trying to read the news headlines on people's papers as they wait on the platforms; are the people in shorts and sunglasses, or wrapped up in scarves and hats, or standing dejectedly with dripping umbrellas? Is the pigeon with the stumpy leg still about …? All these things. And then off at the bus station to walk up through town, under Christmas lights, or in the warm, early morning sunshine, when the air is full of birdsong and the smell of fresh bread. And, of course, the tantalising promise of seeing Lucie opening her curtains, or – in latter days – blowing kisses to me – or not seeing her at all, which could make or break my day.

I smile sadly at the irony: I wanted Lucie, and, previously, I wanted Charlotte – I wanted to be the father of her baby, not my best mate, Dave, who she was seeing behind my back. And now I have Lucie and am about to be a father – now I'm living with Lucie and discussing baby names on the way to work – the glitter has fallen off, and I want my old life back. I miss my Stetson. I can't believe no one found it and gave it back to me. Unless it got crushed. Unless whoever came in and cleaned up after the riot just chucked everything in a skip. Unless someone found it and decided to keep it. My palms are clammy with sweat, and I have to concentrate on my breathing.

I look out of the window. We've passed the highest point of the A396, near Silverton, and I can see right the way down the Esk Valley, which is now in full bloom. The sky is a happy, hazy blue, and there isn't a cloud to be seen. The trees and hills throw their shadows in patches over the verdant scene, buzzards circle high above, and flocks of goldfinch flit up like puffs of dandelion seeds from the hedges. I catch glimpses of the Esk, reflecting the sky as it meanders along, and the fields are dotted with fluffy white sheep. It's an idyllic scene, and I feel my body becoming calmer. I'm a lucky man. And I have an important job to do – I have to contact the police somehow, but avoid Superintendent Parker, and I have to find out what's happened to Eleanor, and get her back to work – and apologise for getting her into this mess – and I have to get justice for the lost foetuses and for Geoff Kerslake. I have a beautiful and capable woman at my side – we'll find a way …

"I'll pick up some milk once I've dropped you off. What do you want for tea tonight?"

Lucie pulls in just outside the Gazette offices. I can see Marie through the window, talking to Derek. Or, rather, Derek's talking at her. They're behind the reception desk, and Lucie's talking to me at the same time, so I'm not sure exactly what's going on, but from their posture, I'd say Derek was … threatening her?

"So, pie, mash and peas, then. Is that okay? I'll cook something proper tomorrow, but Tony's on a late one tonight so I won't be home in time to prepare anything. Oh, God! I've just thought! Do you want to wait for me to come back through town and pick you up, or do you just want to get the bus back?"

Lucie looks so innocent. She has absolutely no idea what's been going through my head during our journey, and she has no idea that right now I'm trying to look through the fuzzy halo of her tangled hair to try to work out why Derek is so close to Marie, looming over her.

"Erm, I'll get the bus back, thanks, love. I don't want you to be worrying about me being cross and waiting in the Half Moon for ages, if Tony's held up. And I can put the dinner on then, if you phone me and let me know when you're leaving." I smile and kiss her quickly on the cheek.

She flushes, pulls my face back closer to hers, and kisses me deeply. Yesterday, I would have wanted a moment like this to be unending, but today, I wrench myself away, and peck her quickly on the lips. "Gotta go, love – Derek's on the warpath already!" I say, nodding towards the offices.

"Oh! Okay, yeah, have a good day, then!" She glances at the office window, but I don't know how much she's taken in.

"Yep, you, too!" I grab my holdall, flash her a grin, slam the car door and hurry into reception. I never go through reception. The newsdesk staff go through the side door. I make to back out, but it's too late. The door clangs a bit behind me, and Derek's face whips round. He's livid. His expression is frightening. Marie's clearly crying and doesn't meet my eyes. Derek steps deliberately away from Marie, saying, "Good morning, Simon. Marie here is having a bad day – *women's troubles,*" he mouths the last bit at me and rolls his eyes. "Best you go on up and start work. And put the kettle on, would you?"

As I walk across to the dark blue door, I realise I haven't waved at Lucie, and when I look out of the window, of course, she's not there. And did I really just call her *love*?

As soon as I open the door, I know something is wrong. I can hear water gushing, but I can't work out where it's coming from. My shoes squish – the square of blue carpet between the doors and the stairs is sodden. I dash upstairs, but no one else is in the office. I poke my head round both toilet doors and shout *hello? Is anyone in there?* But there's no answer. I check my watch – it's not yet eight o'clock. I hadn't realised Lucie and I were that early. So what time did Marie get in? And what's she done to annoy Derek? Then it hits me. I bet someone's told him she's pregnant, and he's cross because she didn't inform him first so he could fire her without everyone knowing the reason why. Marie won't be such an attraction all fat and bloated and emotional. I cringe – is this how I feel about Lucie? She's done her job, she's making a new human, so let's leave her to it and go onto the next one?

But the water. I'm dashing about not really doing anything significant, and I'm light-headed and a bit shaky, so I run back down to reception and yell for Derek.

"What?!" he snaps from the door. I can see Marie hurrying away up Bampton Street, head down, obviously upset.

"What's the matter with Marie? Has she gone home?" I step into reception again, and notice a runnel of dirty water slowly reaching into the room. I let the stairwell door close behind me. Derek storms over, stopping far too close to me for comfort.

"I told you what was wrong with Marie, Simon, didn't I? Women's troubles. And yes, I've sent her home," he hisses. "Now." He steps back. He's struggling to control himself. "What on earth are you shouting about?"

"I can hear …"

The stairwell door bursts open, and Mickey springs through it. "Si, Derek, quick! There's water all over the place!"

Derek meets my eyes for a millisecond. They're lucid, but not with panic and horror. They're lucid with triumph.

"Where's the stopcock? We've got to turn the water off!"

Mickey and I are dashing about the building, turning off the electrics, looking in the toilets, around the kitchen areas, anywhere for a stopcock. We've got the door to the side entrance open now, and water's running in rivulets out onto the pavement. Trish runs in, splashing over the soggy carpet, slipping on the wood floor of reception, leans over and grabs the phone. "I'm calling the water board! Heather, go next door and tell them in the post office – it might come through their walls!"

"What's the code for the darkroom?" I yell to Trish.

"C1999X!"

"It's not opening!"

"Try again!"

"I have!"

"He must have changed the bloody code!" Trish stares at me. "Bash the door down and get his stuff out!" She turns and hurries to reception. "Where *is* Lee?!"

Steve, newly arrived at work, is standing on the pavement, open-mouthed. "Derek gave him the morning off to get his car MOTd." Trish and I pause, looking at the YTS lad, then Mickey shouts, "Steve! Help me shift this stuff off the floor!"

"Where's the fucking stopcock?!"

Trish dashes back in, phone in hand, "It's in the darkroom! Get that door down!"

"Where the fuck is Lee?!" I mutter, looking for something heavy.

"Where the fuck is Derek?!" Mickey snarls, struggling up the stairs with boxes of paper.

There's a fire extinguisher in the corner by the side door. "Get out the way!" I heave it out of its stand and run at the darkroom door, smashing it with as much force as I can muster against the number lock. Nothing happens. I try again. Wood splinters. I bash the bottom of the extinguisher at the weakened point. The lock doesn't budge, but there's a dent in the wood. I pull back, panting a bit, but Mickey grabs the cannister from me and slams it into the door repeatedly until there's a hole. He drops the fire extinguisher onto the wet carpet, and reaches his arm in, up to his neck, trying to reach the lock and open the door from the inside. The door clicks, Mickey pulls it open, and a swarm of black flies sweeps out, getting in our faces and mouths as we shout.

Trish shudders and yells, "Under the sink!" Mickey – his shape obscured by flies – rips the cupboard doors open, and in seconds, the gushing of the water stops.

The absence of the noise is shocking. All that remains is a dripping and the sounds of our disgust as we spit out and try to swat the remaining flies. Mickey appears in the doorway, cringing, slapping at the insects on his clothes, sweeping his hands through his hair. We look around. The whole of the ground floor is a mess. Footsteps make the floorboards above creak, so as one, we look up. Derek is coming downstairs, brandishing a slip of paper. "I found the code for the darkroom door," he says, smiling.

We look at each other in disbelief. Then there's a voice from the street. "Hello? South West Water?"

"He must be in shock," Trish murmurs to me, nodding in Derek's direction. We're all sitting wherever we can that's dry in reception, drinking coffee. Derek's given Heather some petty cash, and she's gone down to the bakery for doughnuts.

"He looks fine to me," I mutter back.

"Simon. Come on. He's been editor here for years. This place is his life. He wouldn't want anything bad to happen here! You need to chill out a bit, or people are going to start thinking you really are a conspiracy theorist!" She says it kindly, but she's also saying it as a warning. I'm on dangerous ground. Something occurs to me – that's it! And then my heart sinks and I know it's all over.

"The cellar."

"What?" Trish turns to me, confused, concerned.

"We put all our archives and research in the cellar the other day because Derek wanted to revamp the office."

I pull back the heavy, sodden blue carpet so Mickey can lift the hatch which is the cellar door. The galvanised steps shine as usual, but you can't see the floor, and it's not just because of the darkness. It looks like Swansbourne Water down there. Light reflects intermittently off what can only be floodwater. I swing my legs down the hole and onto the first step. Mickey hands me a torch, and I go down. Water soaks through my shoes and up my legs before I know it, so I wave the beam of light around. It's just water. Must be over three feet deep. It must have been running all night. I shine the light at fixed spots where I think I remember putting my boxes, to see if I can make out a shadow. Nothing. Slowly, I sweep the beam of yellow light across the water, wall to wall. There's something on the surface! "I think I can see our stack of back-copies!" I shout up. Then I step down until my feet touch the cellar floor, and wade over to the stack. It's like wading through treacle. Except it isn't like wading through treacle, because it's cold, and the thickness only comes in places. I go to pick up sheets of paper lying on and just below the surface of the water, but my fingers go right through them. It's like paper mâché down here. I'm almost at the stacks now – I can see the wooden framework that holds the newspapers together. Somewhere in this stack is the copy of the Gazette that holds my first bylined story – the one about the driver who got his lorry stuck in a tree at the Walrons.

There are clods of saturated paper floating around the area, but the newspaper at the top seems to be intact. As I try to drag the wooden framework and whatever it still holds towards the steps, I wonder if Marie had caught Derek bashing the pipe that had caused the leak. I don't think I'll see her again, that's for sure – whether he threatened her, fired her or what. I expect he'll make an announcement that she left because she was pregnant. All I have to decide is whether I should leave on moral grounds, or whether it's best to keep your enemies close.

Mickey and I wrestle the stack of disintegrating newspapers up the cellar steps. There's not a lot left. We manoeuvre it into reception. Derek has taken the rest of newsdesk upstairs to carry on with our work as best we can, which will entail an awful lot of calling people back and apologising for not calling them or being with them, when we said we would. It also involves Steve doing his first front-page story – the one about this morning's disaster. Lee turns up at midday, wondering what on earth has happened, and expressing his guilt at taking the morning off. When I ask him if his car made it through its MOT, he doesn't know what I'm talking about. He said Derek had offered him the morning off in lieu – to make up for the evening he spent with me taking pictures out at Willand.

I shake my head and smile at this further evidence that Derek had rigged the whole thing. I'm about to push my theory further by slyly commenting that it was a bad time for Lee to have changed the code to the darkroom door, when Lee says, "I still don't understand why you had to bash a hole in my door, though. Why didn't Trish just tell you the code? It wasn't like I kept the bloody crown jewels in there!"

"She did. It didn't work. Someone had changed it." I watch my conclusion dawn on him.

Somehow, the only things of his that suffered any major damage were the flies. Downstairs is a mess and is now covered in *closed* and *no entry* signs, and there's a team of men in overalls pumping the water out of the cellar. Trish has been tasked with the job of finding professional cleaners and decorators. She's already got an electrician – the aptly named Jason Sparky – checking the place over, making hissing noises and shaking his head. His name would be amusing, but everyone's too busy and preoccupied to laugh. Mickey and I leave the stack to dry. The ink's run, and we can't get pages unstuck from pages without ripping them.

"What's so important about these old papers, anyway?" Mickey asks. "I'm surprised Derek wanted to hang on to them. Surely if we needed to reread one, they hold copies at Plymouth?"

"You'd think so, wouldn't you? But no. They don't. Unless anyone's got a copy at home, that's that."

"Why don't you ask?" Mickey says, sparking up a cigarette.

"Because they'd find out and have it destroyed."

"'They'?"

"The people who are trying to cover up what happened at Willand."

"Oh, bloody hell, Si! Nothing happened at Willand! Nothing ever happens at Willand! It was just a load of bollocks Geoff Kerslake made up to get his own back on the guy who was shagging his missus!"

"John Barton?"

"Are you having a laugh?! It was Derek, you dozy bastard!"

I storm up to newsdesk, leaving Mickey to his cigarette. There's the usual cacophony in the office, and the door to Derek's office is closed. I stride over and wrench it open.

"You fucking bastard!" I yell at Derek. "How much did you get for this, eh? How much money did they give you for making this happen?!"

My fists are on his desk, the office door is open. The office is suddenly silent. Derek puts the receiver of his phone back in its cradle, lights another cigarette, and then looks up at me.

"Oh dear, Simon. Not this again, surely." He stands and shakes his head slowly. "I've given you chance after chance, but you're still allowing your psychiatric issues to get the better of you."

"What bloody 'psychiatric issues'?!"

"Simon, we've all seen you struggling. We've all seen you walk past the office a hundred times before you feel able to come in. Your previous editor on the *Swansbourne Gazette* did warn me your empathy and compassion sometimes caused you problems, but I thought the step up might be good for you. It seems you might have been better off staying in Swansbourne after all." Derek has moved round and out from behind his desk while he's been speaking, and now I find myself following him out into the main office.

"What the fuck are you talking about?!"

"The stress, Simon! Of seeing a body hanging from a tree! Of becoming involved with the girl whose brother started this whole fantasy off in the first place! Of finding yourself unexpectedly expecting a baby! At your age! And now you've accidentally flooded your office!"

"What do you mean, I flooded the office?! It wasn't me! The place was under water when I got in here this morning!"

"The last time Lee had a fly disaster, it was you who helped clear up, wasn't it?"

"Yes! It's always me who helps clear up! I'm always the first one in, other than you!"

"Yes, you are. And it's commendable. However, it seems someone pushed the freezer back too far and cracked the pipe. A tiny, but catastrophic crack."

Derek is smiling, and I'm aware that everyone in the office is looking at me. I know that he's lying, putting on a show, but I'm feeling light-headed and off-kilter. I look at my colleagues. Trish's eyes are full of concern, and she stands up and puts a hand on my shoulder. I can't work out what is happening. I'm sweating. I need to get out of here, need to get out of here, grab my coat, can't find my hat, Derek's talking, something about more compassionate leave, I'm stumbling down the stairs, the men have gone, I open the door, a hand on my shoulder, guiding me into a van …

One of the first stories I covered when I joined the Gazette was one about a lorry that had somehow ended up on the narrow road behind the wide grass verge that runs parallel with the A396 at the Walrons (a housing estate on the outskirts of Eskwich, that almost joins up with Ashley). It was too tall to pass beneath the cherry and rowan trees that dot the grass, and had ended up with a thick branch stuck between its cab and its cargo. When I arrived on scene, the driver was out of his lorry, sitting down with his back against the tree, drinking a mug of tea that one of the residents had made him. Loads of kids were out on the grass, pointing and laughing, along with a group of adults – presumably the parents – some of whom were snapping pictures with their cameras. The story was to be a kind of feel-good, comical one, that would lift the paper from its usual opening stories about unemployment levels and business closures. Eventually, a team of council workers arrived and severed the branch from the trunk, freeing the lorry; but it transpired that the driver had put so much force into trying to free it himself before he realised how stuck in the tree his vehicle actually was, that he'd loosened the trunk from its roots. The council came back a few days later and cut it down, but for reasons best known to the workers, they left the fallen tree on the grass next to its stump for several days. Then, one day, Lee was driving me out to Ashley Tip to cover a story about a truck of stolen Ming vases that had been dumped there. It was springtime, and I smiled sadly at the cherry trees that had turned into clouds of candyfloss-pink blossom, thinking about their fallen friend a few hundred yards up the road, but as we drew closer to it, I could see that it was as covered in blossom as the rest of them. I was so amazed, I asked Lee to pull over and take a picture of it, which he duly did. I tried to get Derek to put that story in the next edition, as a kind of light relief from the story of the stolen Ming vases, but he wasn't entertaining it. "Those trees come out in blossom every bloody year, Simon! There is no story!" he said, and that was that, even though he'd completely missed the point.

News *stories,* we call them. Stories. It seems ironic to me, because they are always presented as fact. And when we're trained up, we're told to *get at the facts.* The trouble is, one person's fact is another person's fiction. Or hearsay. Or interpretation. And even us – the reporters – are never impartial. We might be a fresh pair of eyes on the situation, but we'll make our own interpretation of the news we gather. How many things do we miss? And where does a story start, anyway? And even when you've written it up, it's the editor's call as to the headline and its position in the paper. Will the audience you had in mind even see it? And those who do read it – what will they make of it? They'll see what they want to see, I suppose. We all do it.

The fallen blossom tree thing turned out to be a few stories within stories. Yes, it was funny seeing a lorry stuck in what is essentially an ornamental tree. It was miraculous to me that the tree blossomed even though it had been cut down. The first, Derek decided should go in the paper. The second not – he didn't see anything in it. But there was a third story that didn't make the paper. I didn't think too much of it at the time – I was a rookie: I'd been headhunted, and I was desperate to impress. Arguing with my boss about what should be a story and what shouldn't – or, rather, what should make the paper and what shouldn't – was not something I was going to do. He had twice my age in journalistic experience alone. What did I know? And, anyway, if I played my cards right, maybe I could have his job one day.

The story that didn't make the grade, was this. The driver of the lorry was a local man named Geoff Kerslake. He was a train driver, really, but his family had been hit hard by Mrs Thatcher's policies, so he had taken on another job to make ends meet.

Geoff had been delivering anything from animal feed to building supplies. When he'd picked up his lorry that morning, it had been packed and covered and was ready to go. Naturally, he'd asked what his load was, and had been told that it was *stuff for the railway.* He was to transport it from the depo in Exeter to Eskwich Junction, let the staff there unload it, and then bring the lorry back so it could be filled with something else.

He told me all this after the council had cut the branch and the neighbours had dispersed. I'd hung around, because he'd seemed a bit off. I mean, crashing a lorry – especially publicly – is never going to look good in the eyes of your employer, but that didn't account for the look in his eyes. So I asked him. He'd heard something on the CB in his cab that he shouldn't have heard. Two men were speaking – his boss, and an American. They'd said something about the *stuff* he was carrying. It was a weedkiller, apparently. Geoff had grabbed his CB and asked why, if he was carrying weedkiller, he wasn't driving a tanker built for purpose. He'd seen the grass verge separating the main road from a residents-only parking one and had pulled over. There had been silence first, then his boss had come on and told him that a tanker hadn't been available, and the delivery had been urgent, that there was nothing to worry about, and he should just make his delivery as he would any other. But Geoff hadn't been happy about it. There had been an argument. In the end, his boss had told him that he either had to make the delivery, or look for a new job, and what choice did Geoff have? And he'd misjudged the height of the vehicle and got it caught in a tree.

Derek had told me that it wasn't a story, because it was just an argument between a worker and his boss – it, like trees blossoming – happened all the time.

Nia, 2022.

It's almost December. I've been to see Misty, in Eskwich, and am driving back to Exeter along the valley road. It's been raining for days, and the sky is a thick, soft blue-grey this late afternoon. I've turned my music off, so all I can hear is the rumble of my car's engine and the splash of its tyres through puddles on the tarmac. The trees just beyond Ashley have lost pretty much all their leaves, but the ones that remain are deep reds, oranges and yellows, and their wet branches glint in my headlights. To my left, the low fields are partially covered in a thick mist coming off the river, and the woods on the hills behind are ruddy in what's left of the light. As I cross Bickleigh bridge, the river foams and surges beneath, only inches from the beer garden of the Heron. Up in the hills approaching Butterleigh and Silverton, the sun manages to burn a pinprick of yellow through the fog. It's all so utterly beautiful, I wish I was just *Driving Home for Christmas,* singing along to my Christmas mix, my only stress working out what on earth I could get as a present for Matt.

Instead, I've had to turn my music off so I can try to make sense of what Misty told me. It had been a bloody difficult conversation to have. In fact, it had been bloody difficult to get her to talk to me at all. I rang the bell and watched the blurry shape of her getting closer to the door, through the opaque glass. She paused a couple of feet before she got to the door, and I knew she knew it was me, and I knew she knew that I knew she didn't want to speak to me. She paused for so long that I thought she was just going to go back into the house, and I wondered whether calling through the letterbox would help, but I didn't know what to say. But she moved forward, unlocked the door and stood in front of me, her expression like that of a bouncer outside a nightclub, facing off a gang of underaged kids.

"Misty. I'm sorry about the other day. Matt's sorry, too – he's not here, by the way …". I expected her to say something, but she just stood there, waiting for me to justify myself.

"Look, Misty. My mum's died, I've jacked my job in, I'm in a mess, and it's nearly Christmas …"

Misty gives a hollow laugh. "'Nearly Christmas'?! What the bloody hell does Christmas have to do with anything?! Why is it people are expected to do anything for anyone just because there's a bloody tree up by the clock tower, and everyone's wearing Santa hats?! All this bloody 'be kind' bollocks! No one's good to anyone unless there's something in it for them. *Be kind when it suits you,* is what they mean! I …"

Misty breaks off, her face starting to crack. She looks away, then glances up at me, her eyes defiant but wet. I stare back, pleading. "I need to know what happened to my dad, Misty. It's eating me alive."

Misty sobs, whips round, and stalks back into the house, leaving the door open for me. I step into the porch, softly closing the door behind me. The house doesn't smell of brownies today. It smells of polish and over-fragrant laundry. Her robot hoover is gliding over the hall carpet. I wonder how much it cost, and the thought makes me shiver.

The sound of the kettle boiling guides me to the kitchen, where Misty is spooning coffee into two mugs. I pull out a chair and sit at the table. The house feels strangely empty and quiet; or, rather, *full* and quiet, although there's no one here but the two of us. This room is packed to the rafters with ghosts. Then something occurs to me.

"Misty, is Danny in right now?"

"Danny?!" She almost laughs. "No, Danny's not here! Danny should never have been here! I kicked him out."

"Why?!" I'm shocked, although I can't say why.

"Why?! Do you really need to ask, Nia? Because he's got a daughter who he rarely sees, because he's been hanging round here playing the poor, hard-done-by! He needs to stop playing with his bloody train sets and go and sort his life out! I'm sick to the back teeth of mothering him! He needed a kick up the backside, and now he needs to grow a pair of balls!"

Misty slams the mugs of steaming coffee on the table, and we look at each other in silence. The anger in her eyes dies. She's given up. "Bloody fathers!" she jokes, but the defiance in her stance is gone, and she's slouching. She smiles. "Tell me what you know about your dad, Nia, and I'll tell you if it's true. We'll go from there."

I push my shock at her outburst down, and return her smile. If she's in the mood to talk, I need to play along. "I know that Dad was a journalist on the Esky Gazette. I know that you used to work in reception there. You must have known him." Misty nods. "And I know that Derek Locke is Matt's dad, and that he pays for everything for you, but that you don't get on." She nods again. "I don't *know* anything else." I pause. "That's not true. I know that Matt's dad was the editor on the Gazette when you and Simon worked there. And that my dad disappeared before I was born. I *think* that something happened to him because of a story he was working on. And I *think* you've got a pretty good idea what that something was." I look her in the eyes, and try to get the aggression out of my gaze.

Misty pushes her chair back a bit from the table, and recrosses her legs. She takes a big gulp of her coffee, then cradles the mug in her hands as if she were cold.

Staring into the liquid, she says, "And that's literally all it is – an *idea*. So I can't say anything, because I don't *know* anything for sure."

"Please tell me what you think, Misty. I need to know what happened to my dad. I *deserve* to know what happened to my dad. You must see that. And I can tell it's killing you, too."

Misty's eyes fill with tears. "When I said I can't say anything, that's exactly what I meant. I *can't* say anything." She stops, and stares into her coffee again.

"Misty."

"For Christ's sake, Lavinia! My name's Marie!"

I don't say anything. I just wait for her to look at me. A tear drips from her face into her drink, and she slams the mug on the table and wipes her eyes with the sleeve of her Joules jumper.

"If I say anything, Derek will ruin me. And I've got nothing, without him, and neither has Matthew!"

"*Derek* will ruin you? What do you mean?"

"He'll chuck me out of the house, empty my bank account! I'll be homeless! And what will happen to Matt?!"

"Why, though?" I say, almost silently. "Has Derek got something to do with my dad going missing?" I shiver again. The robot hoover butts against the strip of metal marking the kitchen from the hall, making me jump.

"I need a cigarette." Misty – Marie – stands abruptly, and flounces out, almost tripping over the hoover as she does so.

I stay put. I finish my coffee and take in the pristine kitchen. It's like I'm sitting in an advert in one of those country house-type magazines. I know Misty's been doing her housework today, so it's not the sparkle and the slight smell of bleach that gives me this impression: it's the complete lack of anything personal. There are no photos or notes stuck to the fridge – there are no fridge magnets. There's no *wonderful mum* mug – in fact, all the mugs are from a set that looks like it's been bought in John Lewis. I pick up my empty mug, and sure enough, there's the John Lewis stamp on the bottom. There's nothing personal anywhere. Except Misty's Radley handbag.

I know I'm going to look inside, even though I don't know what I'm looking for, and even though I fill the kettle with water and switch it on again and rinse the mugs out, and pretend to myself that I've only got up to make another drink.

With a furtive but completely redundant glance out of the kitchen doorway – it gives a view of the side of the staircase and nothing else – I peer into Misty's unclasped red bag. It's a hideous thing. It reminds me of a blood clot and has the look of what I hope is fake crocodile skin. There are three compartments: two gaping ones on either side of a zipped one. I don't know what I'm looking for, let alone where to find it, and I'm trying to suppress the feeling of guilt that is creeping through me. I *think* Misty's going to tell me what she knows, but she might just have gone for a cigarette to collect herself and concoct a lie. I nip out of the kitchen and glance down the hall. Through the opaque glass, I can make out the shape of Misty standing just outside the porch, arm bent at the elbow, cigarette glowing.

Back in the kitchen, I pull her purse out of one of the gaping compartments. It's shiny black, and I flip it open, trying to avoid touching the polished bronze Scotty dog on the front. More compartments, and loads of cards in their slots. Instinct makes me open the zipped one in the middle. As I imagined, it's stuffed with little bits of paper. I pull them all out carefully, and flip through them. Most of them are business cards for artists that she must have picked up at a craft fair or something. A few are photos of Matt in various stages of life, and I can't help but smile to see that Misty's got the same one as me: a picture of Matt and me as kids, waving from the open carriage of a miniature railway train. One of a semi-naked, much younger Misty, posing for the camera in lacy underwear, surprises me. Matt wasn't lying about her having been a model. The edges of the photo are dog-eared, the layers of paper fraying. I tear my eyes from it and carry on flipping.

People always say, when they find something they've been searching for, that it's *always in the last place you look.* In fact, I think a famous comedian made a joke about that. It might have been Rhod Gilbert. He made the point that if it was in the first place you looked, you wouldn't keep looking, which I remember had made me laugh. What I've found, I don't understand, but I know it's what I was looking for. It's an ID card. A British Rail ID card, and a very old one. What on earth would Misty be doing with an old ID card for a Geoffrey Kerslake?

The front door clicks closed, and I hear Misty's footsteps down the hall. When the smell of her cigarette smoke reaches me, I'm pouring boiling water into our mugs.

"Oh, thanks, Nia," she says, taking the milk out of the fridge. "I was going to make another once I'd had my smoke."

I turn and take the milk from her, smiling. She sounds normal, although it's only my guilt causing me to examine her tone. She drops her packet of cigarettes and a tarnished Zippo lighter back into her bag, frowns and sits down.

I put the mugs on the table, and we both cup our hands round them, mirroring one another. It is cold in here. Misty laughs when she notices, and says, "I'll switch the thermostat up to twenty-five!"

"You'll have to remortgage the house!" I call after her, before cringing at what's just come out of my mouth, but she laughs again, albeit from her mouth and not her soul.

When she returns, her face is hard. "I do what I do to survive, Lavinia. Same as you do. But you can give me back the item you stole from my handbag. Stealing isn't nice. And I was going to tell you. In fact, I'm still going to tell you. But now – because of what you did – I'm going to give you the brutal truth."

I'm blushing and shaking. I put the ID card on the table in front of her. "I'm sorry," I murmur. "How did you know?"

"I have a Ring doorbell, Nia. And a camera that I can place anywhere in the house, and watch through an app on my phone. You underestimate me.

"Now. I think you've got a pretty good idea what I'm going to tell you, and you can believe what you want. Your father was unwell. Mental health wasn't a thing in the 80s, like it is now. Simon had PTSD, and developed delusions. Derek and I found him hanging from a tree – like Geoff Kerslake, a man he was obsessed with – in the grounds at Redbank. Your mum didn't know his family, and we had no forwarding details, so he was cremated in the same way a homeless person would have been. Lucie and I sprinkled his ashes into the sea at Orcombe Point in Exmouth. She didn't want to tell you when you were little, that he'd chickened out and killed himself, and after a while, what with you going off the rails, it was easier to let you believe the lie. I mean, it wasn't really a lie, was it? To all intents and purposes, he did disappear."

"Bollocks."

Misty erupts into hysterical laughter. "Fine, then, believe what you like, Nia. All anyone's ever done is try to make things easier for you! But, before you invest all your inheritance in that cafe you're planning to run with Matt, I suggest you ask him about the secret model railway in the woods at Redbank, and ask him why – as your best – or is it only? – friend – poor sod, he'll never accept it'll never be lover! – he chose to make out he knew nothing about it. Money and sex, Nia. Money and sex. That's what makes the world go round. You're just like your dad – naïve and idealistic. And just like your dad, you just needed to play the game. That's all you need to do to survive in the world – play the game. And cover your tracks."

"Matt, where are you? I keep calling, but all I'm getting is your bloody answerphone! Look, I met up with your mum today, and now I'm going to see your dad. I'm going to sort this out once and for all. So bloody call me back!" I throw myself into my car and slam the door. Then I set off for Redbank Court.

Derek adjusts his tie and looks me straight in the eye.

"You'll never get your so-called 'justice', Lavinia. It's a case of the survival of the fittest; and the survival of the 'fittest' doesn't mean the survival of the 'nicest'."

I know he's about to launch into some kind of speech, so I just stand there and let him do it. I look at him while he's speaking, but I let my eyes glaze over. This room doesn't scare me any more – not even the glass-eyed heads of the murdered deer nailed high up on the walls. This house is pretending to be something it's not, and this tyrant in front of me – he's just a sad old man in a faded brown suit. He might have lots of money, and a few friends in high places, but he's just another guy whose life didn't turn out as he'd hoped. I almost feel sorry for him. Almost.

"There's no such thing as utopia, Nia," he begins, stretching back in his armchair, gesturing me to sit down. I decline. "It's like the baby owls on *Springwatch*. To have the best chance of survival, a chick must kill its sibling. Have any of your namby-pamby friendships ever got you anywhere? I made my connections wisely, not 'morally'. I was asked to do someone a favour, and I did it with the connections and influence I had. I didn't mean for those people to lose their baby. And the meat in the factory clearly wasn't poisoned. In fact, if the wind had been blowing the other way that day, no one would have known about it. Job done, and I get to support a woman and a child I love, without being called a pervert.

"Misty was – is – an attractive girl, and I like her. I know how it would have been portrayed if I'd asked her to marry me. I would have lost my friends and my job, and Misty would have been branded a gold-digger. So I did what I did. Survival of the fittest.

"But, whatever you say, I'll be okay. The charges will be dropped. Or, if they get me as far as prison, I'll be exonerated within the week. And then there'll be the next scandal. They'll decide to close Esky 'Spoons because it's not making the shareholders enough money, and there'll be staff protests, the alcoholics will have nowhere to go; Broadoaks will get taken over, or they'll get robots in and all the Esky Polish will be out of jobs; someone will attack someone else with a machete in a pub over drugs or a girl. And my sad little story will be forgotten.

"What's done is done, Nia. Say what you like to whom you like – it's of no consequence to me. Look at Boris Johnson! People like you can't 'win', because life isn't a game. You just survive, or you go under. All this is dead and gone, so why don't you go off and do something that makes you feel happy? Your dad was just the weakest chick in the nest, that's all. It's nature."

His oration evidently finished, Derek picks up a newspaper, effectively dismissing me. I smile, although he doesn't notice, because he's opened the broadsheet wide, and covered his face. Then I sit down in the same sofa I sat in that day with Matt. I'm just about to ask Derek where Vera is, when the front door booms closed, and someone runs down the tiled floor, then along the corridor. They're wearing trainers or something similar, and they're running fast. Fear floods through me, so I grab the stalk of the iron lampstand on the table next to me, hoping I can wrench its plug out of the electrical socket if I need to defend myself. I glance at Derek, who remains immobile. Then I see why.

Matt, pale, and dripping with nervous sweat, stands in the doorway, panting.

"Nia!" he breathes, and he bumbles over to the couch and flops down beside me. He stinks of alcohol, and envelops me in a sloppy hug. I move away, but the arm of the sofa blocks me. Reluctantly, I stare into his bloated, reddened face. "Nia!" he slurs again. "I'm so sorry. I …"

"Matthew!" Derek's bark jolts us to attention. "Go upstairs, go to your room, and tidy yourself up! Lavinia is just leaving."

I'm both propping Matt up and pushing him off me as we leave Derek's lounge.

"Sorry, Nia, I'm a mess," Matt slurs, stumbling along the corridor.

"Yes, you are," I reply. At this moment, I find him repulsive. All I want to do is run out of this fucked-up place and drive as far away from it as I can, but Matt's stopped talking, he's let go of me, his head's stooped and he looks utterly dejected. He's been my friend for years, and he needs help right now, not anger. "Look. We'll sort you out, okay?" I say, holding him by the shoulders and trying to smile. "I'll help you up to your room, wherever it is, you lie down, I'll find you some water, then you sleep this off, call me in the morning, and we'll talk it out, okay?"

Matt nods, tears now in his eyes, and we go up the wide staircase, Matt pulling himself up by the banister, me walking very close to him in case he falls. We pass along more *Scooby Doo*-esque corridors, but I don't feel frightened or even weirded out any more. It's just sad. Matt pushes a door open, and falls onto the springy, single bed at the far end of a room that's about as big as my kitchen. The bed's in the corner, under the window, and is made up with a quilt and a pillow in a plain, dark blue duvet set that looks like it was from a bargain home store. There's a half-empty litre bottle of water on the wooden desk, next to a six-pack of cheese and onion crisps. Under the bed is a pair of Matt's trainers, a rucksack, and some kind of fancy-dress cowboy hat. The pictures on the walls in this room are all of steam trains, and there's a pile of *Railway Modeller* magazines and a disposable vape on top of a plastic storage box that's doubling up as a bedside table. So, this is Matt's room when he's round his dad's. I never knew he even stayed here overnight, let alone had his own room.

I take the bottle of water over to Matt, but he's asleep already, face down, drooling onto his pillow, so I leave it next to the magazines, and leave. As soon as I've pulled Matt's bedroom door closed, fear floods me again. I don't want to bump into Derek, or Vera, or anyone else. I pad along the corridor and down the stairs, holding my breath, and I don't let it out until I've banged the front door closed behind me. It's all very well being blasé about the place when I'm with Matt, but alone, Redbank Court is bloody terrifying.

I wake up cold in my bed, to the sound of the early Penzance to London train whizzing past. Picking up my phone, I'm disappointed but not surprised to find that Matt hasn't called. I wish I knew what was going on with him. Yes, we all used to have a drink that got messy from time to time when we were younger, but this is twice I've seen him absolutely bladdered at odd times of the day, on his own. I wonder if he's supposed to be in work today, and I almost call him in case he needs waking up and reminding, but I don't hit the green call button. Matt's his own person and his own responsibility; I asked him to call me, and if he doesn't, that's up to him; and if I'm honest, the image of his blubbery, drunken face is still in my mind, along with his alcoholic breath, and I shudder with revulsion. I get myself up and dressed, make a coffee, and start sorting out the rest of the house – the sooner I get it cleared and cleaned, the sooner I can sell it. Or make it my own.

Matt calls at about half past two, which is the time of day that I am at my worst, and when I answer the phone, I know it shows in my voice.

"Look, Nia, I'm sorry, okay? I said I was sorry yesterday, so let's just drop it and move on, okay?"

"You …"

Matt cuts me off. "I've had an idea. About how we can maybe find out about what happened with your dad."

"What …"

"Nia, just listen. We'll use the Platform Five Boys YouTube channel. We have almost a million subscribers, right, so if we re-enact what Al said happened out by the chicken factory, maybe someone who knows something will get in touch via social media or something."

I'm silent for a bit. So's Matt. "So, what? You set up a scene? Do they make model abattoirs and model weedkilling trains? And, what, you paint *Agent Orange* on the side of the truck …"

"I haven't worked out the details yet, but don't you think it's worth a shot? I mean, I don't want to tempt fate, but what's the worst that could happen? No one notices anything, and it's just another shunting mission. The railway community's a pretty close thing, Nia, and it's a pretty iconic scene: five bridges in a row, an abattoir, then Esky loop and the old railway buildings; someone will recognise it." Matt pauses for a second. "Yeah! What we could do is set up several scenes – Esky Junction, Southampton docks, Clapham Junction, Liverpool Lime Street, Crewe – then we could give people points for the engines they recognise, and the places! Oh my God, why didn't I think of this before!"

He's buzzing. He sounds like the Matt I know again. And it's a great idea. I tell him to get on his group chat right now, and let me know after. In all my excitement, I completely forget to ask him what he was sorry about. This is the second time he's apologised for nothing. Unless he has done something. But he's never been anything but a brilliant friend to me. Maybe it's because he gave me some home truths the other day. Maybe it's because he loves me and he knows I don't love him, in which case I should be the one who's sorry, shouldn't I? Maybe it's just him being drunk.

There's a steam special on Saturday – the last one of the year – and now most of the bulldozers and cranes have finished their work repairing the track and sea wall at Swansbourne, Matt and Danny want to see it on its way to Penzance from the bridge by Kennaway Tunnel, and, when he mentions it to me, I remember the night on third bridge when he told me about it. I doubt he remembers, though, so I just say I'm doing nothing that day and could do with some sea air, and that I'll tag along too, as it's been windy and rainy for the last couple of weeks, and the sea would either be hammering the sea wall and coming up over the track when the Scotsman comes through, or will be that beautiful, glassy, after-storm sapphire. Either way, the opportunities for great photos are unsurpassed, so Leon, Crofty and Jason say they'll come along, too. So it will be the Platform Five Boys, and little old me. Matt tells me he'll pick me up on his way through, and it'll have to be early, as it's an iconic view that makes it into railway magazines nearly every month, so it'll be hard enough to get on the bridge, let alone get a good spot.

The morning dawns clear and cold, with ominous dark grey streaks of cloud. Coming from his place in Exmouth, Matt has to go all the way up the Esk Estuary to Exeter, then all the way down the other side to get to

Swansbourne. In the car on the second leg of the journey, I ask Matt why he didn't go by train – the whole route is picturesque – and he replies that he wanted to be sure of getting there in good time. You can't rely on the rail service – sorry, services – in this country. We haven't been able to pretty much since Thatcher privatised British Rail. It's sickeningly ironic.

In its predominantly clear blue sky, the sun gives everything a rosy-golden glow, and the raindrops left on the leaves glitter. Swansbourne is a strange place, and the supermarket and new housing estates they've built and are building on what used to be the outskirts by Langdon Hospital are totally incongruous with the tiny street that makes up the town centre, with its failing cafes, charity and souvenir shops. Yes, the green is nice, and the stream that runs through the town in a nice straight line all the way to the sea, bedecked with permanent Christmas lights, is nice, and the duck sanctuary is nice, and the black swans are nice, but to me, the whole place is twee, and a good fifty to one hundred years out of date. There is nothing for young people here, bar a tacky arcade that's okay if you're about twelve. Yes, it's all quite pretty and innocuous, and if all you want to do in the summer is be on the beach somewhere cheap with your kids, then yes, come to

Swansbourne, but why anyone would choose to live here, I have no idea. I know it gets a good tourist trade, but out of season, it's just depressing.

Matt parks up on Marine Parade – a street that runs parallel with the railway line, which in turn, runs parallel with the shoreline – and we walk over to the suitably depressing-looking pub – the Marine Tavern. We're supposed to be meeting everyone here, but there's the caveat that if it gets close to the time we should be putting our beach towels down – as it were – on the bridge, and not everyone has arrived, it's every man for himself. Standing outside the beer garden, Matt points out the bridge. It's wrought iron, quite flimsy looking, and, he says, leads you from Marine Parade, over the railway line, and onto the sea wall, from which you can walk along either back into town or the short distance to Cardinal's Cove. The steep cliff face can only be twenty feet or so away from the bridge. Matt says that's why he loves the line so much – you pass in and out of the cliffs, via little coves, all the way to Tamehaven, and if you're watching a steam special coming the other way, you get the steam billowing out of the tunnel in the engine's wake. I can hear the sea, but I can't see it. It all feels a bit wild.

Matt's phone buzzes. He takes it out of his pocket, looks at it, then waves at a black BMW that's parked further up the road. Leon and Crofty emerge from it and saunter over to us, while Jason – who's clearly driven them both – fiddles about on his phone and scans around for a parking meter. He grins, or grimaces, I can't tell which from this distance, at us, and gestures for us all to go in.

The interior of the Marine Tavern looks as if it hasn't been done up since the 1990s. It's a pretty big space, with lots of tables, and the bar stretches halfway along the far wall. The beer garden was packed with tables, too, and I see from a notice on the bar that there's a balcony area too – presumably giving a sea view – or a railway view, depending on what you're in Swansbourne for. "Shall we go up?" I ask Matt, pointing at the sign.

"Nah, we might be standing on the bridge for ages, so we may as well stay warm while we can," he replies. "What do you fancy to drink?"

"An oat milk latte, please," I say, but the barman, who's staring at me, shakes his head and laughs.

"You'll have a hard time finding oat milk in Swansbourne!" he says.

"Just an Americano, then, please," I say to Matt. "With loads of sugar."

"What are we all having, then?" Jason brings a rush of cold, briny air in with him, and stands just behind me and Matt. Danny and the others order coffee and bacon sandwiches – it's assumed, in a friendly kind of way, that Jason will pay for it all. I guess it's because he's that much older than us – about twenty years, probably – and he does tend to take on the role of dad of the group. I suppose it's just another instance of us being *perpetual teenagers,* as Danny calls us. We're all approaching forty – we should be able to pay for our own breakfasts by now.

As if he's read my mind, Matt says, "No, Jase, I'll get this," and we all turn to him in surprise.

"Are you sure? It's going to be a lot with all six of us," Jason says.

"Yep, it's no problem. You always shout us, Jase. And I got paid yesterday."

"Okay, thanks, mate." That's Jason. The other three have gone off to find a big enough table.

"Anything for the lady?" says the barman.

I force my glare into a smile, and tell him nothing to eat, thanks. It seems that it's not just the decor that's stuck in the 90s.

"Right, guys," says Matt, pulling his chair as far forward as it will comfortably go. "I've had an idea for Platform Five."

"Live feeds?" That's Crofty. "I think it's the way forward. We could have it all going, and do a spontaneous kind of chat, like a podcast. We could make it really interactive – people could be chatting with us. Like, one of us sits out and watches the chat, and butts in with stuff on behalf of whoever's watching …"

Matt cuts him off. "To be honest, I've been thinking about that, too, mate, but that's not what I was going to say …"

"Yeah! Live feeds would be awesome," says Danny. "We could even do it from Bishop's Lyd, and get on the station when the trains come in. Yeah! We could ask the drivers if we could film from the footplate, or something …"

"Ahh, I've not been on a footplate for ages," says Leon. "In fact, the last time I was on an out-of-service, it was in this diesel at the South Devon …"

"What, when you were six, and your mum had taken you to Day Out With Thomas?!"

"Fuck off, Crofty! You were there, too, remember? We went down on the off chance, but there were no locos running so we did the museum and that, just so we wouldn't look like a couple of twats."

"Oh yeah. Dan, you ought to get Gwen down to see the otters."

"That's a non sequitur!" says Danny, through a mouthful of sandwich.

"No, there's the otter and butterfly sanctuary opposite the station, remember?"

"Is there? Me and Kerry took Gwen down that day, and she was so scared of the engines, we just got in the car and went back home. Bloody expensive twenty minutes that was!"

Exasperated, Matt shouts, "Guys!" and everyone stares at him. He explains his idea for the shunting mission.

The guys exchange looks. Then Danny comments, "Well, yeah, it sounds nice, but it's hardly revolutionary, is it?"

"Yeah, the fuss you made, I thought something big was happening, like Netflix wanted us, or something!"

Matt looks awkwardly at me. With his eyes, he's asking if he can tell them. I shrug.

Then Jason, pale-faced, and sounding a little off, says, "What's going on? Why Eskwich Junction, and why 1980s weedkiller trains? What do you … what do you …?"

"Why? What do *you* know?" snaps Matt.

A silence descends. It can only have lasted for a couple of seconds, max, but it feels like fifteen years. There's a cold rush of air, and someone shouts, "It's running a bloody hour early!"

I hadn't noticed, but the Tavern has become decidedly busier while we've all been eating and talking, and suddenly there's an exodus. Matt and Jason are still staring at each other, but Danny and Leon have joined the rush for the door, and ultimately, the bridge, while Crofty's standing checking his phone. "Yep, it's on Real Time!" He grabs the camera bag I didn't notice he'd been carrying, and heads off, muttering, "I can't believe I've been distracted by a fucking bacon sandwich!"

I stand, placing my hand on Matt's shoulder, but looking at Jason. I can't read his expression, and I feel a bit light-headed. "Come on, you two," I say, only vaguely aware of the cringeworthiness of my words, "we can chat about this later, but the train's coming!"

As soon as I'm out of the door, I'm blasted by the gale coming off the sea. My hair's being whipped about like crazy, so using the hairband that lives on my wrist, I try to tie it back. The salt in the air has already made it thick and rough, and strands pull on my scalp as I twist the band tight. There are already people on the bridge, and I'm surprised to see that everyone's cramming into the near-side corner rather than standing in the middle. There's a low, loud whistle away in the distance, and lights inching towards us. Then I see why everyone's vying for the side – it's to get a good angle for a photo. The tang of smoke wafts on the wind, and suddenly, the iconic Flying Scotsman is speeding through Swansbourne Station, an enormous plume of thick, white smoke streaming behind it. Matt and I are in the middle of the bridge, and I'm suddenly aware of how thin and fragile it seems. Glancing behind me, the dark mouth of Kennaway Tunnel gapes scarily, so I whip my face back to the monstrous engine powering its way towards us. The wind has whipped up the waves, and they are crashing up over the sea wall, the spray hitting the tracks, drops of it hitting us. I grip the bridge's iron handrail and turn to Matt, who's grinning at me. The smokebox is about to smash us, the engine's chugging, its power vibrating through the metal I'm holding, and so bloody loud! And then we're engulfed in thick smoke and the bridge is shaking and people are shouting and laughing, and the massive locomotive passes beneath us with a deafening whistle, and when the smoke clears and I am coughing it out of my lungs, I watch the carriage roofs zip by, and the whistle fades into the tunnel, and we all turn 180 degrees, and all that's left is a shadow and a cloud of smoke.

I find myself laughing, and Matt's arm around me. "Told you it was fun!" he says.

Railway photographers disperse as soon as the train is out of sight, but the Platform Five Boys and I stay on the bridge. Crofty and Leon are still facing the tunnel, chatting, but Danny is staring over the tumultuous ocean. The sky is gloomy, but the only water in the air is salty sea spray, and Exmouth is still visible over the estuary. The lights of Swansbourne Station sparkle, and I have a craving for a hot meal and a pint. I'm about to voice this to Matt when I notice Jason on the sea wall. I nudge Matt, who shouts down to him, and Jason turns and waves at us to join him. Danny is already clomping down the wet steps, and Leon and Crofty fall in with us.

"Well, that was worth rushing for, wasn't it?" laughs Jason, his voice almost lost on the wind. It's as if that awkward moment with Matt had never happened.

"Yeah," says Matt, flatly. "What are you doing down here?"

"Watching that seal," Jason replies.

"That's not a seal! It's someone's dog!" says Crofty, shrugging his camera bag over his shoulder.

"Bit far out to be a dog," says Leon, digging in his pocket. He pulls out a tiny pair of binoculars.

"Still doing a bit of birdwatching on the sly, are we, Leo?"

"Yeah, but it depends what you mean by 'bird'," Danny jokes.

"Fuck off, Dan. I just don't see the point of being out in the middle of nowhere waiting for a train, just scrolling through your phone or constantly refreshing Real Time. I've seen woodpeckers and all sorts with these. You should try it – you might learn something. It is a seal, by the way. Look."

Danny and Jason have a go with the binoculars, but I'm starving, so I head off in the direction of the Marine Tavern with Matt, and they catch us up.

"Back so soon?" asks the barman. Something about the way he's looking at me gives me the creeps, and I'm really glad when he tells us they're not doing food today because the chef's got Covid. We trudge back out into the beer garden, and Jason says, "Fish and chips all round then?"

"To be honest, I don't fancy it." The words are out of my mouth before I've thought about it. It was nice of him to offer. "I want to sit down somewhere nice and have a pint. Shall we look for another pub?"

"You could go back in and ask your mate," suggests Danny, with a smirk, but Matt's already Googling.

"We could try the White Hart," he says.

"No!" says Jason. We all look at him. "Sorry!" He looks nervous and embarrassed. "I used to live in Swansbourne, back in the day, and no one ever went in the White Hart but the hardcore locals who'd start on the whiskey as soon as the doors opened. It's a right dump, a tiny little place next to the laundrette."

"Says here, it's recently been taken over and expanded, and the food looks great." Matt looks at us all and shrugs. "I think we should give it a go."

Jason can't really argue with this – it's got to be twenty-odd years since he lived here, so that's where we head.

"I didn't know you lived in Swansbourne," says Matt.

"Why would you?" Jason counters. "I'm a lot older than you lot, and I've lived all over the place. I used to rent that flat up there." He points at a large, off-white building on the corner of the main street, opposite the station. "Good view of the sea and the railway," he says, by way of an explanation. "Anyway, it was a long time ago." And he leads us away from the sea and the street, and along a path that runs all the way along the stream. "May as well take the scenic route! I'll show you the duck sanctuary, Danny. You could bring Gwen down in the spring when the chicks are hatching."

Danny nods and smiles but says nothing. I think he looks sad, but no one else seems to notice. I can't actually remember ever having seen Gwen. Maybe he doesn't get much access now he and Kerry have split up. Another dadless kid in the world.

We see the ornamental ducks, we see the lawn bowls club and the green, and we're right at the end of the main street. There's a library and a few cafes, and just on a corner, there's the White Hart, in the middle of a long terrace of old, white houses. There's no laundrette, so, presumably, the new owners extended into it. It's clearly more of a gastro pub than an old local now, all grey and white with shining wooden highlights. I see Jason glance up at the licensee names above the door: John and Sue Barton. Jason smirks, and I wonder why.

Inside is lovely. There's a real log fire burning, it's warm, and as well as mismatched wooden tables – all highly polished – there's an area by the fire with tartan-covered armchairs and a sofa. Without thinking, I plonk myself down into one of the chairs.

"Make yourself at home, then," laughs Matt. He grabs a couple of menus from the holder on the bar, and everyone sits down.

"I'll get the drinks in," says Jason, and he walks slowly back to the bar, admiring the old oil paintings on the walls. I wonder if he's into art as well as steam trains. He's a funny bloke: kind, generous and affable, but there's something off about him that I catch every so often and can't put my finger on.

"Actually, could I have a glass of wine instead of a pint, please, Jase?" I call over.

"Red or white?"

"Umm, white please. A Pinot or a Sav Blanc." I smile. "Thanks, Jason."

"Simon?"

The landlady serves the coffees she's been making and moves over to Jason as if she's known him for years.

Maybe she has. Maybe that's why he smiled at the sign outside.

Jason flushes red and backs away a bit.

"It's me, Jackie! Very long time no see!"

"Ahh, ex-girlfriend," Danny whispers. "That's why he didn't want to come here. Older woman, too, sly dog!"

"Sorry, I think you've got me confused with someone," Jason's saying. "My name's Jason. Could I order some drinks, please?"

The woman, Jackie, is clearly thrown by this. "Oh. Oh. I'm sorry," she says, peering at him. "You just remind me of someone, that's all." She starts getting our drinks on autopilot, glancing at Jason as she does so. "Are you sure we've never met before?"

"No. Well, I lived in Swansbourne for a bit when I was young," he says, "when I was at school, I mean. Maybe I look a bit like my dad, and he may have come in here? Presuming you used to work in here back then! But his name's Ernest, anyway."

"Do you mean Ernest Hemmingway?" asks Jackie, with a grin. Jason laughs, shaking his head, and they both glance over to us. Danny must be right – Jackie's an old flame, and Jason's embarrassed.

While we wait for our food, Matt brings up the shunting mission again.

"Well, yeah, if you want to do it for a bit of 80s nostalgia and try to grab some other followers, then, yeah, why not?" Leon says. "But I think live feeds are the way to go."

"So, what were you talking about earlier, Jason?" asks Matt, nipping any tangents in the bud. Also, he stresses Jason's name. He only ever calls him Jase.

"Oh, nothing. It was just Al was telling me about that Willand thing, and I remember it being on the news, that's all."

"Really? Because you sounded … odd." Matt's pushing.

"Sorry," says Jason. "It's just … well … a friend of mine lived behind the house that backs onto that line, and his wife lost her baby. You know, after the weedkiller went down. We all just thought it was … odd, you know. But apparently the whole story was made up, so it must just have been coincidence. But you looked quite … involved, Nia."

Now I'm in the spotlight, and for some reason I'm reluctant to tell Jason my story, which is crazy because he's linked to it, too, and, thankfully, a lad who looks as if he's about twelve starts to bring our food out.

"I think Jason's my dad."

Matt almost steers the car into Cockwood Harbour, and he has to brake so he doesn't hit a group of cyclists coming round the corner.

"What are you talking about, Lavinia?"

"Since when have I been Lavinia to you, and why are you shouting?" I find myself shouting back. The atmosphere in the car reminds me of the last time we were in a car for a long time together, and although I don't want to fall out with my best friend again, it feels inevitable.

"He's not your dad, Nia."

"How do you know?"

"Oh my God. You're clinging to straws, Nia! Just because someone has a link to the same mystery as you, and has the same colour hair as you, doesn't make you related!"

"Jason doesn't have the same colour hair as me. He's bald."

"No, he's not! He just shaves his head! You must have noticed he sometimes has a gingery beard!"

"No. No, I've never noticed that. Oh my God. He is my dad!" Tears prick my eyes, and I start laughing. I want to jump up and down! I want to hug Matt! I want to cry! I want to go and find Jason!

"Nia!" Matt really shouts. He's throwing us round the twisty A road back to Exeter, and I find myself grabbing the handle above the door.

"Seriously! Matt! You have to stop the car! You have to go and find Jason! Which way did he go? Was he dropping Danny off in Eskwich on the way back to Bishop's?"

Matt hauls the car off the road and into the layby under the motorway bridge just outside Exminster.

"Jesus, Matt! What are you doing?!"

Matt turns the engine off and rips himself free of his seatbelt. His face is a picture of agony, and his eyes are wet. "Nia!" He puts a hand on my leg, and I brush it off. "And that's why!" he says, exasperated. "That's why I kept my dad's fucking secret for my whole fucking life, and look where it's got me!"

"What are you talking about, Matt?" We're staring at each other with emotions I can't name.

"Jason isn't your dad, Nia, and I know he's not your dad, because your dad is buried in the woods at Redbank. My dad had him killed, and I kept his secret because I knew if I told you what I knew, you wouldn't want anything to do with me, let alone love me. But you were never going to love me anyway, were you? You don't love anyone. You're fucking frigid."

The silence that follows rings in my ears, and I'm light-headed again.

"No, he's not." I murmur, willing my words into truth, and shutting out everything else Matt said.

"Yes, he is. That's why we couldn't play in the woods as kids. And I have his hat under my bed at Dad's."

I stand, reeling and numb, under the motorway bridge.
Matt's long gone. Realising I'm cold, I scurry up the
concrete bank to where the bottom of the road meets the
support, like a small rodent seeking a hiding place. I watch
vehicles pass, some at speed, all with their wipers going, in
both directions. I twist my phone about in my pocket. No
calls, but who on earth would be calling? I don't know why
I don't call the police. I know I ought to call the police.
Matt's dad is a murderer, and Matt's complicit. How can he
profess to love me, and yet lie to me for God knows how
long about the thing that has always mattered to me most –
my dad?! Hot, angry tears spill down my face as I find
Danny in my contacts. When he picks up, with no
preamble, I ask him for Jason's number. They're all still in
the car, and I listen to Jason reciting his number to Danny,
who recites it to me. He could just have WhatsApped it, but
hearing Jason so willing to give it to me without any kind
of explanation means a lot. He must know the truth about
my dad.

Simon, 2022.

I've reached the tipping point. Critical mass. I haven't
heard from anyone, nor have I attempted to make contact.

It's okay, you're in control; it's okay, you're in control I chant to myself as I pace around my room, light-headed and sweating. And I am in control. It's just that I am torn. Do I face the bull and fight it? My mind is so warped now, I don't even know which side of the argument the bull is supposed to represent. I take my battered copy of *The Sun Also Rises* off the windowsill, and leaf through it. Another fragment of its spine comes away, and I watch it float to the floor like it's in slow motion.

The next time I'm truly conscious, I'm driving out to second bridge. Real Time Trains has informed me that one of the old HSTs – that still have decades of life in them – will be passing through around lunchtime on its way to be scrapped. They're being replaced with new, American engines, for no apparent reason. For all the twenty-first century's ostensible eco-consciousness, our government have seen fit to scrap hundreds of perfectly good engines again. It's history repeating. We wear poppies at this time of year to remember the so-called war to end all wars, yet no one's called a ceasefire in Ukraine. Nor will they – war is too lucrative for some. As a species, we have achieved so much – just look at the railway infrastructure in Britain as one example – yet every generation is useless. We talk about changing things. We have comprehensive discourses on everything from the climate crisis to neurodivergence, and everyone has a voice on social media – as much as The Algorithm allows. And it's this – The Algorithm that's my problem. I could bring the Willand Incident to light again, easily, but to what end? Everyone's truth is different. I could get Misty and Eleanor to testify, and Tony and Anna could have closure. Maybe they'd get some monetary compensation. Maybe Derek and his cronies would be publicly disgraced. Maybe Geoff Kerslake's kids would have closure. But, more than likely, it would reopen old wounds, and to what end? It's over, gone. We should look forward, not back. And sometimes not knowing is easier, because you don't have anything to deal with. There's always pain, but there's always hope. Like Schrodinger's cat. It might be alive, it might be dead, but no one has to deal with a consequence if no one knows. No one has to take responsibility for anything. I've been watching people all my life. They think they want the truth, but really, they just want an easy life. Take me, for example. I'd have to explain to Nia why I chose to stay so close to her but so very far away all her life. I'd have to explain that although I tried my hardest to do good in the world, no one took me seriously. It's survival of the fittest, and the nice people aren't the fittest. Simon Hulme was a failure, and they killed him off. You have to close yourself off and lie. Look after number one. Do what you have do to survive. It's nature.

Nia, 2022.

I could walk the short distance to Exminster, stand outside someone's house and call a taxi, but I decide to walk home, in spite of the rain. I don't feel like talking to anyone, and besides, I need time to think. I'm itching to call Jason, but I know he'll still be driving; also, Danny's in the passenger seat. I have to wait until I can talk to him alone, and it would probably be better to arrange to meet him, and speak in person so I can watch his reactions.

Thick clouds have darkened the sky so much everyone's driving with their headlights on. I'm too scared to use the subway under Exe Bridges roundabout, so I walk the long way round and take my chances with the pedestrian crossings. I stop on the bridge for a moment and watch people walking along the concrete banks of the overflow channel, and the swans gliding through the calm water. Behind me, over four rows of traffic and a bus lane, stand the red ruins of Exeter city wall, along with some bits of a building that I think was the castle. I leave it all and continue home, wet, cold and hungry. I could stop in Burger King, or even drown my sorrows at the bar in the Kings Head, but a train rattles along the viaduct, reminding me of Matt. I go home, put the kettle on, run a bath, then get straight into bed. I have no idea what time it is.

When I wake, it's properly dark. I find my phone on the bathroom floor with my wet clothes, and call Jason's number. It rings for a long time, but when the posh woman's voice welcomes me to the answerphone service and informs me that the person I want to speak to is unavailable, I'm silent after the beep. I don't know what to say.

I dress, brush my teeth and my hair, and put a coffee on. I try Jason again, willing him to pick up after the next ring. Voicemail again. I ring off before the beeps. I tidy the house, then ring again. I put the washing on, telling myself he's probably busy, or at work, or driving. Maybe he has a landline and is talking to someone else on that. I should leave a message, or text him so he knows who it is – he probably doesn't recognise my number. I don't. I just ring again. I should leave it for today and call him in the morning. Anyway, if he picks his phone up and sees he has three missed calls, he'll probably call the number to see who it is. But I want to know about my dad. I can feel myself getting wound up. I'm about to cry. I'm frustrated and angry. I'm pacing the ground floor of my house. I feel shaky. Everything seems a bit unreal.

And all this is because of Matt. He's broken the law, and he's betrayed me. He's betrayed me for fucking years, all because he wants a shag. And my dad is dead. Murdered. My mind races. I wonder what they did to him. I wonder if he'd been scared, or if his death had come out of the blue. And my whole life was fucked-up, and it's Matt's fault. I throw myself down on the floor, crying and screaming, punching and kicking and thrashing about. Like a toddler having a tantrum, and what an apt simile that is, except the anger doesn't dissipate.

Eventually, I'm still, and aware of the sound of a train moving slowly. It's about to stop at St Thomas'. I get up and absently wipe my face. I'm vaguely aware that it's stinging because of all the salt, but I don't care, because I find myself moving very quickly. My dad is dead. He's not coming back. I'll get the police to dig up the wood at Redbank Court, his body will be found, Matt and his dad will be sentenced, justice will be done, and everyone will move on. Everyone apart from me. I slam my car door and rev the engine.

Matt is not at his flat. Matt is not at his mum's. Matt must be in his special, secret place. The place where he spent time with his dad. His murdering bastard of a dad. So that's where I'm going to go. Whichever way the wind's blowing.

Simon, 2022.

Real Time Trains shows me that the special is running very late. I drive to McDonald's in Eskwich, have some food, and go to the loo. I sit at the table in the greasy-smelling restaurant and watch people. A chip falls from my hand, and automatically, I attempt to catch it. I fail, and it falls in the corner of the low, narrow windowsill, just below my knee. There's dust, grease and spiders' webs down there – the cleaners clearly only wipe down the tables and run a brush and a mop over the floor. I watch a tiny fly wobble its way through the air to my chip. It stops, seemingly in mid-air, and its little wings blur, but they're too small to make enough sound to reach my ears. A big, dark brown spider rushes out from somewhere. Its meal will be small, but it's easily gained. I check my app again. The sky's darkened while I've been in here. I ought to go.

The HST's headlights glow from where it waits in Eskwich loop. Ironically, it's waiting for another of its kind to pass – this one carrying what might turn out to be its last passengers. The lights from the 2 Sisters complex illuminate the scene well enough, and I'm not photographing this engine. It's more like I'm taking my proverbial hat off to it, in respect. Then I hear shouts from behind me. I look down the line and see figures moving on third bridge. That bridge is illuminated by the light from the gypsy camp, and I know that not far down the line behind it, fourth bridge is illuminated by the streetlights from the main road. There's no real darkness any more. The two people are arguing, pushing each other around, but I can't make out their words because of the perpetual hum from the abattoir behind me, but I do hear the engine of the HST start up.

I turn and watch it pull away and gather speed as it sets off on the final leg of its final journey. As soon as it passes under the bridge, I race across to the other side, like a six-year-old waving it off, and I'm just in time to see one of the third bridge figures shove the other, and that other loses its balance on the crumbly stone of third bridge, and the figure falls. The bang isn't loud, but it's palpable. The brakes of the HST screech, but it speeds on regardless. I don't see where it stops. I don't see where it stops because I'm running, running to third bridge, running to third bridge just in time to see Nia fling herself into her car and drive off. I know she can see me in her rear-view mirror, because I, too am illuminated by the security lights from the gypsy camp.

It's presented in the papers as a lovers' tiff. But now Nia's running. History repeating. I wonder what choices she'll make. But no one's looking any more. This is over and gone; look forward, not back. Just cover your tracks.

Milton Keynes UK
Ingram Content Group UK Ltd.
UKHW022202260624
444703UK00007B/67